Blues

He's an alcoholic. Oliver remembers reading that somewhere in a magazine. Man with a big problem.

Must be fifteen years older than Elora.

Sleeping with her.

Somehow this C. C. Gilley had convinced her of his love and vilely seduced her. How could she do this to her dad, lose her innocence to this animal? He should never have let her go off to the city. She was naive, unready.

Don't a lot of these rock stars shoot heroin? If C. C. Gilley has AIDS, Oliver will kill him.

Standing by his window as dawn fills the eastern sky, he stares out at the trailer. She's sleeping with him in there. Next to his body.

It's an infatuation, no question, not love, Oliver has seen the girls go through it with other pop stars. *I so love you, Van. Oh, Michael, do you even know I exist?* Most of this at the age of ten, however.

He'll sober up, he'll realize he's been on a bender, and go home after coffee. Elora-less. If God is just.

Books by William Deverell

Needles
High Crimes
Mecca
The Dance of Shiva

William Deverell

Platinum
Blues

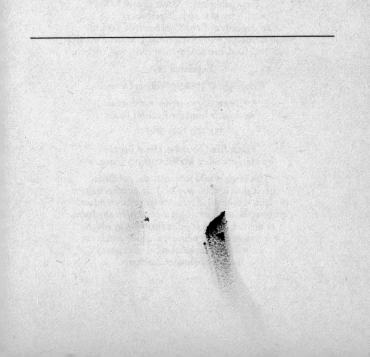

A Mandarin Paperback

PLATINUM BLUES

First published in Great Britain 1990
by Mandarin Paperbacks
an imprints of Reed Consumer Books Ltd
Michelin House, 81 Fulham Road, London SW3 6RB
and Auckland, Melbourne, Singapore and Toronto

Reprinted 1994

Copyright © 1988 by William Deverell

A CIP catalogue record for this title
is available from the British Library

ISBN 0 7493 0191 0

Printed and bound in Great Britain
by HarperCollins Manufacturing, Glasgow

With love to Daniel and Tamara,
who keep me in tune
with the times.

ACKNOWLEDGMENTS

I spent several traumatic days and nights traveling the Pacific Coast with the Bryan Adams tour, bunking in the crew bus, a kind of Animal House on wheels. I survived that to spend a few more days with Loverboy during a Los Angeles video shoot, and received some cogent advice from Paul Dean on the art of songwriting. Special thanks are owed to talent manager Bruce Allen for opening doors and smoothing my way.

Gil Friesen, president of A&M Records, kindly gave me the run of his company's offices, plant, and studios in Hollywood, and my research there was assisted by many of A&M's top-flight music people. Jeffrey Glenn and Howard Berman, attorneys in San Francisco, helped guide me through the byways of U.S. civil procedure. Art Bergman and Taylor Little of the Vancouver band, "Poisoned," helped me see the world from the musician's point of view.

I was introduced to both the topside and the underside of the rock music world by various musicians and songwriters who, although of small and local renown, are all, as far as I'm concerned, stars.

My varied sources provided me with a feast of verisimilitude, but I warn emphatically that none of the novel's characters or events are in any way drawn (or plagiarized) from real events and people.

William Deverell

Platinum
Blues

▶ ▶ ▶

"My code name is Sergeant Pepper. I'm with the organization."

"The organization?"

"You know the one."

"Uh, jes' a minute, lemme think. Hey, man, I got it. The Lonely Hearts Club Band. Ringo sent you, right?"

"I can't release names. It's top security. High places."

"Sounds like you is definitely at some high place right now. What you been mainlining, goofballs?"

"What's your name?"

"Code name's Mr. Elliott Goodweather."

"Are you in the organization?"

"Well, I'm not actual an organization man, just a purveyor of quality spice and herbs, mainly from the Orient. Unbeknownst to me, some rascal went an' hid opium in the saffron and thus, I, innocent, face trial in an hour."

"Yes. So do I."

"What they do you for, sergeant?"

"Murder one."

"Oh, hey, you mus' be the dude that shot up that restaurant in Hollywood, I heard you was coming up for trial."

"I was acting under orders."

"I got it. The ol' reliable insanity defense. Used it in front of the draft board myself once. All the brothers heading off to Nam to be kilt, I decided, I'm hearin' God talkin' to me, God Hisself, passing down instructions to earth through the agency of Elliott Goodweather."

"They'll be coming for me."

"The organization?"

"Yes."

"Ask them to pick me up on their way out, okay, Sarge? Else I get buried. This is my fifth and I'm looking at twenty."

■ ■ ■

CHAPTER

1

Raquel asks, "Warm you up, Mr. Gulliver?"

Oliver tries to think of something flip and teasing to say to her - words should fall trippingly from a lawyer's tongue - but the best he can do is a crooked smile and a "Call me Oliver."

"How about sugar?"

"No, just plain Oliver is fine."

She laughs. Her little tank-topped tits move to six inches from his nose. He sucks in the fragrances, a nosegay of tart armpit over coffee freshly dripped, as she leans across him to refill the chief of police.

If he could find the strength to move his head a few inches, he'd see one of her nipples. Her hair is orange and butch. It doesn't seem right for a waitress in the Paradise Cafe.

The chief, Jesse Gonzales, says, "I gotta go, I got the travail of ten men to do." But he lets her fill his cup.

The head of Foolsgold's one-man police force, Jesse had two guys with him in better times. He uses words like travail, which comes from being self-taught but widely read. Oliver likes him: behind the grumpy crust hides a two-hundred pound teddy bear, full of soft stuffing. He has a thin, wimpy moustache he's been trying to bring to flower for two decades.

"You look like you could stand a little sweetening," Raquel tells the chief. She drops half a dozen paper sugar pads in front of him and gambols away, deserting the two men in their window booth. Raquel has just shown up here from San Francisco, likes the small-town life, she says. What's this brassy young thing doing in pokey, hokey Foolsgold? She won't last long. Kids never do here. Foolsgold is a decaying bush town on the California North Coast, and Oliver V. Gulliver happens to be its mayor. No honor.

His daughter Elora is in San Francisco, the city of AIDS. She's eighteen, almost Raquel's age, yet he has been composing hot fantasies of making out with this new waitress. Whence comes this sudden impurity of mind?

Another facet of his late mid-life crisis.

Oliver is a worrier, it's what he does best in life, he holds the Guinness record. Mainly it comes from being single parent to Elora and Lindy, who has reached fifteen, an age of formidable danger. When Madelaine died eight years ago, in awful cancerous agony, not yet forty, Oliver declined the aid of grandparents, of relatives, of friends, and with stoic unease shouldered alone the task of ushering the girls into womanhood.

Oliver looks outside, into the brightness of the day, across the street and along the weathered redwood storefronts of Madrona Street. Faithless for six months, the sun has finally routed the clouds of spring, and this morning it kisses Foolsgold, population 1,420, down from over 2,500, now just a circle with a dot in it on the Exxon road map.

But maybe this will be a good year, a turnaround in lumber, they're already talking about a rise in house starts.

"Here comes a pain in the fundament," Jesse says.

Ernie Bolestero, The Competition, turning on his simulated smile as he enters the cafe. He joshes with Raquel at the counter.

He's Foolsgold's other lawyer, five-six, a ferret, neatly double-breasted compared to Oliver in his baggy old suit. He came here from Orange County five years ago, just before the bottom dropped out of lumber, and now they had two lawyers in a town big enough to support one, this young schemer always undercutting Oliver, hustling his clients.

3

"I love it," he says, joining them, "that pious little porkchop walking in and there's this guy getting gobbled on the screen."

Jesse Gonzales looks at him blankly. "Gobbled on the screen?" Oliver isn't sure either.

"You guys haven't heard? It's all over town." Ernie leans forward, looking pleased with his news. "You know the preacher Sybil McGuid has gone dotty for?"

. "Reverend Blythe," says Oliver. A fleecer of lambs from Ohio who has been operating from a hired hall down in Eureka.

"He was up visiting Sybil last night, staying over, and he decided for some reason to take a stroll at one in the morning, saw all the cars parked around by the Opera House, and the lights on inside. He walked in as the heroine was taking it in the mouth in living color."

"Clarence," says Oliver, with a slowly sinking heart.

Clarence, Oliver's late wife's brother, the bad news bear of Foolsgold. Clarence Boggs, proprietor of Boggs Insurance Agency. Who also works evenings as projectionist at the Opera House.

Ernie chuckles. "Way I get the story, for about the last ten nights Clarence has been running porno flicks after the bars close. I gather he laid in a stockpile of product from L.A. Last night's main feature was called *The Harder They Come*."

Jesse Gonzales says with relish: "Let me get this straight. Pastor Wilfrid Blythe of the True Word Pentecostal Assembly walks into the Foolsgold Opera House last night as some guy is getting his joint consumed on the screen?" He pounds the table and guffaws, and Mrs. Chong pokes her head from the kitchen door.

Oliver isn't finding this funny, not at all.

"Has Sybil found out?" he says. Sybil McGuid, who owns half of Foolsgold including the Opera House, provides most of the bread Oliver butters for his family.

Conversation stops as Clarence Boggs himself enters the restaurant, avoiding everyone, sitting down at the counter. The Paradise Cafe is the only place in Foolsgold you can get a beer in the morning, Oliver should have expected him.

4

"Excuse me, gentlemen," says Oliver, getting up.

"Better tell him to get rid of the evidence," Jesse says.

Oliver brings his coffee over and sits beside Clarence, a tall, disconnected oddity. It is hard to believe he came out of the same womb as Madelaine. He has large eyes and a small nose, irregular features scattered across a slack, lazy face, and is wearing his trademark blue suit and red bow tie.

"Jesus, get me a beer," he says to Raquel.

"What kind?"

"Any kind. After I finish it get me another. I'm trying to work up enough courage to hang myself."

"Beer and a rope, comin' up," she says.

Clarence says in a dismal voice, "I just talked to her, tried to apologize. She's gonna close down the Opera House, and she's talking about taking her insurance business to some State Farm guy in Eureka."

Oliver steadies his coffee cup before bringing it to his lips. The rainy season had made him demented, co-signing that note for Clarence. A hundred and twenty thousand from the Savings and Loan to buy old Tomlinson's insurance agency, a doomed ship with Clarence at the helm. Oliver hadn't been able to say no to his deceased wife's kid brother. He is quietly, icily furious.

"I'm tits up if she pulls her accounts. The policies on the mill, the plywood plant – shit, half the town – out the window. No one else pays any insurance premiums here worth a wet fart. We're dying. The cheap lumber from Canada is murdering us. You got to feel it in your practice, too."

The worst scenario is this: Clarence will fold his business and steal away like a desert Arab, saddling Oliver with a lifetime of debt.

Raquel brings the beer and flits off to the cash to get Jesse and Ernie, who have seen the storm on Oliver's face and are leaving.

Clarence rambles on, not daring to look at Oliver. "I been thinking, if I could get a new start somewhere without this millstone hanging around my neck, I could be back in Foolsgold

5

in five or six years and pay off the bank in one fell swoop. Around L.A., that's where you make the boola boola. Film industry."

Oliver has struggled for everything he's got, three acres, three-bedroom house with a terrific view, 1985 Chrysler Le-Baron, 1979 Toyota four-wheel pickup, Bel-Air Model 24 Camperhome, fishing cabin up the Foolsgold River. And three big mortgages.

Clarence, at thirty-eight, has, on the other hand, already fulfilled early promise of being a glad-handing layabout. As a lawyer, Oliver wouldn't have advised John Paul Getty to co-sign that note.

"Let's face it, God's great but invisible plan doesn't have me in there as an insurance agent."

Oliver finds his voice. It's loud and ill-humored. "Look, you asshole, if you lose Sybil McGuid's accounts and then stiff me with that loan, I'm going to find you in your sleep one night and I'm going to be armed with a baseball bat and I'm going to split open both your kneecaps."

By the end of this speech, Oliver is almost shouting. The silence is long and hard. Oliver listens to Mrs. Chong stifle a cough by the kitchen door. Another silence.

"We're gonna have to cut that guy's coffee off," says Raquel from somewhere.

Clarence tries for a nervous smile to make it light, but Oliver's cold eyes hold him like hooks, and the smile dies.

"Okay," he says. "I'll work something out with her."

*   *   *

From his upstairs office in the Foolsgold Savings and Loan Building, Oliver allows his gaze to travel across Madrona Street, up the fronts of the Paradise Cafe and the post office, beyond to the spire of the Methodist church, then distantly to the redwood forests running to the seacliffs, fingers of fog speeding in from the ocean, a horizon lost in a gauze of mist.

The truly beautiful thing to see is the Foolsgold River,

6

which curls and falls down a valley to the sea. Back upstream twenty miles lurk fat rainbow trout. Yes, maybe this weekend. He sees one rising sideways from the water, furious and on the hook.

"Oliver, if you wouldn't mind coming back into this world for a few seconds, here are two foreclosures just came in from the Savings and Loan." Mrs. Plymm, his secretary, has snuck in behind him. "Daydreaming. Gracious, one of these days you'll go someplace and never come back." She hands him the new files.

"I wasn't daydreaming. I often meditate."

"Oh, honestly." Mrs. Plymm knows him, she's been with him for twenty years. She's sixty-four and plump and full of cheer.

"Foreclosures," says Oliver. "More people to kick out of their houses. It fills you with a sense of power." He looks over the files with dread.

Foreclosures, wills, separation agreements, speeding tickets. It's what he's done all his working life and it's what he'll do until he dies. What happened to those youthful dreams of being a courtroom counsel, getting his name in the TV news? He's fifty, still dreaming, but the former dreams of glory have become the pointless reveries of a foolish romancer trudging down the lonely road past middle age toward senility.

He's feeling sour. The scene with Clarence has put him permanently on edge for the day. He wants to escape to his nest, to Lindy, his dog, his gentle three acres.

He glances outside again and sees Sybil McGuid's 1981 Cadillac Brougham crawling around Two Street to Madrona. It angle-parks in front of his building, below him. Oliver watches her unbuckle Jamey, who is twenty-five, 250 pounds, and retarded. Sybil McGuid's only child and heir, he dwarfs his mother, sixty, tiny, starched, her hair in a severe bun.

Oliver turns around. "She's here."

"I'll put tea on."

Sybil walks in without knocking, it doesn't matter, he could be taking instructions from the president of Chase Manhattan

7

Bank and she'd come in and tell the guy to wait outside. It's like being owned. When Oliver took over his father's practice fifteen years ago, he told himself, this is it, the independent G.P., never going to be beholden to anyone. But times are tough, and Sybil McGuid keeps the fridge full, and Ernie Bolestero lurks in the wings . . .

She has left his office door open. In the waiting room he can hear Jamey and his mouth organ, a nice tune, he knows it from the radio, the Hit Parade, or whatever they call it these days.

"Jamey, don't bother Mrs. Plymm," Sybil says.

"Oh, he can serenade me all day long, Sybil," Mrs. Plymm calls.

Jamey has a basement full of musical instruments and plays them all. Someone read God's recipe wrong, didn't put in enough eggs and added too much flour, and Jamey is a musical *idiot savant*. Born out of wedlock, he was sired in mystery, perhaps by an itinerant kazoo salesman.

Sybil fetches him, points him to the big horsehair chair he likes, and he plumps into it. "Hullo, Mr. Gulliver."

Jamey shakes the spit from his harmonica, batting it into the palm of his other hand, and Sybil shrieks, "Jamey!"

"It's what they all do," Jamey says. "Mick Jagger, I seen him do that on the TV."

She hands him a clean hanky. "Wipe it." To Oliver, she says, "I suppose you've heard. Poor Pastor Blythe, he was *so* shocked."

"You can't close the Opera House down, that's unfair," Oliver says. The Opera House, Foolsgold's single architectural treasure, has been run as a movie theater for the last twenty years. It was built in 1901 when it looked like Foolsgold was about to go somewhere. Instead, the lumber barons chose Eureka, south of here, which likes to crow about its preserved Old Town.

"We used to have touring companies," she says, a little wistful. "*Brigadoon, Naughty Marietta*." She snaps to. "Now it's a place where layabouts pay Clarence Boggs to see filthy, filthy movies. I intend to put the theater to a more godly use. Pastor

8

Blythe hopes to start a permanent congregation here. This town is full of Satan's work, Oliver. The pastor will have his hands full."

"I'm going to get you deprogrammed, Sybil, before you start signing everything over to him."

She huffs. "You don't know him. Oliver, he is *so* good. I'm almost in tears when I think of how I failed Jesus all those years." She takes a determined, business-like breath. "The Opera House is a beautiful building and we're going to keep it intact, but add a few decorations. Pastor Blythe will want it this Sunday. Only twenty-three came out last Sabbath, but, really, that awful hall in Eureka."

Her father, from whom she had inherited everything, had been a beer-drinking galoot of a forest baron. It was predictable, Oliver supposes, that Sybil would ultimately find solace in old-time religion.

"I'm adamant. I've announced it to the *Inquirer*."

Oliver sighs. "I'll draw up a lease." He'll stall for time, drag it out.

"I trust Pastor Blythe."

"I'll draw up a lease. And I'll ask Clarence to make sure you've got the right coverage, it's a priceless building."

She doesn't respond right away. Jamey provides background music, humming.

"I will *never* forgive him, running those evil movies in *my* theater."

"It was a prank. My God, you've known him since he was a baby. He pulls that stuff all the time."

"I am absolutely mortified, Oliver. And he's *your* brother-in-law. Madelaine was such a jewel, I can't believe God created them as sister and brother."

Oliver looks at Jamey, who gives him a big, reassuring smile. Clarence likes to kid Jamey, make him laugh. Jamey likes Clarence.

Oliver takes a deep breath. "Look, Sybil, I'm not talking as his brother-in-law or anything, he's got to make it on his own, but don't you think you should be supporting local business

9

instead of going to Eureka? That agent there doesn't have a feel for the local conditions. It means you'll bankrupt Clarence, he owes bills all over town. He's just going through a phase, he's lonely, that's the trouble, especially after his girlfriend left him. What do you think, Jamey? We have to look after our own, don't we?"

"I like Clarence," he says.

This seems to soften Sybil. "Hmnf. I'll think about it. He'd better smarten up. If Clarence is lonely, we all know where there's a Friend."

Mrs. Plymm brings in tea and cookies.

CHAPTER

2

Tennyson, mostly Irish setter, does an old dog's tailwag dance around Oliver's feet as he steps from his car and onto the driveway in front of a meandering redwood split-level, *casa Gulliver*. It's on a hill and gets the setting sun over the ocean, a sun that is now threading rays through gaps in the fog, and painting below, golden and pretty, the town of Foolsgold.

He parks the LeBaron in the garage beside his pickup, and walks around to the back, to the cherry orchard where stands forlornly his grand old Bel-Air Camperhome, in which he and Madelaine and the kids when they were small used to tool around to places like Yosemite and Yellowstone.

Lindy, his fifteen year old, offers less warmth than Tennyson, a limpid wave from the hammock, an expenditure of point zero zero two calories. Oliver can hear the bass thump of the Walkman she's plugged into as she leafs through one of her sister's Italian fashion magazines. Oliver's looked at some of them, nowadays models have to show their tits.

"Picked up some fresh crab at the wharf," she says. "Made a salad. In the fridge."

"Did Elora call?"

"Nope."

"Write?"

"No, Dad."

"Not a letter in four days," Oliver says. "She doesn't think I worry, or what?" He tries not to think of that serial killer down in Marin County, the guy who breaks into homes. "When she does write, she gives us chickenfeed. I don't believe all she does is windowshop and ride cable cars."

Lindy says, "If she wrote and said she was having fun, boy *then* you'd get uptight."

San Francisco gets Oliver uptight.

It's Friday, end of the working week. A sunny day in June. Unwind.

"Sybil McGuid's closing down the old Opera House," he says.

Lindy climbs from the hammock, abandoning the magazine and radio. "I heard. Mrs. McGuid is just a dried-up old prune."

"Lindy!" Oliver says.

"Jeez, Dad, that's all the kids have in the winter, the movies." She arranges some plates and silverware on the picnic table.

"Yeah, and too much to do the rest of the year," Oliver says. "Who's your boyfriend for the beach party tonight? New one each week. Tell me it's not Greasy Grissom."

Lindy wanders over to the garden and plucks some radishes and takes them to the outdoor tap. "*Gregory* Grissom just happens to be one of the people in my group. Kids have groups now, they don't have boyfriends and girlfriends. Just because back in your Victoria era or whatever, you and Mom went steady doesn't set the pattern for all of history."

"You bet we went steady, from when we were at college," Oliver says. "That's pretty sick, I guess, by your modern casual standards, a relationship lasting more than two seconds."

The unceasing parade of acned faces, gangly boys hot for his daughters. He will keep them at bay, he'll get Lindy with her straight A's into college if it kills him. When Elora quit Humboldt State six weeks ago, she wounded him. Modeling. San Francisco.

"Who's going to be at this thing?" he asks. He remembers the beach parties when he was a kid, the snuggling, the blankets around the driftwood fire.

12

"You know, my friends."

"There had better not be any of those drugged-out beach bozos."

Walking Tennyson around the flats last week, he had found a flaccid, spent condom on the sand. Before Lindy goes, he will instruct her: Don't do anything stupid.

But maybe what is stupid is no condom.

His graceful, sprouting fawn dances up to him, and pops a little radish into his mouth. "Whatever befalls me tonight, Dad, I hope you'll remember me fondly."

He doesn't like this humor, thinks of the serial killer again. "Twelve midnight," he says. "Not a microsecond later."

He goes inside to shower.

The Oliver Gulliver in the bathroom mirror surprises him, a friendly face not revealing his many cares. Balding, but from the forehead up, at least. Five foot eleven spread fairly even, but he's got to take a couple of pounds off, start jogging again. You can see where the girls get their looks, not taking anything away from Madelaine, a stunner. When he smiles, a good, square-chinned American face greets you like a handshake. Mayor Gulliver, elected by acclamation four times running.

But the handsome, happy face belies the worried man within. He doesn't want to tell Lindy about her uncle's threats to weigh anchor from Foolsgold and leave them debt-ridden.

*   *   *

Oliver lies in bed, braced by pillows, watching the news, Channel Three, Eureka, on the fourteen-inch set on top of the bureau. More layoffs in the forests. They should blockade the border before Canadian softwood completes the destruction of Foolsgold. But the Great Communicator's for free trade. We've got to get those crazies out of the White House this year. Strange how northern Humboldt County is so Reaganized after all he's never done for us. Jeez, terrible accident on the 97 near Fort Dick, a lumber truck squashes a vw van, looks like an accordion, thank God there was only one passenger, the late wrong-way William Numickie of Coos Bay, Oregon.

Was Raquel coming on to him in the cafe, or what? You can't tell about modern girls, sometimes they're just being friendly. Guilt assails him. He's done nothing to deserve it, unless you count this recent wave of randy imaginings.

It's his middle-age crisis. Three months ago he reached the big five-oh. It's a downhill stumble from here. The crisis comes complete with an itch for the flesh which he cannot scratch away. After eight years of repose, Oliver's manhood has arisen from its torpor, and he has added scenes of lust to the incessant daydreams. Walking determinedly in Lust's shadow is his ever-present companion, Guilt. Why is that pest hanging around? You can't betray the dead. The girls aren't impressed by his loyalty to a memory. Lindy recently ended an argument with, "You're uptight, Dad, you need to go out somewhere and get lucky."

Okay, there *was* that Christmas party a few years ago, in the back of Harvey Sweet's van, with Harvey Sweet's wife, an ugly, grunting incident fueled by California Chardonnay, a comedy turned tragedy when one of the local kids saw him crawling out of there, buckling his pants. And doubtless ratted to his daughters, though they said nothing. Totally mortified, paralyzed by a fear he'd lost the girls' respect, he swore celibacy to the end of time.

Madelaine said, dying there, "Don't be lonely. Find someone." He can't, it will always feel like adultery, a befouling of her memory. He sees her wasting, cancerous cells wolfing healthy ones. Eight years, still this pain.

Also eating away at him is the empty nest syndrome, the girls growing, leaving him to mourn the dying self of his own youth. It's a long, long while from May to December, and the days grow short when you reach September. What has he really accomplished in his fifty years? Name one case, one trial of note.

The late movie will erase sad thoughts, *Last Ditch Creek*, a

14

Byron Jones western, he's Oliver's favorite actor, he comes from Wales via the Royal Shakespeare Company and he out-Coopers Gary and outEastwoods Clint.

Early into it, a quarter past midnight – it's how they test you, grabbing another fifteen minutes – there's a soft chugging of untuned engine outside.

It's Greasy Grissom with his old Chev half-ton.

The engine cuts and afterwards Oliver thinks he hears urgent whisperings at the door. What? *Are my clothes on straight? Can you smell the beer on my breath?* The front door opens and closes, the hallway corridor creaks, and outside the engine starts.

Oliver feels released, returns to his movie, he becomes Byron Jones tracking Clarence Boggs across the sun-washed deserts of New Mexico.

Daydream merges with nightdream, and it's hours later that the frozen fragile surface of his unconsciousness is broken. By kitchen sounds, whump of fridge door closing, clatter of silverware, something worse, words, guttural, male.

Oliver is awake, tingling. The television screen is a blur of buzzing light.

He finds his pants and feels a little braver with them on. More silverware clatter. A sound like a laugh. Thieves of the night looting the sterling? Escapees from Humboldt jail, desperate and bold. Or maybe that serial killer, looking for the butcher knife. As he sneaks from the bedroom, Oliver hears more fragmented mutterings from the fluorescent-lit kitchen. How many men?

Quickly he's into the den and finds the phone. They hadn't cut the line. After two rings, the good sound of Chief Gonzales' sleepy grunt.

Oliver cups his mouth with his hand. "Jesse, it's Oliver. Someone's in my house."

"Wuh, wuh, Oliver?"

"Person or persons unknown. In. My. Kitchen."

"Be right down, don't do anything."

Oliver will not confront them, but he's emboldened now, and sidles behind the half-open kitchen door. Try to identify them in case they bolt.

Nose to the door-hinge, Oliver sees it's only one man, at the counter, digging into a jar of peanut butter with a spoon, and swabbing it on a slice of brown bread. His hair is a wild, unbrushed russet bush, and he has rings in his ears. He's skinny, gives up forty pounds to Oliver.

He sings, "I got the peanut butter, baby, but I ain't got the jam," the words coming as if burned from his throat. He staggers, grabs the lip of the counter. "Hey, babe, slow down for the curve."

Fried to the gills, Oliver sees. Not dangerous, armed only with a spoon. As the man steps into the kitchen, he staggers again, then catches his balance with a little dance step, and he spots Oliver. His eyes are like glints of starlight, but red and bagged beneath a bony face of narrow planes and angles. He stares bleakly at Oliver.

"You room service?" he says.

"No, I'm not."

"Where we playin' tonight? I forget. Been on the road too long."

"I'll show you where the road is," says Oliver.

"You my driver?" He pauses in thought. "No, I ain't been on the road, I been in the Graham F. Harley Detox. . ." He squints around, trying to focus, staggers back. "This ain't the detox center, it's a trailer camp. You got a nice one here, ours is kinda small, eh? I'm fucking starvin', man." He starts going at his bread and peanut butter like a wolf.

"Let me understand this," Oliver says softly. "You were hungry so you came into my home to eat."

"Whazzat? Sorry, I'm a little pissed."

"At whom?"

"Pissed, inebrelated . . . inebriated. Hey, jus' a minute, it's coming back, eh?"

The *eh*, the little Canadianism, concerns Oliver. Maybe it's

16

the custom in Canada, people have to share their kitchens with any drunken hophead who walks in.

"I'm in a town called Foolsburg."

"Foolsgold."

"I'm gonna live with a family here, a lawyer. . ."

Oliver's anus muscles clench.

"No, wait, I fell in love, that's it, I fell in love with a chick. Fuckin' A, that's why I feel weird and happy, I'm in love. Some more pieces are comin' together – I'm in your house, right?"

"Correct." He chokes on the word, has to clear his windpipe.

"You gotta be her father."

Through the window, Oliver sees lights go on in the Bel-Air Camperhome.

The creature in the kitchen lurches forward, stretching his hand out in greeting, a hand smeared brown with a mis-hit gob of peanut butter.

Oliver is gone, outside the kitchen door, into the back yard, striding in panic to where Elora is removing suitcases from a battered old Mercedes. Her hair is magenta and short. She looks tough and wise. Her hug is joyous.

"We just drove. I didn't know how to call you, to tell you. Oh, Dad, I'm so excited!"

"What do they want him for?"

"He's a little loaded, I drove most of the way. God, I told him to be quiet, did he wake you?" The words bubble out as she hauls a couple of guitar cases from the back of the car. "I thought we'd bed down in the trailer. I was going to explain everything in the morning."

Oliver's brain races, tries to assess the extent of her break-down.

Here he comes, stumbling outside through the kitchen doorway.

"This guy is a friend of yours. That's what you're saying?"

"He had a collapse a few months ago, you probably read about it."

Oliver stares at her blankly. He looks at the old Mercedes,

about a '65. It has a peace symbol stenciled on the back. The bumper sticker reads, "Happiness is Coming."

"Dad, he's C.C. Gilley."

Somewhere he'd heard the name.

"C.C. Gilley, I went head over heels for him when I was twelve. For God's sake, Dad, C.C. Gilley. That poster above my bed."

Yes, above her bed, the same creature as on the lawn. In the poster he was back-lit, half-naked, tortured and powerful, flailing at a guitar. Oliver looks away from Elora, his first-born, to the all-too-real version of C.C. Gilley, weaving toward them.

"He's burned out," Elora says. "I'm going to nurse him back to health." She adds, "We're in love. It's an utter mindblaster."

Jesse Gonzales' four-wheel Scout sweeps around the driveway into the orchard, and he steps out with gun raised.

Tennyson the watchdog finally comes wandering out, curious.

"It's okay, Jesse," Oliver says.

"Well, what's the trouble?" He's nervous.

"A mistake," Oliver says. "Elora came back suddenly. Surprised me."

Jesse eyes C.C. Gilley, who seems to have lost purpose and is wandering aimlessly toward a cherry tree. "You sure?"

Oliver puts his arm around his friend's shoulders, tries to urge him back to his vehicle. "Gee, I'm sorry about this, he's a friend of Elora's, we're going to put him up for a few days. He's been sick."

Jesse turns around, looks one last time at Gilley. "You do not speak in jest."

C.C. Gilley is on his hands and knees, vomiting bread and peanut butter onto the grass.

CHAPTER

3

Oliver is unable to return to the womb of sleep that night. After Elora put Gilley to bed in the camperhome, Oliver suggested she might prefer to stay in the house. *Don't be old-fashioned, Dad.*

He's an alcoholic, Oliver remembers reading that somewhere in a magazine. Man with a big problem.

Must be fifteen years older than Elora.

Sleeping with her.

Somehow this C.C. Gilley had convinced her of his love and vilely seduced her. How could she do this to her dad, lose her innocence to this animal? He should never have let her go off to the city. She was naive, unready.

Don't a lot of these rock stars shoot heroin? If C.C. Gilley has AIDS, Oliver will kill him.

Standing by his window as dawn fills the eastern sky, he stares out at the trailer. She's sleeping with him in there. Next to his body.

It's an infatuation, no question, not love, Oliver has seen the girls go through it with other pop stars. *I so love you, Van. Oh, Michael, do you even know I exist?* Most of this at the age of ten, however.

He'll sober up, he'll realize he's been on a bender, and go home after coffee. Elora-less. If God is just.

An infatuation, not the real thing.

His perfect daughter, Elora, a groupie to a washed-out drunk. The good burghers of Foolsgold will be clucking and cooing over the news: hey, Mabel, guess what the mayor's kitten dragged home.

How would Madelaine have dealt with this? Is there anything in the manuals about eighteen-year-old innocents bringing home an alcoholic rock and roll singer?

Oliver will talk to her. He has been planning his speech. *I know you think you're in love, and you're probably pretty charged-up emotionally, and sometimes that makes it hard to think things through...* He'd be calm, understanding, eloquent, he would let her know he loves her, but that she must hear him out, he's her father, and wise.

It is not until mid-morning that Elora – she's in long pyjamas at least – yawns her way from the trailer to the house, where Oliver waits in the kitchen, furiously quaffing coffee.

Elora plants a kiss on his forehead. "You're losing more hair. Makes you look sexy."

"Sit down."

"Oh-oh. A heart-to-heart."

"You've got that right."

"You have some things to say to me for my own good." She goes to the stove and pours herself a coffee. She carries herself with a sureness he's never seen before, the sureness of lost virginity, of womanhood.

Only six weeks from home, completely ruined, he's failed Madelaine.

What did he do wrong?

Calm thyself, act confident. But into his speech, he loses his false cool, and his voice cracks. "Look, I know you think you're in love, and you're probably finding it a great goddamn burden to think clearly, if you can think at all, but you've just bought a big problem. C.C. Gilley may be a pop star, but he's also a soak. You want a guy that's going to end up like old Gus Pritchard, who you see every Sunday morning drunk out in front of the

Seven Street Bar with his pants half off? He's twenty years older –"

"Fourteen."

". . . He probably shoots junk, he's probably gone to bed with ten thousand schoolgirl whores with every disease known in the panoply of medicine, and he's a *drunk*."

He can tell he's getting red in the face. Slow down. The coffee is jangling through him, it feels like he's backed into an electric fence. Softer: "He'll cause you pain."

Her voice has empathy, as if she understands. "I sense a parental crisis."

He gets up and pours another coffee. She follows him, takes his arm. "Dad, contrary to what you want to believe, I'm growing up. Growing up people fall in love. Yes, I do have sex with him."

"You using anything?" he mumbles. Condoms preferably, he can't say it.

"I'm not trying to get pregnant, if that's got you worried."

"Will you listen me out? Really concentrate, because if I have to say I told you so, I want you to remember."

"Dad, I know about people with drinking problems. I had two summers working in that hostel. I'm going to make him stop drinking. I can do it."

"With the power of your love. You're infatuated, suddenly you're Wonder Woman. Elora, there's a difference between love and infatuation. Love is what you feel for members of your own species. This guy's from another galaxy. If you're honest with yourself, you'll see it as an old unfulfilled adolescent dream. But I hear her talking about growing up."

Elora flares a little. "Well, I think you're just jealous. Single father loses daughter, I read about it in *Psychology Today*, it's a big crisis."

"She's become a pop psychologist."

He slumps back into his chair, and Elora pursues him, kneels on the floor, sets her chin on his knee and stares at him with the tolerance one reserves for a stubborn child. "It'll be different when you get to know him."

"He's not what I think."

"No, he's not, Dad. He's not a phony. He's caring. I know he seems a little rough around the edges at first look, but when you get to know him you'll get to like him. If you stop blocking."

Oliver's coffee tastes sour, like defeat. How much hurt will she endure before this is over?

"He's in love with me, Dad. He really is. It's something you just know."

"The great expert on love." Oliver finds his eyes dampening. He can't let her see him cry. He twists away from her unyielding gaze and pretends to stare soulfully out the window. But she reads him, and takes his hand.

"You didn't raise a brainless older daughter, Father. I know I'm not as smart as Lindy, but I do have, you know, *common* sense? That comes from you, I've inherited it. I mean, everyone says I've pretty well been created in your image, in terms of personality. Real conservative. Don't make mistakes."

"I'm hardly a conservative." He's a civil libertarian, a Democrat.

Yes, okay, he'll give this Gilley the presumption of innocence. Before he runs him off the property.

Lindy comes in sleepy-eyed from her bedroom and sees her sister.

"Elora!"

"Wait 'til you see what I brought home."

*   *   *

The big Husqvarna growls with a full throat, then screams with the kill as it bites. Oliver eases the chain out, then makes the back cut, and the thirty-foot fir topples neatly between two plum trees. The saw chuffs on idle as Oliver sizes up his next victim. These firs are choking the sun from the orchard. He'd been putting this off. He should have done it in April, when the plums were blossoming.

22

Elora comes racing barefoot across the lawn. "Dad, he's still sleeping."

"It's a quarter of four, he's been in there for thirteen hours. Anyone checked to see if he's breathing?"

"He hasn't slept for a while."

"I can't let the world stop because I've got a rock star in the back yard."

Oliver sees she's looking past him. Her expression softens, and Oliver feels a rush of tenderness toward her.

He turns to see Gilley at the trailer door, in underpants, gaping about him in total bewilderment. But when his eyes set on Elora, his face breaks into a crooked, crazy smile.

*   *   *

"This is the place to work up some songs," Gilley says, knocking back the last of his red wine. "Starting tomorrow. Tomorrow my manager comes up, Jodie Brown, with a little four-track studio. It'll just go nicely into the trailer there. May want hang some baffles up, sounds like a transistor radio down a hole in there."

How many weeks are you planning to stay? Oliver would like to ask. He pokes at his food.

Gilley pats his belly. "As cooks, you ladies are outa control, man." He refills his glass and raises it in a toast. "Lindy and Elora."

Lindy toasts back. "To love."

Elora throws a slice of garlic toast at her. The girls have been carrying on all day, whispering excitedly in the kitchen. Lindy is on the side of love, Oliver feels deserted and alone. They sit side by side, The Lovers, holding hands under the table.

"This is absurd, man," Gilley says. "For twelve years I been writing love songs. Fakin' it." He leans toward Lindy. "I'm gonna tell you something. I never been in love before."

"Honest?"

"It's the weirdest feeling." He turns smilingly to Oliver. "Look, Mr. Gulliver – "

"Call me Oliver."

"Oliver. Look, I know you got some second feelings about Elora and me –"

"Gil-*ley*!" Elora wails.

"Naw, your dad wants to be out in the open, and we'll both feel better that way. I have a drinking problem. I know this, eh? I'm gonna stop. Midnight tonight. I'm gonna write songs. I'm gonna get healthy." He sips his wine and beams at them. "This is what I been missing out of life – a family scene." A family scene, Oliver learns, is what Gilley has not known since his adopting parents split up. When he was eight.

Oliver learns a lot about Gilley this night. The young man becomes garrulous as he gets into Oliver's stash of Napa Valley Zinfandel. There is a guileless openness about him, that Oliver will reluctantly add to the inconsiderable positive side of the ledger.

After the dishes go in, they retreat to the living room, and Oliver makes a fire and listens to Gilley relate his stories of the hard life and the high life. Being sixteen, pasting together his first neighborhood band, playing cinderblock high school gyms where it sounds like a firecracker in a tin can. On the road in an old Ford van, travelling by Arkansas credit card – a siphon and a pail – scratching and clawing for gigs. "Bubble gum music, the songs are for shit, Credence Clearwater, Sedaka, but you cover them all, if you play something different you start a stampede to the bar."

When he started getting dates in the good clubs in Vancouver, Baceda's, Oil Can Harry's, a scout for Oriole Records discovered him, their legal department engineering a contract that tied him up for ten years in options. Gilley is bitter about this, he sees himself as a downtrodden victim of the record bosses. The capitalist pigs of the L.A. record industry suck everything they can out of a guy, then say, "Next."

Still Oriole Records made him a star. "Plain Brown Wrapper," his first hit, instant rocket, number one, a million copies. But Oriole Records had him hooked into that miserly contract, fifty grand for a platinum record. He earned better on

24

the road, backing up for the Flying Burrito Brothers first time out. Then the headliners, North America, Australia and Europe. Nobody worked a building like Gilley, he tells them. Nobody got the crowd going like him.

Oliver adds arrogance to the negative column. Still, it's not the overweening self-importance he expected of your typical so-called rock idol. But where are the stories of the skinny teenaged tramps that board the bus at the end of the show? What about the drugs, does not cocaine flow like lava?

Gilley gets a little drunk and starts railing again at his record company. It was the unfair contract that did him in. Hoping to break it he sabotaged Oriole with two bad records, political and angry.

The records killed his crowds. Bitter, he hit the bottle hard. Maybe he was a drunk before that, but it never affected his performance. He failed to make tour dates, he collapsed six months ago. It's history. He tells them he understands his problem, he'll be off the booze tomorrow.

After the wine runs out, Gilley and Elora return to the trailer. But he doesn't go to bed.

He sits on the redwood deck outside the trailer door, singing to an acoustic guitar, drinking cognac until the cold stars fade into dawn.

CHAPTER

4

All night, blues from the cracked, ravaged voice of C.C. Gilley made Oliver's dreams depressing. In the morning, feeling worn, Oliver sent Lindy off to wheel her grandma to the Sunday service at the Methodist Church. By early afternoon, neither Elora nor Gilley are stirring in the trailer. Oliver, lapping stain on the trailer deck, has all senses attuned for emanations from within.

He's staying two months, he announced, long enough to write an album of songs. We'll see how long he lasts, Oliver thinks. He will play saboteur, a subtle terrorist to this unblest love affair.

Gilley and Elora don't make a match. They're too different. She's an innocent, he's blighted, he's seen too much of ·the world.

Still, he's something different from the usual routine, interesting, like an extraterrestrial in the orchard. He's a big star, Foolsgold is abuzz.

He's an alcoholic, it'll end in massive hurt for her.

As he begins to work open another can of stain with a screwdriver, he hears thudding from within the trailer. He turns to stone, immobile, listening to a pounding that is also loudly in his heart, a sound that continues for cruel minutes. A long, sweet moan: Elora. Gilley gasping, then, "I love you!"

"Oh, Gilley!"

"Sweet Jesus!" Gilley bellows like a stricken bull.

She utters a sharp: "Oh."

Silence. Oliver, his face the color of a ripe tomato, quietly slips his brush into the paint thinner and creeps back to the house.

He wanders anxiously about the kitchen for a while, putting things in the dishwasher, wiping the counter down, then goes to the den to study the budget the town secretary-treasurer sent up to him. Maybe he should find the money for the policing estimates, get Chief Gonzales an inexpensive rookie cop, the Five Street sewer can wait a year. On the other hand, there's very little crime in Foolsgold. His mind drifts worriedly to Elora.

He wishes Madelaine were here. It's not easy to be a single parent.

He starts as Elora's hands circle his face from behind him. She touches her lips, cool and moist, to his forehead, and says, "We gonna be pals?"

Oliver's not some rabid redneck when it comes to child-rearing. He's read the progressive manuals.

"I love you, kid. Just keep your head on straight, don't make any rash decisions like engaging him or something, and we'll take it day by day."

"He wants to marry me."

Oh, God.

"But I told him, he has to win your approval. That's the deal."

*   *   *

Oliver silently steams as he finishes staining the deck. Gilley had greeted him at the trailer door, grinning behind dark glasses . . . brandy on his breath. Oliver will get him alone, away from Elora, hand him the walking papers. That's it, he's had his chance.

Gilley sits under a nearby tree with Lindy, showing her a few chords on an acoustic guitar. "Like this, eh, one note's gotta

27

blend into the next, no hard pickin' to chop it up." Gilley takes the guitar from her, plays a few bars, a melody so gentle it soothes the savage beast in Oliver's heart. "You barely touch the strings, the light touch, like Hendrix."

"That's really pretty," Lindy says.

"Pretty in the city," says Gilley, and he starts singing, "Pretty small-town girl in the city, won't you take pity, I'm a fool of the city. And I am to blame, don't laugh at my pain."

"I think that is utterly brill."

Gilley talks as he plays the tune again. "Came to me about ten days after I met her. Two days after we fell in love." He looks up at Oliver, who retreats from eye contact, from Gilley's smile, and goes back to his brush.

"There I was hidin' out from the fascist running dogs of the Graham F. Harley Detoxification Center, sittin' on the bed of her little apartment, watchin' her dress, lovin' her, so gentle and real and sweet. Music fairy touched a wand to me, and I leaped outa bed and went racin' for the guitar." He closes his eyes and sings, "Oh, pretty small-town girl in the city, ain't you got pity, for a fool from the city. She's pretty eyes, she's pretty wise, she don't listen to my lies."

Oliver stops working again. A curious energy seems to issue from Gilley, narcotic, haunting, yet poignant, it pulls you to him despite everything. . .

He's a drunk.

"Don't laugh at my pain. Who's impressed by my fame? Who can guess at my shame?"

Oliver catches on – it's Gilley's autobiography, a confession to a small-town girl he met in San Francisco. Oliver hears in it the loneliness of a long-distance slide, Gilley's fall from rock god to rock bottom. "I was idolized, but she don't sympathize. She sees behind my thin disguise."

It's a love song to his daughter, a ballad you'd call it, bluesy, pained, honest. Good tune, catchy lyrics. Oliver has what his daughters deride as middle-of-the-road ears, but there's some rock and roll he likes, Simon and Garfunkel, John Denver. And this isn't bad either, he hates to admit it.

Gilley seems to slide within himself, vanishing inside his music, his eyes closed, his mouth shaping silent words, his hands caressing the guitar like a sexual thing as he explores his melody, improvises. After a while he's seems not here any more, no longer on the property. Lindy looks captivated, hugging her knees on the grass.

Elora comes from the house wiping her hands on her apron, and she stands facing Gilley, thoughtful.

It is a long time before he looks up and sees her. "How long've you been here?" he says.

"Fifteen minutes. Where were you?"

"Man, I'm not sure," He sings the verse again, "She's a small-town girl in the city, she's so pretty, pretty small-town girl in the city." He laughs, plays his guitar and talks. "Met her on the Mason Street cable car. She told me she don't date guys she don't know." He comes down hard across the strings, damps them with the heel of his hand. "She don't *know* me. I had number one and six videos in 1984, she don't know me."

"He was wearing a suit. I couldn't believe it was C.C. Gilley."

Oliver watches Gilley's fingertips bubble across the strings, a clear, romantic line, a different tune.

"That's how I smuggled myself outa the detox unit," he tells them. "Borrowed the counselor's suit, eh." He plays an escape jig. "On the cable car, I says to Elora, you don't date guys you don't know, how do I get an introduction?"

He puts the guitar down and reaches a hand up and pulls Elora gently down beside him and kisses her. "Yeah, small-town girl in the city. I figured I had to save her from its cruel maws."

Elora pulls a little away from him, wrinkling her nose. "Gilley, you've been drinking," Elora says softly. "This is Day One, remember?"

"Just a little eye-opener."

"Please, Gilley." Her tone is serious.

He turns to Oliver as if seeking escape. "Oliver, I need some advice. I'm being sued by my record company for breach of contract. Also by my booking agent, my manager, my previous lawyer and eighteen hockey and basketball arenas. I want to hire you as my new lawyer."

A long, strained silence as Elora stares down at him, hurt.

"I had just one. Listen, I got to face Jodie Brown today. I need the strength. And speak of the devil."

Gilley gets up, hands the guitar to Lindy, as a fat old Dodge van swings around the driveway, circles through the cherry trees to the trailer, and lurches to a halt.

Jodie Brown climbs from the truck, looks around. She's chunky, with a squashed face like a wrestler's. She doesn't look happy. She brushes Gilley away as he tries to kiss her.

"I wanna plow you, that's my first reaction on seeing you," she says. "I can smell your bad habit on your breath."

"You ain't lost weight," says Gilley. "On the other hands you ain't lost your looks neither." He announces, "Okay, my manager Jodie Brown, this is Elora's kid sister, Lindy, playing lead guitar, and Mr. Gulliver."

"Call me Oliver."

"An honest lawyer, I had to go to Foolsgold to find one."

"And the little Japanese genius in the van is named Yamaha," Jodie says. She opens the back doors and they look inside at Gilley's new high-tech portable recording studio.

"Four tracks, computer memory," she says. "Loads of outboard, search and find, presets, fuzz tones, phase-shifting, reverbs and echo-send. It cost twenty-five grand. Let's see, that on top of the twenty-five you already owe me comes to a nice round fifty."

"Soon as I sign a record contract," Gilley says.

"You got a record contract," she says.

"And I got some songs happening." He gets into the van and Oliver helps him unload the portable studio. "But I ain't giving them to Oriole Records. I'm not going to crawl around their feet eatin' their scraps no more. I'm going to an independent."

"You got a place we can talk?" Jodie gives everyone an apologetic look.

"In here." Gilley grabs Oliver's arm and leads him to the

trailer. "I don't go nowhere without my solicitor." He throws some clothes off a couple of chairs and sits Oliver down. Jodie stays outside for a minute, conferring with Elora. Oliver sees them through the window, the two women talking gravely, as if plotting.

"She makes me nervous." Gilley is looking at the opened bottle of Remy Martin on the counter by the sink. "I'm gonna ease off the drinking, tailor it down a little each day. If I go absolute cold turkey I won't be able to work." He pours himself an inch into a tumbler.

"I won't allow Elora to play second fiddle to a bottle," Oliver says fiercely. The strength is in him now, he's finally alone with the foe. "You don't kick it, I'm kicking your ass out of here."

Gilley holds the glass waist-high, like a gun he doesn't dare draw.

"Listen, I'm gonna taper off, that's the plan."

"You take one more sip and I'm packing you back with your manager."

At this, Jodie Brown joins them, picking up the tension, looking at Gilley with his glass of cognac.

"You told me you were coming up here to dry out and write songs." She shuts the door, and studies him, an object of disgust.

"Jodie, I need a small advance. I can't expect to scunge off the Gullivers."

"You're getting no more from me."

Oliver shifts uncomfortably in his chair. He's broke. Great. A simplifying factor in any lingering debate in Oliver's mind.

"I don't see any royalty checks coming in. Why is that, do you think?"

"I, uh. . ." Gilley has a guilty look. "You know how it works. You assign your songs for a bunch of money. You spend the money. Some fat imperialist in an office collects the royalties." He shrugs, just holding that glass of cognac, white-knuckling it.

"You sold your best songs, huh?" Jodie shakes her head. "You don't feel like such a big rock star with your head in the toilet, I bet. V.S.O.P. may be okay as an addiction to a big star, but it's too good for a bum." She grabs the glass from Gilley's hand and pours the cognac down the sink. "You're a drunk."

"You're a fairy princess," he says stiffly. "How are the guys?"

Jodie turns to Oliver. "His career came to an end at Madison Square Gardens a year ago. When they booed him he urinated onto the front row. You can't keep your fans when you piss on them."

"How are the guys, I asked."

"Kelly Lagrange is doing some sessions work in L.A., keyboard dubs. He's waiting. Buddy-Joe Boogie Bronson is playing drums for J. Geils, filling in for a few weeks. He's waiting. Winston Ogumbo has been admitted to the Zen monastery in Carmel, and he's taken a five-year vow of silence. But he's waiting."

"Blinkie?"

"Blinkie Smith, forget it. You need another bass player. He's just signed up with a new band. Long Tom Slider and the Joy Flakes. It's a built-up pomp rock band. Great talent except for this six-and-a-half-foot blow job as singer. He's a real space cowboy, Tom Slider, useta play around Indiana as Flush Gordon and the Plumbers."

A muttered curse. "I always figured he'd let me down. Defected to a glitter band? One of those like Queen, they all wear costumes?"

"Yeah, there's still money in schlock. Blinkie couldn't handle your act, pal. Says he won't work no more with a juicehead."

Jodie pauses to light a cigarillo, and it fills the trailer with heavy smoke. "You heard Royalty Distillers just bought out Oriole, your old record company. They're going to put out a hip new wine cooler, Long Tom Slider and Blinkie Smith and the Joy Flakes are gonna tour it, and it's a megabuck campaign."

"Yeah, it's the music business all snuggled up in bed with corporate momma these days, ain't it? Bands hyping cigarets and beer and Crapsi-cola, Madison Avenue fucks art in the ass every time. Blinkie's actually gonna take part in that? Blinkie? Wearing makeup?"

"Big bucks for him."

"Well, there's a thousand starvin' bass players out there, eh. Find me one and tell the other guys just keep waitin'."

"What is everyone waiting for?"

"The songs are comin' like crazy," Gilley says. "This is corn-ball, Jodie, and I know you're too emotionally fucked-up to understand it, but ever since I fell in love, songs have been rollin' off me like sweat. I got one, it's like a gentle kiss between the cheeks, it'll be a moonshot."

"You got it written out?"

"You mean like on one of those papers with lines?" He snorts. "Sheet music is for people who don't have no ears. I got it written in here." He points to his head. " 'Small-Town Girl in the City.' Nobody hears my songs until I finish my demo tape." He draws his tongue around his dry lips.

"So I tell Oriole to be patient."

"You tell Oriole to suck. They're not getting these songs."

"You're behind on two albums and you'll owe them another next year. It's a shitty contract, but back then you were too smart to need an agent, huh, Gilley?"

"Where is that contract?" Oliver says. He'll be a lawyer, look for loopholes.

Jodie digs into her briefcase and gives Oliver the contract. Oliver first looks to see if it was signed right. You can sludge through a thirty-page agreement looking for unenforceable clauses, and then find staring you in the face that someone forgot to sign it.

"Just tell the guys to hang in, I gotta have a couple of months' solitude. Then we'll tour the bejeezus out of the U.S. and Canada. Just a couple of months. I'll come up with ten big hard diamonds."

Oliver sees it. "Their last renewal letter isn't signed."

Jodie comes over and looks. "There's a signature."

"That's the witness, probably a secretary. It's in the name of the president, Benjamin Ford, but he didn't sign." Oliver's proud of himself.

"I mean, is that major?" Jodie says.

Oliver riffles through the boilerplate language at the back of the contract. It'll be here, a standard clause. He reads, "Clause 42, paragraph bracket f, 'A renewal of option is valid only if in writing, signed by a person authorized.'"

Gilley claps his hands.

"You don't owe them any records," Oliver says.

Jodie is thoughtful. "Never noticed that. You need two more months, huh, Gilley?"

"Jodie, believe me."

"But you owe me, sweetie, fifty big ones, money I went to the bank for."

"And I'll pay it back."

"Okay, let's have a bet. Fifty G's you ain't got the balls to last two months without taking a drink."

Oliver senses that the main challenge is to manhood, the money is symbolic.

"Oliver here has already had the graciousness to tell me he's gonna ride my bum outa town. He don't approve of the relationship." Gilley shakes his head sadly. "Elora wants his blessing."

Jodie says, "And he ain't giving it, I can tell."

Gilley pulls out a wan smile from somewhere, and turns to Oliver. "Let's add some oomph to the bet. You wanna get in for a piece?"

"How much?"

"Your goddamn approval. All of it. If I get by two months without a drink, you pay off with your consent. 'Cause I'm gonna be proposing marriage to your daughter."

As Oliver tries to come to grips with the sudden menace of this dilemma, Elora opens the door and pops her head in. "Dad, Mrs. McGuid is here, with that minister. To sign a lease for the Opera House."

Oliver remembers, he'd told them to come by. He looks outside – Mrs. McGuid is taking Gilley's guitar away from Jamey, slapping his hand. That smiling cherub, Reverend Blythe, is looking around the grounds as if adding up Oliver's assets. Oliver, doing inner battle, turns back to Gilley.

"Okay, you're on." It's Oliver's own hoarse voice.

Feeling wobbly, he gets up to follow Elora out to the guests, but Jodie grabs his elbow.

"Stick around for ten seconds, Oliver, let's see if he can last that long." She pours an inch of Remy into a glass. She moves to a position in front of Gilley, and she swirls the cognac. He stares defiantly back.

"So smooth," she says. "Doesn't bite the nostrils."

"You can't jerk me off."

She takes a sip, barely touches her tongue to it. Gilley looks outside, as if pretending something out the window has distracted him.

Jodie doesn't move, hovers like a vulture. She takes another sip, rolls it around her mouth, and swallows.

"You ain't got the testicles to quit. You're a spineless coward."

Gilley stands up with fury on his face. Oliver sees fist fight possibilities, he better usher the visitors into the house. He goes outside and closes the door.

He is five steps from the trailer, putting his best smile on, when he hears the sound of a glass smashing, and Gilley's muffled roar, "Get outa here, you dirty old dike!"

Jodie opens the door and marches savagely toward her van, barely looking at Blythe, who has been sneaking up to eavesdrop.

Gilley charges after her, bowling over the little preacher, who falls back onto his rump on the grass. "You're fired, you ugly shit!"

"You won't make it, pisstank!" She climbs into the van.

"Stuff it up your glory hole!" Gilley screams at the top of his lungs.

The van moves around some trees, then onto the driveway and down the hill.

Gilley looks around, as if coming to, finding himself standing in a deep and utter silence surrounded by three Gullivers, little old Sybil, fat Jamey and pastor Blythe checking his pants for grass stains.

"Jeez, I'm sorry," Gilley mumbles.

35

Oliver works up a brave, hearty laugh. "Uh, this is a friend of Elora's, C.C. Gilley."

The pastor's eyes are hard little slits as he looks Gilley over, assessing him. Is this him finally, Satan incarnate?

"Your name isn't unknown," Blythe says.

Gilley looks for rescue to Oliver, who comes up with an awkward little handclap. "Well, now who's for coffee or tea?"

Silence. The reverend is looking at Gilley's bumper sticker, "Happiness is Coming." He says, "Sister Sybil and I have to get back for evening service. We'll just sign the lease."

Jamey is again playing with Gilley's guitar. "Put that down," says Mrs. McGuid. "You don't know what diseases." She turns to Oliver. "I'm rather pleased to tell you, Oliver, that your late wife's brother was at the service this morning."

"Clarence *Boggs*?"

"Brother Clarence has confessed Jesus as his Savior," says Blythe. "He came forward on his knees. Praise the Lord."

A warm glow suffuses Oliver. "Praise the Lord," he says.

▶ ▶ ▶

"This organization you speak of. What's its purpose?"

"To protect us from the mind-enslavers."

"Who are?"

"The media. They're controlled by a mental telepathy device the Russians operate from a radar station near the Arctic Circle. I can't tell you any more than that."

"This is a sort of paramilitary spy group?"

"Maybe."

"Did they issue you any identification?"

"Of course not."

"Nothing in the name of Sergeant Pepper?"

"That's just my code name."

"And they sent you on a mission, you say."

"Yes."

"To kill?"

"My brain was joined to theirs."

"And how does the organization give orders to you?"

"I can't say more than this: on some record albums one finds secret messages."

"Who is at the head of the organization?"

"I'm not empowered to say that."

"Where is it based?"

"Washington."

"Has it something to do with the government?"

"Of course."

"The White House?"

"The President doesn't know. We've had to protect him."

"The military? The Pentagon?"

"There is contact. I can't tell you any more."

"Because it's all hokum, isn't it, witness?"

"Objection. Argumentive."

"This is proper cross-examination, your honor."

"Yes. Objection overruled."

"You've created a delusion conveniently barren of detail, some secret organization that you fabricated to excuse murder. I put it

37

to you this is all just an imposture."

"Believe what you want."

"You want us to believe you're insane, yes?"

"No."

"What then?"

"I want you to believe I am not insane."

"So you were of sound mind when you shot those two persons?"

"Of course. The organization doesn't take on anyone with missing gears."

■ ■ ■

CHAPTER

5

Oliver Gulliver dreams a silky dream of Raquel unclothed, moving toward him, desperate for his body. . .

A horn blares, and he swerves hard right to avoid being squashed like a bug by a loaded logging truck barreling out of the mist down the middle of the road. It's dangerous to day-dream here on the Redwood Highway, where trucks and trees loom suddenly out at you from the sea-fog.

He feels fine, strapped into his Chrysler LeBaron, heading south to home. Maybe he's not Melvin Belli, he's not a grandstand show, but he wins his share, including the drunk driving this afternoon in Crescent City. Pretty good for a small-town lawyer. He caught a cop in a dumb falsehood, contradicted him with his own notes, and old Judge Cotter threw it out in disgust. It's good to know your local judges, that's where that smartass lawyer up from Sacramento blew it, got his client six months for stealing from an honor box. The savagery of it all captured old Cotter's imagination.

Near the Trinidad exit, the sun pierces the mist and he glimpses a girl in brief shorts and long hair, a guitar case over her shoulder and her thumb in the air. Oliver slows. She's pretty, a smile, a flash of sun on her face. Then he sees her bearded boyfriend hidden like a radar trap behind the salal bush, and as Oliver accelerates he sees his tattoos. Punks. The boy gives Oliver a finger as he passes.

Oliver gets enough of freaks, a month of C.C. Gilley in the back yard, the first two weeks of which were the literal screaming meemies. But he hung in, the alcoholic sweats are gone. Oliver gives the guy credit – but more credit to Elora and her calm ministerings. They're still in love, rapturous and blind, and it's beautiful to see in a way, but frightening, too, and Oliver keeps asking: how can this be happening to him?

For Gilley, need to write songs has replaced need for drink. He composes with urgency, repressing his addiction. All night you can hear him and his guitar, the words coming scorched from his ruined throat. He's not regulated by the sun like normal people.

It's all a nourishing bone for the townsfolk of Foolsgold to gnaw on, gossip being the major industry after trees, but no business lost. He has persuaded Sybil he's a man of good deed, he's saving a poor wretch's soul from the hell of alcoholism.

But does he wish this young man success in his struggle against whatever demons of his mind haunted him into alcoholism? Is not the payoff of this two-month bet a little too rich for Oliver's blood? Mrs. Elora Gilley, God forbid. Oliver should have bargained better, he should have held out for two years of drinklessness.

Continued good news on the Clarence front. His conniving brother-in-law is still finding Jesus every Sunday at the True Word Pentecostal Hall, the ex-Opera House, a place for which he holds the insurance account. He has not spoken again to Oliver those unspeakable thoughts about running off to Los Angeles.

Here's the little gravel road that leads to the little cabin wherein lives Raquel. Maybe it's her day off. Maybe she's outside on the grass, lying in the sun. Maybe he should . . . No.

He slows at the town limit as C.C. Gilley's 1965 Mercedes comes down the hill from the right, from Oliver's house, not stopping for the sign. Once in a while after he wakes up, the guy goes for a drive, his stereo blaring. *The only important music is music in a movin' car, eh?* Now he can see Gilley is singing into a microphone which plugs into his custom-built two-track dashboard recorder. He's always revising lyrics. Gilley waves to Oliver, a cigaret pinched between his fingers. His Mercedes roars past, receding, a sweet whiff of pot, and the car wallows into the rear-view mirror and grows small.

Oliver assumes cannabis is safer than booze, you don't become so hooked or get quite as stupid. Gilley says he's smoked grass since he was ten. Oliver can't say no, all the kids around here do it, this is Humboldt County, Oliver's even tried it. But Gilley better not try turning the girls onto crack or something.

Oliver is still figuring him out. He offers surprising moments of vulnerability, he's open, gregarious, roguish. Behind the buffoonery he seems wise and tricky. He's too flip, hiding something. His caring for Elora seems genuine, Oliver's got to admit it, and she's happier than he's even known her to be. She's strong, she'll survive the inevitable crash. Oliver will wait it out and be there.

Oliver turns off the highway, churns up the hill to his place, and now he can see the Town of Foolsgold, and now the log-piled shore and the crags and cliffs and the endless patterned ocean and the distant wake of fishing boats. Melancholy foghorns hoot. All things considered, including the occasional wafts from the pulp mill, the cold, wet winters, plus C.C. Gilley, middle age and unrelenting horniness, things could be worse, he could be just one more ant in the ant pile. He can enjoy imagined greatness in his daydreams, but meanwhile he's mayor of Foolsgold, king of Castle Gulliver.

For a second, he thinks it's Madelaine in the kitchen, and he has a moment of heartache. Lindy turns around in an apron covered with flour, it's a big oatmeal cookie operation. She gives him a peck on the cheek.

"I saw Gilley take off south," Oliver says. "I guess it's too much to hope he'll keep on going."

"Dad." A chiding tone.

"He owes us for about five hundred dollars worth of phone calls. The guy claims he used to take home fifty thousand from

41

a concert. Where did all that go, did he ever buy a savings bond?"

"Don't be such a grump. I'm making some stuff for the party."

"What party?"

"Last Friday in July Day. Remember?"

A local rite the Foolsgold kids celebrate. Oliver forgot, this year it's at his place.

"Gilley's going to play for us," says Elora, behind him.

Oliver turns around. What had she heard? Her eyes are wet and hurt.

"Sorry," says Oliver. A pause. "It's ticks me off that he doesn't seem to appreciate. He settles into this place like I owe it to him, he's gracious enough not to complain when the ice cream runs out." He rumples Elora's hair. "Sorry. Hey, I *like* him." Don't get pregnant, is all Oliver asks. Just let the thing burn to an end and gently gutter out.

"Well, he really loves you, you know, he takes you for granted because he treats you like a father, that's what fathers are for, he never had his own." Elora tosses her hair. "Whatever you think of him, you're helping a great artist, Dad, comparable in your day, say, to Bing Cosby."

"Bing Crosby," he says.

"Three platinums and eight gold. Almost all songs he wrote himself. And he hadn't written a song in two years before he met me. I've helped him, we've all helped, and his music is coming, six songs this month. He wants eleven or twelve, he's halfway there."

She stands proudly away from her father.

"We're getting him back on his feet."

*   *   *

Oliver looks out the bathroom window while shaving and sees C.C. Gilley's returned Mercedes. The two hitchhikers Oliver had passed on the road emerge from the car with packsacks, tents, and guitar cases.

Oliver strides through the kitchen wiping shaving cream off his face and neck. "Squatters. He's going to try to turn this place into some kind of a hippy colony."

"Oh, be cool, Dad," Lindy says. She and Elora are still organizing party food.

Oliver goes out back to where Gilley is saying, "Here he is now. This ain't like the city, eh, people are friendly here, you can walk off with their right arm. Hey, Oliver, these are a couple of musicians, we're going to jam a little."

The hitchhikers look a little in awe of Gilley. "What's your names, I forget," he says.

"I'm Garson," says the punk.

"Everyone calls me Splint," says the girl, smiling brightly at him.

Oliver and Garson can't look each other in the eye. The punk had insulted Oliver on the highway. Oliver had accelerated away. Why does he feel guilt? Garson had been pimping in the weeds, offering his girlfriend. He's mid-twenties, she's five years younger, she doesn't look so pretty close up, more tarty. She has a man's undershirt on, with nothing underneath it. Splint catches him staring, and he glances away.

"I'm going out," Oliver says, "but there's some cold cuts the girls fixed up if you want to get some food happening." *Get some food happening.* He's hip.

Splint protests. "Oh, no, no, please, we don't want to be a nuisance, we just ate at a burger joint."

"There's food for an army," Gilley says. "You guys can stay in the trailer, or Oliver's got a spare room in the basement."

"Actually, if we can just pitch our tent," Splint says.

"Yeah, sure, that'll be fine," Oliver says quickly.

He follows Gilley into the house, down the basement steps to the roughed-in bathroom there.

"Do you know these people?" Oliver asks.

"They're musicians, eh, that's all you gotta know." He pisses into the toilet while Oliver stands in the doorway. "They ain't members of the union, they play the streets, that's where you start."

"This Garson looks like he could clean your house out like a whistle and be gone in five minutes."

"You're a mean mistruster, Oliver. They're from Vancouver, my home town, they haven't grown up in crime-ridden fuckin' America, they never learned to steal. They're on a spiritual journey to San Francisco." He sings as he zips up. " 'Wear some flowers in your hair.' I was a fucking precocious hippy looking for God on the Haight. Twelve years old. Got kicked outa school, went home and told my mom I was going to California. She said I'll pack you a lunch."

Gilley, washing his hands, stares at his lean, wrecked face in the mirror.

"I'm thirty-two," he says. "I lost my youth somewhere."

"I'm fifty and my best years are ahead of me," Oliver says, wanting to believe it. "I figure there's justice there somehow. God evens us out."

"I seen God." He splashes water on his face. "God comes when you're out in front of thirty thousand people, suckin' in their high and giving it back to them, and wanting your guitar to eat you alive. It's a form of communion."

"I didn't think you were religious," Oliver says.

"Well, I'm a sort of evangelical reformed Buddhist. And whatever else is goin'."

*   *   *

Oliver picks up a bucket of chicken from the Mister Rooster's and a case of beer from the liquor store and goes over to Jesse's house, just as glad to be out of the kids' hair. The two Gonzales boys are grown and gone, and Friday nights Jesse's wife is usually at ladies' bowling, so Oliver and Jesse traditionally kick back, checkers or crib or a game on TV or just bullshitting about Foolsgold, America, and funding the Contras.

"Sure Bush was in on it," Jesse is saying. "Sure Reagan knew the basic idea. Sometimes in the national interest, if you're the president, you've got to take the law in your own hands."

"They *broke* the law!"

44

"So assign me to the case. I'll bust them for contempt of Congress. I need a big crime, I'm going stale. Say, ain't you discomforted about all those kids at your place?"

Discomfitted, yes, he is, and he realizes he's been wrangling over politics nervously, keeping his mind off things at home. He has extracted conditions, no underage drinkers, everyone outdoors, no one in the house. He doesn't want Garson and Splint in there packing up his appliances.

They go from politics to family, and after his fourth beer Oliver finds himself talking about Elora, his doubts about Gilley, his consuming concern about what Madelaine would have advised. Jesse asks him why doesn't he find a female "concert" to help run things at home.

"The girls wouldn't be able to adjust to it."

At about eleven, as they're planning an August weekend up at Oliver's fishing cabin, the phone rings. It's Ernie Bolestero.

"A fire?" Jesse says.

Fire, the word hits you in the belly. His house, the kids on a drunken, Gilley-inspired rampage.

The chief looks white. "The Opera House. It burned down, just like that, in an hour."

Oliver's thoughts are suddenly on insurance, on Clarence. There better not have been any mistakes with that policy.

A few miles out of Foolsgold the horizon glows sickly, and in the cloudless sky smoke obscures the stars. On Madrona Street barriers are up, and volunteer firemen are hosing down embers.

Mayor Gulliver looks dejectedly at this latest cruelty to Foolsgold, the glowing ashes of this grand old building. The Opera House, a legacy of his past, gone. Maybe God didn't want it desecrated by the scheming Reverend Blythe. He doesn't see the pastor or Sybil McGuid among the red-shining faces of forty solemn friends and neighbors still here.

Ernie Bolestero comes up to Oliver and Jesse. "Some of the guys say gasoline, it went up so fast," Ernie says.

"Who the hell," Oliver mumbles.

"Kids, maybe," the chief says sadly, "there's been no end of perturbation about closing the movies down."

"It won't be kids from this town," Bolestero says. "No way, right, Oliver?"

What's the client-napping Bolestero doing out so late? Probably working the busy streets, passing out cards. "Sybil McGuid been around?" Oliver says.

"Her and Jamey and Reverend Blythe," Ernie says. "I did my best to calm her down." Always in like a dirty shirt.

Where's Clarence? Oliver wonders. Hopefully he's with the good Reverend Blythe, helping console Sister Sybil.

CHAPTER

6

At one AM, Oliver, tense and fretful, wanders from the house. He'll try to be with it, hang out with the kids on the lawn, while Gilley, on the campervan doorstep, serenades them with some of his old songs. The hitchhikers, Garson and Splint, had long ago stopped trying to keep up with him. Oliver could tell they weren't much good as musicians. But big, fat, sashaying Jamey is up on the deck, playing bass guitar, he knows all the songs. They play into mikes, amplified and pretty loud.

Where the *hell* is Clarence? Nobody saw him at the fire. Oliver went to his house, the lights were on, and his Tempo was still in the carport, but no one home.

Lindy comes up to him and hands him a beer. Gesturing at Jamey, Oliver says, "What's *he* doing here?"

"He kind of hitched a ride up with some of the kids who went down to check out the fire. It's okay, he's happy."

He'll have to drive Jamey home. Sybil will be having an aneurysm.

"It's a kind of down party, isn't it?" Lindy says.

There's a weight of sadness. Apparently everyone left the party for the fire, and about thirty of the older kids reassembled here just before Oliver returned. Where's Clarence?

He looks around for delectable Raquel, but she's not about, a loner.

47

Here's hot stuff, though, Splint, thin legs and shorts, dancing barefoot on the grass.

Lindy wanders off, and he dreams guiltily about lust with Splint under a cherry tree. After a while he can't take it any more. Maybe he'll go to bed.

"Play us one of your new ones," someone says.

"I don't know," Gilley says, "I think it's bad luck. Mainly because you get song pirates, man. Lurkin' in the tulies."

"Aw, come on."

Lindy says, "Sing 'Small-Town Girl.'"

"Anyone got any tape recorders, I want 'em produced in front of me."

Elora, sitting by his knees, says, "Honey, they're friends."

"Listen, I love you folks, but I get psychotic about my songs, eh. It's blues, Jamey, we're in C for four bars, then F, just do this riff, if you dig it." Gilley twangs a few chords. Jamey has the beat, nothing to it. "And you do dig it. Far fuckin' out, man, whip it up, you're the total cat's ass, Jamey."

His guitar drowns his voice as it picks out "Small-Town Girl in the City," and he starts singing the verse, "Oh, pretty small-town girl in the city, ain't you got pity, I'm a fool of the city. . ." You kind of get used to his voice after a while, it's ragged, almost harsh, but there's something compelling, it's raw and real. Singers don't sound like Vaughn Monroe any more.

Oliver will take Jamey home after this song. He wanders up to the driveway in front of the house, and sees the lights of Foolsgold like a checkerboard below him. In the center, a red and blistered tooth gap, is the gutted Opera House. Who did it? Why?

Garson the punk joins him, stands beside him with his beer, staring down at the great rectangle of embers. Garson, who had stink-fingered him, a little drunk now. There's a skull tattooed on his left bicep.

"It's spiritual, man," he says. "Religious. The dance of Shiva, the destroyer. I love it when things burn."

A grade-A creep. Oliver walks away, goes to get Jamey. But Splint comes barefooting up to him.

48

"You a lawyer?" she says.

"That's my bag," he says. Her undershirt sticks to her from her dancing. She smells like ginger and salt, different from Raquel. Hairy armpits.

"Can I talk to you for a minute?"

Oliver doesn't like giving advice free. "Okay, sure," he says.

He lets her lead him around the driveway and behind a hedge, where it's dark and the noise is muted.

"God, what a blast," she says. "Imagine you're hitchin' rides and C.C. Gilley comes along. In the middle of fuckin' nowhere."

Fuckin' nowhere is Foolsgold. Oliver resents this. "What's the problem?"

"Like, I'm wondering if I can get deported, like? Back to Canada?"

"Why should you?"

"Okay, like I kind of skipped out on a beef in Vancouver. Would that be enough?"

"A warrant for what?"

She moves closer to him, her nipples bulbing from her wet undershirt. "Like, uh, for hooking?"

"Prostitution." The word sits pompously in the air.

"I was a little broke, like? I turned a few tricks and the cops made me on one."

These are the honest Canadians Gilley brings home. A hustler and her pimp. Oliver thinks of diseases, herpes, AIDS, but sexual juices are pumping through him. A hooker, it turns him on more knowing this.

"You didn't show up for your trial?"

"Right." She smiles.

"I'd be careful, that's all. They put all these things on a computer line."

"Maybe I better use another name." She steps closer, a touch away. "I'm a Sagittarius, what are you?"

"Aries."

"Oh, that's exciting."

Oliver holds his breath.

"We're broke. Thanks for the food and a place to pitch our

tent. Oh, yeah, and like for the advice, you know?" Then she puts her hand lightly on his arm and whispers close to his ear, "Do you want to fuck me in the tent for fifty dollars?"

Oliver feels compromised by an unbidden erection. "No, ah, that's not . . . no, I wouldn't, no."

"Okay, whatever, I just thought the way you were looking at me. This is for free." Up on her toes, she closes in on him, her arms around his neck, he's paralyzed by her scent, her hot tongue.

Their bodies turn intensely white, spotlit in the headlights of Sybil McGuid's Cadillac as it drifts softly around the curve. Oliver draws away in panic. The car parks twenty feet from them and the headlights go out.

Splint swirls away, dancing toward the orchard.

Darkness and silence. The music has stopped.

Oliver is in shock. His engine is racing but he's not going anywhere.

Car doors open. "Oliver?" Her skritchy voice.

"Hey, I was just on my way to your place, Sybil." He says this without choking. "With Jamey."

"He's here," she says with relief.

"Praise God," comes the voice of Reverend Blythe.

"Clarence with you?"

"No," she says.

He finds them and leads them to a knoll, where there is light. Nothing is said about what they have witnessed, but Oliver sees Sybil staring at Splint dancing amid the bundled bodies. Sodom and Gomorrah in the Gullivers' back yard.

Oliver will pretend they were hallucinating. He shows a calm, unflappable exterior. "Did you make contact with Clarence, Sybil?"

"Clarence has disappeared. No hide, nor hair. And he hasn't given me a copy of the policy on the Opera House. Or on any of my other properties for that matter."

A trap door swings open beneath Oliver's intestines.

"If he's run off with the premiums, I'm putting the blame right on your head, Oliver Gulliver."

"He was talking about going fishing," Oliver says. Is this true? Hadn't Clarence said something like that last week? *L.A., that's where you make the boola boola.*

"We shouldn't think the worst," says Blythe. "Clarence has given himself to the Savior."

"I think he is a confidence trickster." Sybil marches down to the party, looking for her son.

"Jamey's in the trailer, Mrs. McGuid," Lindy calls to her. "We've been taking extra care of him."

Oliver regains use of his muscles, races toward the trailer to try to head Sybil off. By now he has no reason to expect that a final calamity has not been planned for him. At the trailer door, he smells it, pungent, powerful, Gilley calls it his Mendocino Mind-Fuck. But Sybil is already inside, taking it in with her hawk-like eyes:

Gilley rolling another joint and passing it to Garson. And Jamey, his fingertips at his fat, puckered lips, sucking in the sweet smoke from a thick roach. They may be too stoned to notice Sybil, immobile there, as if struck by lightning.

"This weed is a fuckin' *mother*, man, you ain't ever got off like this before. I'll lay some on you, a few reefers."

Sybil lets everything go in one screech. "Jamey!"

As he turns and sees her, his eyes pop out, and he lets go the smoke from his lungs with a great whoosh, like one of those wind gods in the old atlases.

"Oh, boy, trouble city," he says.

CHAPTER 7

Oliver blinks awake, tries to shred the morose fog of his dream. He remembers recent Foolsgold history, and reality is worse than nightmare.

"Scumbag dirt chutes!"

Oliver feels a thousand-pound weight sitting on his chest, pinning him to the bed.

"Handknobs! Wanks!"

Gilley. Outside. A terrible sigh. "Je-sus Kee-rist."

Oliver drives himself to a sitting position and looks out the window. Gilley is in his undershorts standing about where his 1965 Mercedes used to be.

Walking outside, buttoning up his shirt, Oliver discerns that Garson and Splint have struck their tent and ripped off, it would seem, Gilley's wheels. He checks the garage and finds his LeBaron and the pickup safely inside. He'd made sure to lock them up. The mean mistruster finds irony here, it's bound to be the one light moment of the day. The mystic pimp and his dancing whore, *they're musicians, that's all you gotta know, eh?*

Elora is standing in pyjamas at the trailer door. "I remember thinking there was something weird about them."

"When did they leave?" Oliver asks.

"I dunno," Gilley says. "I was worn, I went to bed early,

about three, the car was still here. I wake up to take a piss, and it's gone. How do I get ahold of the local Gestapo? We gotta stop them at the border."

Oliver remembers Splint's tongue hot in his mouth, the two of them impaled in Sybil McGuid's headlights. He's feeling nauseated.

"Right," says Gilley. "Nothin' tastes so sweet in the throat as the words, 'I told you so.' Oliver, it's like a cross you carry when you been at the top. 'Hey, man, we ripped off C.C. Gilley's wheels,' that'll be their only fame. Man, I got half my tapes in there, my early Hendrix, collector's items, my. . ."

Gilley doesn't complete for several seconds.

"My songs! I was rehearsing them when I picked them rip-off artists up. My songs, my new songs!" He starts screaming again: "Wank-ers!"

"Better get down to the police station. I'll phone ahead." Oliver gives Gilley the keys to the pickup and goes inside and phones Jesse Gonzales with a description of the car and the probable occupants. Then he calls Clarence's number at home. No answer.

Lindy bounds downstairs. "Wow, what's the racket? Dad, you look like the torment of the damned."

She doesn't know her dad is stuck on a defalcated loan for a hundred and twenty thousand dollars that he signed during a day of dementia.

Oliver chokes down a couple of pieces of toast, then takes a drive across town to the little stucco house Clarence used to share with a girl from Kindleman's Hardware who finally left him, like a string of others.

If Clarence has gone on the lam, why is his Tempo still in the carport? He finds the house key where Clarence usually keeps it, behind the eaves, and inside he finds clothes and papers strewn about. Maybe there was a struggle, an incredibly stupid gang of kidnappers has taken Clarence for ransom. An empty suitcase open on the bed. In the kitchen, a three-quarters empty fifth of Old Crow. On the living-room table, his daybook.

Nothing much in it except, last Thursday, at ten-thirty AM, an appointment with "E.B." – Ernie Bolestero? Was Clarence, too, retaining the Competition?

Outside, he finds the keys to the Tempo still in the ignition and the battery dead.

He drives over to check Clarence's office, angle-parks in front of the Paradise Cafe. As he steps onto the sidewalk, Ernie Bolestero bangs on the glass of a window booth. Oliver has Bolestero on his list of people he doesn't want to see this morning, but he goes in.

Raquel, at the cash, looks up from a paperback. "Hullo, Mr. Mayor. You look like someone dragged you through a bush backward." From beside her, Mollie Chong's portable radio, sad country music issues.

"See the fire?"

"Yeah, it totaled me. Got depressed, went home, drank a bottle of wine and flaked. Heard there was a hot time up at your place, too. Make out okay?"

"What do you mean?"

"You know." She smiles too confidingly. The word of his unwilled encounter with Splint is out, a brushfire around Foolsgold. "The usual, double cream?"

"I'll manage." Oliver pours a cupful of coffee from the pot on the warmer and goes to Bolestero's table. Ernie looks wan and sleepless, and gives off an unwashed odor.

"I was up at the police station," he says. "Your daughter's boyfriend was filing a complaint about a stolen car. That must've been quite the party you threw."

"I didn't throw it."

"I heard you were there."

From Blythe? Ernie's been up and around, spreading mean gossip. Oliver is too weary to defend himself.

"I'll tell you who *didn't* set the fire," Bolestero says. "Your brother-in-law. How do I know that?" He leans toward Oliver and says softly and urgently, "I'm going to lay this on you, and it's heavy, so listen. What I was doing in the cop shop was filing charges against Clarence."

54

Oliver feels an Arctic chill. "Who made the complaint?"

Bolestero doesn't answer yet. "Sam Holden at the bank says Clarence moved about thirty-five grand over to a branch in Eureka last week. The manager there says the money was withdrawn on Wednesday."

Oliver brings the cup to his numbed lips, manages not to spill any.

"The thirty-five grand represents the policy premiums on Mrs. McGuid's properties, I know that for a fact. When the fire happened he panicked, skipped. Someone thought they saw him getting on the night bus to Portland, it left about half an hour after the fire started. So I been asked to lay charges."

"By whom?"

"Well, Sybil McGuid and Pastor Blythe, they asked."

Oliver hasn't had a chance to rise for the count and Bolestero is ripping off his clients.

"I told her I can't take instructions from you, Oliver's your lawyer, but she says she can't very well retain you to sue your own brother-in-law." Bolestero shakes his head sadly. "She's pretty sore at you, I'm afraid, she thinks you're to blame in some way. I said, no, maybe Clarence is a rotten apple, Oliver's a saint. I told her, I don't want your other business, Oliver's been doing it for years, and a damn good job, but I'll take on this one case. And since I'm going to be the pastor's lawyer anyway..." He shrugs.

Oliver's brain calculates. A hundred and twenty thousand dollars on Clarence's loan to repay. Losing Sybil McGuid to Bolestero, that's nearly two thirds of his income. What he earns doesn't even pay his mortgages. He's bankrupt.

As he drops some change in front of Raquel, she says, "Have a good day."

8

"Small-town life is not for me."

Oliver lowers his newspaper, the *Eureka Times-Standard*. He's in the Paradise Cafe, the townsfolk are gossiping happily at nearby tables, and drifting around him are the spicey scents of the fresh coffee and the pretty waitress. Oliver is about as cheery as a man waiting for the hangman's trapdoor to drop.

"What did you say?" Oliver asks Raquel as she fills his cup and drops two creamers on the saucer.

"At least life in *this* small town isn't for me. The movie's too wacky. Features not only the town drunk and the village idiot, but the broken-down rock star and the totally depressing mayor."

"You quitting?"

"Moving on."

"Oh."

She stares down at the pitiful hunched form. "Well . . . keep smiling."

She leaves. He studies her languid, rolling ass, and tries to imagine, but he can't get it up for Raquel any more, things are that bad, the fact of her bading Foolsgold farewell adds only negligibly to his collected misery.

After many frozen days of immobility following Clarence's flight and his own financial collapse, Oliver decided on Reaganomics: cut back to the bone, sell his bonds and his few stocks, advertise the fishing cabin, the Bel-Air Camperhome. That might clear half of Clarence's hundred and twenty thousand dollar debt, but he's still stuck with two mortgages and five mouths to feed, if you include Tennyson and Gilley. All to be maintained on less than half his former income.

His worst fear is that he will have to lay off Mrs. Plymm. No, his worst fear is that he won't be able to send Lindy to college.

Mrs. Chong is in the kitchen, the waitress is chatting with some of the millwrights, a country singer wails about a truant lover, it's ten AM, and Oliver hasn't the heart to go up to the office and face Mrs. Plymm and tell her there's nothing to do. Two divorces and a dog-bite case in the three weeks since Black Friday. What was it, the twenty-ninth of last month, Last Friday in July Day.

C.C. Gilley, a man still enfevered by his work, is one for whom the shattering of Oliver's world deserves only perfunctory concern. *It ain't the collapse of Western civilization.* Gilley knows what it's like to be the victim of fate's fickle finger.

Adding to Oliver's woes, Gilley tonight completes two months without a drink. Midnight is the deadline, according to ground rules solemnly agreed upon. At midnight Gilley threatens to propose to Oliver's first-born, his innocent lambkin.

Although Oliver still stubbornly declines to picture him as his son-in-law, Gilley has kind of sunk into his skin, and for all his excesses the young man is capable of love, which is something, and he truly likes Oliver, and has been able to lift him occasionally from his depressed stupor. He works at his art twelve hours a night, he's not lazy, and he's fought the good fight against drink.

On the other hand, he seems the gremlin behind the recent black events, maybe he possesses evil power. Pastor Blythe: *Your name is not unknown to me.*

If Gilley is Mephistopheles, Jamey is Faust. His corruption continues - Sybil does not know he sneaks out his bedroom window every other night to jam in the Bel-Air Camperhome.

Gilley says Jamey is going to get some credits on the album. They are buddies. Oliver must reluctantly give points to Gilley for that. Big pop star comes to town and befriends the loneliest guy in it. All the locals treat Jamey as if he's not there. His only pal was Clarence. Gilley's good for Jamey, and Oliver isn't going to fink to his mom. But there's talk she's going to send him to a home.

I got to free Jamey from her clutches, I discovered a musical genius here in this weird little town, it's like finding a rough diamond as big as your fist in somebody's back yard.

Ernie Bolestero came by yesterday, apologizing and pillaging, taking off with five more of Sybil McGuid's files. Rev. Blythe has profited, too, Sybil building him a new church on the ashes of the old.

The insurers have had to pay off, stuck with a contract signed by Clarence, their lawful agent.

L.A., that's where the boola boola is. Film industry. Somehow, Oliver will get it all back from Clarence, if he has to skin it off.

Elsewhere on the crime front, although Jesse Gonzales has alerted the state police, neither Gilley's Mercedes nor its thieves have been found. The loss of the car causes Gilley only mild dismay - he has taken custody of Oliver's pickup - but he's much oppressed by thoughts of his tape getting into wrong hands: a Maxell cassette, on the label, in green felt pen, the great composer's signature and the date he recorded it from his portable Yamaha for road-testing. "Gilley, 29-7-88." On it, various versions of "Small-Town Girl," plus a few others of his tunes. The cassette was still in the dashboard recorder when the car was stolen.

Oliver managed to get Gilley's songs registered with the U.S. Copyright Office by August fifth, a week after the theft.

Oliver looks up from his newspaper to see Gilley pulling up outside in the Toyota, Elora beside him. Grinning ear to ear at Oliver, he's triumphantly waving a reel of tape.

Elora stops on the street to talk to some girlfriends. Gilley enters the Paradise Cafe as if he owns it, turns the radio to a rock and roll station, kisses a startled Raquel on the cheek, pours himself a cup of coffee, and sits across from Oliver.

"The good news is I've finished my demo tape." He thrusts it into Oliver's hand. "For you to copyright, counsellor. The bad news is I'll be leaving you for a while. My manager and me are going to L.A. to cast my music like pearls before the swine. I'm not signing any contract until you tell me it's safe, eh. If I'd of found you years ago, I wouldn't have got tangled up in all those option clauses."

Gilley checks his watch.

"It says here, Friday, August nineteenth, golly, gee whiz, that's two months to the day we made a bet. Cough up the parental consent, Oliver. Give it to me with glowing heart, I don't want you begrudging me."

"Fourteen more hours," says Oliver. "We agreed on midnight."

"Let us not stand on technicality." He chuckles, Oliver's never seen him so ebullient.

"You and Jodie made these foolish bets not knowin' I was made of steel. Yes, I will enjoy to see the expression on her face when I turn up sober on her doorstep with an album that will knock her knickers off. Songs about what nobody understands unless they're there." He sighs, looks out the window at Elora. "Songs from a whacko lovesick mind."

To Raquel, he calls out, "The usual, m'love." He returns to Oliver. "I called the last song 'Paradise Cafe.' Lotsa local content. 'The Fat Lady Don't Sing No More' – it's about the night the Opera House burned down. This is grass-roots America stuff, it'll be like *Born in the U.S.A.*"

Gilley now studies his silent companion closely. "What happened, I stumble into the funeral parlor by mistake? What's with this never-ending anguish of yours, you're like a European movie. Listen, I made unwise investments, I know what it's like to go in the hole. I once had a ranch, mines, all sorts of stuff that got foreclosed. Money ain't important, it can't – "

Oliver interrupts sternly. "If you tell me it can't buy happiness, I'll throw up. It *can* buy happiness, damn it."

Gilley chuckles. "All your troubles happened since I came on

the scene. If you was superstitious you'd think I was to blame."
He reaches across and claps a hand on Oliver's shoulder.

"All right, man, do me a favor and listen. This is important, eh. I come from a homeless home. I been damaged through lack of love. The people that adopted me fought over custody. Neither of them wanted it. It's what made me a drunk, when I look back on it. I was unwanted, and I couldn't handle failure when it came. So this is the first family I ever really had. And I know you kind of like me, even though it's hard taking a steady diet, and you gotta respect me for getting through two months without a drink."

"I'll give you that," Oliver says.

"I got plans on how I'm gonna become an official part of this great American family," Gilley says. "When we launch the tour, you'll give her away in the Superdome." Gilley laughs again, Oliver's being teased. "The point is, don't *worry* about money, man, I ain't gonna let anything happen to you, you took me in when I was down and you'll be under my wing when I'm soarin' again."

"When does this flight take off?"

"You goddamn sourpuss. Listen, I love your daughter, I want to marry her. I got pride, I think I earned your approval. Let's just put that bet aside, and you tell me right now where your head is at about Elora and me."

"It scares me."

"*I* scare you."

"I've known alcoholics."

"I don't need it no more. It's over."

Raquel drops a glass of milk in front of him and floats away.

"Ah, milk, yummy." Gilley takes the glass and downs it.

Elora joins them.

"It's cosmic," says Gilley. "Today I locked in the final mix, and today your dad pays off his gambling debts. We're right now negotiating the terms of surrender."

"Hmnf," she says. "What is this, a slave auction? I'd like to hear a formal proposal before I decide. Anyway, I think I've decided I'm too silly and immature to get married at this time. Dad's right."

Gilley reaches for Elora's hand and armed with that, he squints in close to Oliver, and says, "Tell me you want me to be your grandchildren's father."

Oliver stares at the milk-daubed upper lip of C.C. Gilley, and his gaze travels up the bony and slightly crooked plane of his nose and locks with his hungry eyes. For better or for worse, Oliver thinks.

"I hope you'll be happy," he says.

"I love you, Oliver." Gilley slides off the bench, and leans over and kisses Oliver on the forehead before he can fend him off. Everyone in the restaurant is staring. Elora is laughing.

Gilley slips to his knees in front of her.

"Miss Gulliver, ma'am, I'm hoping it would not be regarded as overly bold of me to offer myself to your lifetime service."

Gilley seems about to say more but Oliver notices his expression alter, focusing elsewhere. Oliver is reminded of the look on Tennyson's face when the dog hears a distant, interesting sound.

But there's not such a sound in the café, aside from everyone's breathing and the radio in the background. Gilley's eyes protrude – Oliver's first thought is he's lost this new family member to a coronary occlusion.

The pop tune on the radio, Oliver realizes. That's what took Gilley away from here. Oliver thinks: many times of late I've heard this melody.

"That's my song," says Elora, breaking the wall of silence. "My *love* song!" She gets up and runs to the counter ands turns the volume up.

Gilley rises, his voice choking. "That's . . . that's 'Small-Town Girl'!"

It is and it isn't. Same tune, different lyrics.

"I'm goin' down for the last time." Raunchy male voice. "Don't pull the rip cord, I'm goin' down, I'm goin' down, I'm free falling for you."

61

They are gathered at the radio. The singer punches out the chorus, heavy and dirty, "Goin' down, goin' down," and a barely audible whisper of soft female voices comes in behind his phrases. "For you" or "on you," it's hard to make out.

"That's 'Small-Town Girl in the City'!" Gilley bellows.

"Goin' down. For you. Goin' down."

Oliver, Gilley, and Elora stand there stunned as the song fades under the D.J.'s voice. "Hey, this is rock and roll all day, boss forty on K-WAC, that was something they just snuck under the door, it's not bad, Long Tom Slider and the Joy Flakes, you're going to hear a lot of it, 'Goin' Down for the Last Time.' We'll go two in a row after this word – "

Gilley drowns out the radio.

"Those wanks that ripped my wheels . . . they were song pirates! I knew it!" He turns to Oliver. "You heard it, it was my song!"

"Yeah, sure sounded like," Oliver says.

"Long Tom Slider," Oliver says, "where did I just see that name?" He returns to his window booth and starts leafing through the newspaper.

"Blinkie," says Gilley, "Blinkie Smith, my ex-bass player, Jodie said he was with a new band, Long Tom Slider and the Joy Flakes. *This* band. What's going on?" He gets up, walks over to Raquel at the counter. "Man, have you got a phone book?"

She brings it out and also passes him the telephone. Everyone else in the restaurant is silent, staring. Mollie Chong, at the kitchen door, calls out, "What the matter, you guys?"

Oliver wonders as he pores over the newspaper: Garson and Splint, hired song pirates? Could they operate so quickly? Gilley's tape was stolen July thirtieth, this is twenty days later, and it's already on the radio.

"All the hits all day all night here at K-WAC, hey, honey, how about that sale down at Ironpants, half price on all summer stock – "

Gilley bellows into the phone. "That song you just played. Who wrote it, give me the D.J."

"Here it is," Oliver says. "Right on the back page. Long Tom Slider."

The full-page ad on the back of the *Times-Standard* features a face right out of whatever modeling agency Marlboro hires from. Tall and manly and relaxed, embracing a guitar, a drink fizzing beside him, nearby the plastic container it was poured from. The copy reads: "His name is Tom Slider. They call him Long Tom. His business is rock. His drink is Tinglewine, made with organically grown Chardonnay grapes and natural sparkling water. Good health to you. From Royalty Distillers."

Gilley's face is black with anger as he hangs up. "He says the songwriting credit is Tom Slider. The lead singer. A blow job and a space case, says Jodie. So somebody tell me what's going on."

Nobody can.

"Look what they did to my song! They raped it!"

▶ ▶ ▶

"Goin' down, goin' down, I'm goin' down for the last time."

"Want to do a thruster, Sergeant Pepper?"

"What's a thruster?"

"A cartwheel. Little yellow pill here?"

"How'd you smuggle those in?"

"You're in the master's presence, my man. I bring them under my foreskin. You notice how they looks up your ass, but they never peels the foreskin back? Try one, kinda like a orgasm without yer arm gettin' tired."

"No, thanks."

"Hey, Sarge, you think the organization's coming soon? My trial ain't going too good, and a screw jes' told me they call my judge Father Time."

"I'm goin' down for the last time, goin' down, goin' down. Don't pull the ripcord."

"You keep singing that, gonna be two crazy people in the holding cells. Are you really a box of animal crackers or is the D.A. right, you're storyin' everybody? Which is it?"

"I'll bet they sent you to spy on me."

"Yes, sir, ol' Goodweather gets a fifteen to twenty-five bounce for pain killer, and the dude that snuffs two people looks to get a nice stay in a rest home. Although maybe not, maybe not. Maybe a short stay in the gas works."

"Goin' down, goin' down."

"Yessir, goin' down to where the prince of darkness presides. I heard tell cyanide smells like peach leaves when it dissolves. Wonder who discovered that? Ain't no one ever reported back."

■ ■ ■

CHAPTER

9

Oliver Gulliver cruises north, on the 199 into Oregon, his Le-Baron sucking expensive gasoline. A dollar a gallon is suddenly a king's ransom.

He's living on credit cards.

To his right, the vast evergreen carpet of the Siskiyou rolls high up into the Coastal mountains as he climbs to Grants Pass. It's an expansive, brilliant August day that were life going well for Oliver, he would notice and enjoy.

At Skorsee College near Medford, southern Oregon, Dr. Aloysius Rigby, the famous composer, writes in residence. "Bring the tapes along," Dr. Rigby said on the phone. "Perhaps I'll be able to write an amusing little paper."

The girls had taped this apparently stolen song, "Goin' Down for the Last Time," and listened to it over and over, comparirg it with Gilley's version. Same chording, tempo and harmony, in verse and chorus. Gilley ranted like a madman. They had stolen his anthem of love to Elora and in changing the lyrics had defiled it, made it evil and lewd.

Oliver's average ear told him the tunes were *almost* the same – some notes were different, not many. But how could this be? Coincidence? They say there is a limited combination of notes that sound well together, and they say a hundred thousand songs are written every year in this country alone. The chance of coincidence must be strong.

Plagiarism . . . it seems unlikely on the facts. After all, Gilley had written the song only two months ago, in late June, and already Long Tom Slider and Oriole Records had a single, an album, and a video on MTV. Slider mashing his pelvis at the screen, the whole performance quirkily obscene. His daughters say, reluctantly, he's a hunk, a natural actor.

Oliver had run a check, and found Oriole Records filed a demo tape of "Goin' Down for the Last Time" with the Copyright Office on Thursday, August fourth, just two weeks ago – and just one day before Oliver registered Gilley's "Small-Town Girl." One day. That gives Slider and Oriole Records a procedural advantage. Their earlier copyright isn't conclusive evidence they own the song, but it puts the onus squarely on Gilley to prove the song stolen and Oriole's copyright invalid.

Gilley says he is as sure as the sun and the stars, Oriole Records, in their latest jihad against him, sent Garson and Splint up to Foolsgold as song pirates to rip off his work of genius. During the early hours of Saturday, July Thirtieth, they stole the car and the tape, and within a couple of days turned over the song to an agent for Oriole Records, which immediately filed for copyright. Long Tom Slider agreed to claim he wrote it.

Oliver is instructed to sue Oriole. Money, says Gilley, is no object.

Thus he spake in one of the semi-lucid moments of an alcoholic epic that is going into its sixth day. He took his first drink on the stroke of midnight that Friday night, sweating through the hours until the bet was officially won. On Saturday night, someone laid him out in the Foolsgold Hotel lounge and he was delivered up to the Gullivers in Johnson's taxi. Slowed him up for a few hours, that's all.

Oliver's suspicious nature has been rewarded with proof. Two dry summer months hadn't been enough to break the back of Gilley's bad habit. Gilley claims this is just a short backslide, he'll be okay when it's over. But Elora is holding firm: if Gilley wishes he can propose again after he stops drinking. It's chaos in the trailer, tears and recriminations and abject apologies.

Oliver realizes he had been hoping hard for something better from Gilley.

The last weeks had been cruel and busy: Oliver's ruin. The Opera House fire, an arson yet unsolved. The theft of the song. Clarence's heist of thirty-five thousand in insurance premiums. A thought keeps niggling at him that somehow all these events are not merely scattered wreckage abandoned by a prankish god. They're connected, there's covert logic here.

*   *   *

Oliver hums "Small-Town Girl" - he can't get it out of his head - as he walks along the corridor of the music building at Scorsee seeking a door marked Dr. Aloysius Rigby. They had looked him up in *Who's Who*. At forty-three, he had won two Pulitzers, composed fifty-seven major orchestral pieces and over a hundred chamber works. Supposed to be one of America's five foremost composers, although frankly Oliver's never heard of him.

He finds his door, pauses. Noises come from within, it sounds like a concerto for strings and cement mixer. He opens the door and gets it full blast, dissonant chords from speakers. A little seated man with a goatee turns from a computer console and brings fanatical eyes to bear on Oliver, then gestures to him to take a seat.

He does, and watches Dr. Aloysius Rigby's fingers attack the console as he intently studies information on the screen. If someone told Oliver these sounds originated in another galaxy, he'd accept it.

After several minutes, the sounds conclude, and Rigby says, "It's called 'Serenata del Fuego.' Do you enjoy art music, Mr. Gulliver?"

No introductions, no coming together by hands. The eyes could be those of an Iranian suicide commando.

"Art music," Oliver says. He's not sure what this means,

67

maybe a kind of classical music. "I'm afraid I've been left behind somewhere. Around Brahms or," - he tries to remember someone more modern - "Mahler."

"Why is it lovers of serious music can never escape the nineteenth century?" says Rigby. "Which is where Mahler belongs."

Oliver can tell he's put his wrong foot forward. "I heard something of yours on Public Radio. It was really interesting, I thought."

"The piece I am currently writing was commissioned by the Portland Symphony. I have been working on it for three months. I will be paid two thousand and five hundred dollars." He begins to raise his voice. "Some cretinous goon who is musically illiterate walks in off the street somewhere and makes two million dollars for a two-minute tune. I have to be subsidized by a bloody college. I am reduced to this, analyzing simple songs for simple minds."

He is barely in control by the end of this speech. He holds out a hand, palm up. Oliver finds the tapes in his briefcase and hands them to Rigby, who plugs one in, C.C. Gilley's version. He continues to talk over the song.

"This great and wonderful country spends more money on music than on movies or pro sports. Twenty billion dollars a year. I saw somewhere our annual sale of pop records in 1986 exceeded the GNP of eighty-two entire countries. At the age of three, I began twenty years of formal music training. I've had another twenty years of composing and conducting since then. I make less than the average American farmer."

He turns the volume down so he can be heard better.

"But America wants garbage, and the record industry is pleased to give it to them, perfect white pap, bee-bop-aloo, music for window cleaners to whistle."

Rigby doesn't even wait for the final chorus of Gilley's song to end. He snaps it out of his cassette player, then clicks in Long Tom Slider's version, and talks through it as well.

"But it's been the same through history. Bartok and Schoenberg in this century, impoverished. Bach and Handel in the eighteenth century, groveling to dukes and princesses for the right to create music. As I grovel to the National Endowment and the foundations. Meanwhile smoke bombs and flashpots explode around some gargoyle in a ripped τ-shirt who stands on a stage smashing τν sets with a sledgehammer and takes away a quarter of a million dollars for a night of music."

Behind him comes Slider, "Goin' down, goin' down."

"It's not only the sickest industry in America, it's the most pornographic. I believe there's a popular group called The Dead Kennedies. Their hit song is called 'Too Drunk To Fuck.' Depraved music that appeals to the crotch. True music must be intellectually understood. Do you agree?"

He clicks off the tape halfway through the song.

Oliver says, "Good music comes better the harder you listen, I always believe."

"You said you were a lover of Mahler, Mr. Gulliver?"

"Well . . . yeah."

He walks to a library of records, fingers through them. "I composed some variations on a theme from "Das Lied von der Erde." He pulls out a record. "This is a limited edition, the St. Louis Symphony. You might find it diverting. On the other side is my 'Agony of the Damned in Twelve Parts.' It won the Hartford Festival last year."

"I'd really be interested."

Rigby takes the record to a turntable.

"By the way," says Oliver, "those two songs, do you want to have a chance to – "

Rigby pauses at his turntable, seeming slightly annoyed at this intrusion, this change of topic.

"The two songs I have just heard," he says, "were composed by the same person."

He goes to a set of electronic keyboards, flexes his fingers, then plays perfect renditions of the chorus and verse of Gilley's song.

"Verse, chorus, and bridge repeat the same melodic characteristics, with some minor and doubtless colorable variations. Both are in the same time and key signatures, and have similar, though commonplace, harmonic structures and rhythm." He plays the chorus again. "That accent is transferred forward by just a quaver in both versions. This discord in the final bar of the verse is tell-tale as well. Musical fingerprints, Mr. Gulliver."

Images flash in front of Oliver of settlement negotiations, of his earning a large but fairly earned contingency fee.

"And what are the chances of your being wrong?" he asks. "If they claim coincidence."

Rigby half smiles, half sneers. "Not a billion monkeys playing a billion harmonicas for a billion years."

Oliver wonders if Rigby is too self-important to make a good witness in court. Opposing counsel could show him up as a bitter smart aleck. But Oliver's excited. "You'll put it in writing?"

"If you leave the tapes with me, I'll do a computer analysis. You will have a twenty-five page report. I am, as you have heard, feeling awkward financially."

Oliver brings out his checkbook. His general account is dangerously low, four thousand and falling, and there are many bills to be paid. He hands Rigby a check for five hundred dollars as agreed by telephone. "And five hundred more when I have the report."

Rigby looks at the check with loving eyes before pocketing it and going back to his turntable. "This was recorded live in St. Louis. There was a flu going around. One day I will compose a piece for orchestra and coughing audience. You have the time?"

"Sure." Oliver endures this, a captive audience of a genius rarely listened to and of music so atonal and unrhythmic as to make him feel his sense of balance is going.

The composer sits and faces his prisoner. Rigby's eyes are dark, intense beads, he's hungry for this small attention to his art.

Oliver is pleased, though, and will take his punishment like a man. This fellow will give a firm, unequivocal report, nothing wishy-washy. Armed with it, he can go to other experts and obtain concurrence.

But he fears ten thousand experts will not be enough to win a judgment in court. Oliver had spent a couple of days in the Humboldt County courthouse library. A terrible word kept rising from the pages of the casebooks. *Access.*

You have to prove access. You have to prove the defendants had access to a recorded or written version of "Small-Town Girl in the City." It means he has to find proof, independent of his expert's opinion, that the song was stolen.

The law of plagiarism in America was forever set on a day in 1924 when Judge Learned Hand pronounced three words in his famous court. "Coincidence makes innocent." And can coincidence ever be impossible? Thus the law says he must link the defendants - Oriole Records and Long Tom Slider - to Gilley's purloined song.

But how? Assume Garson and Splint make the link. How does one track them down - the police haven't found them - and how does one make them talk? He tries to recall his brief conversations with them. Didn't whoring Splint say they were going to San Francisco? Did they then go on to Oriole's head office, in L.A.?

How to contact them? They're street singers, beggars, underworld flotsam.

Is there a link through Blinkie Smith, Gilley's former bass-man, now with the Joy Flakes? But Gilley hasn't been in touch with him for a year. They haven't been on the best of terms.

Oliver closes his eyes and smiles and nods, letting Rigby know he is really into this, it must be eighth, variation of whatever it was that Mahler wrote.

He sees himself in court. The foreman stands. "We find for the plaintiff." The silver-haired judge beams down on Oliver. "Mr. Gulliver, that was the finest work I have seen done in my twenty years on the bench." The courtroom erupts.

Oliver comes out of this with a surge of dissonant strings, and opens his eyes to see Rigby's still on him, accusingly, ripping away all of Oliver's deceits. Oliver knows he doesn't have the courage to take such a trial on. The Federal Court is for him an unchartered water, and the sharks will eat him alive. Oliver's a G.P., a good one, but not an entertainment specialist. A family doctor doesn't do heart transplants.

CHAPTER

10

It's seven AM. Oliver is throwing his bags into the trunk of the Chrysler. Elora is leaning in through the back door giving goodbye kisses to Gilley, who is stretched out there with a pillow. Tennyson is jumping with excitement to see Oliver go.

"Don't come home with some terrible disease, Dad," Lindy says, kissing him on the cheek. "Do you have your calcium tablets?"

"Yes."

"Only drink the bottled water, okay?"

"Yeah, yeah."

Elora says to Gilley, "Don't let anyone give him drugs or something stupid. He likes to impress people with how hip he is."

"He is hip," says Lindy.

"I'm only going for a few days," Oliver says, "don't make it sound like it's the final assault on Everest." He gets in behind the wheel.

Elora closes the door on Gilley and kisses her father through the open driver's window. "You look after yourself, Dad," she says. Then to Gilley, "And you keep an eye on him, okay?"

"Hollywood will be at his feet when I get through with him. I'm gonna make Oliver Gulliver a household word." Gilley is back on the wagon again, and is making energetic promises to stay on it. He has some of his old cheer back.

Oliver edges the car onto the road and down it. They will first stop at Jodie Brown's office in San Francisco, then they're off to an adventure in Los Angeles, that hot pit of hell where the music barons rule their fiefdoms. He has five credit cards and five hundred dollars, and the written opinion of Dr. Aloysius Rigby, and a typewritten memorandum of facts, and a brief on the law. And he has an appointment with Tommy Klein of Klein, Ingle, the big entertainment lawyer. Oliver saw him profiled in *Trial Lawyer Magazine*.

He wants to set the pot aboil, there's no time to waste. "Goin' Down for the Last Time" is hot. Since its release last week it has quickly made it halfway up the Billboard One Hundred. "Bulletting up" is the expression, Oliver learned.

If the song became a million-selling record, what were they looking at in damages? Hundreds of thousands in lost royalties alone. Tommy Klein better not be expecting a retainer up front. What kind of contingency fee would he want? Oliver will try to keep him down to twenty or twenty-five per cent. While Oliver sneaks off to the lawyer's office, Gilley will track down Blinkie Smith and get the inside dope.

Gilley is quiet, unusual for him. Sleeping?

Oliver hasn't told him about Tommy Klein. Gilley claims he doesn't want another lawyer, just Oliver. First human in a suit he's ever trusted, Gilley insisted during one gushing melancholic moment of his drunkathon.

"Tinglewine," comes a voice from the radio, "made from pure Chardonnay grapes and natural sparkling water. Good health – "

"Turn it off," says Gilley.

Oliver does. He stops for the sign, then turns south on the 101. A hitchhiker, it looks like, with a guitar, down by the A&W entrance. And a big suitcase.

Oliver does a double take at the wheel when he recognizes the hitchhiker to be Jamey McGuid. He brakes hard a hundred feet past him. Gilley falls off the back seat and curses.

"What the fuck – "

Oliver reverses as Gilley scrambles up and looks through the rear window.

"It's Jamey," he says. "He's makin' a break for it."

"I have to take him home."

"Bull*shit*!" Gilley leans over the front seat, animated. "Mrs. McGuid's got no papers sayin' she owns him, you told me that. He's twenty-seven, this is America, home of the free, eh. He's a lot smarter than anyone thinks. He can play some licks, too. Why can't he go off and seek his fortune on his own free will?"

Oliver thinks about this, Gilley is eloquent. Jamey has enough together to pack a bag and hitchhike, who's saying Oliver has to deliver him back like a prisoner to his keeper? This is a guy who's managed three or four nights a week to sneak out of his house, from under Sybil's nose, and come and visit Gilley. But can he survive on his own?

Gilley decides the issue by grabbing Jamey's bag and throwing it onto the floor in the back, pulling Jamey into the front seat beside Oliver.

"Where are you off to, Jamey?" says Oliver.

"Hollywood."

Gilley says, "Me and Oliver will be stayin' at a buddy's in Venice, right by the beach, there's lots of room."

He crawls back into his back-seat bed. Oliver drives off.

We got to free Jamey from her clutches. Oliver says, "You set this up, didn't you, Gilley?"

In the rear-view mirror he sees him grinning. "It's me and you and Jamey against the world, Oliver."

*   *   *

Oliver sits on the arm of a sofa in Jodie Brown's office. Gilley is sunk into its cushions. Jamey, beside him, is beaming smiles at everyone.

Leaning back in her swivel chair, her fat ankles crossed on top of a desk blotter, her pug nose stuck out as if she's sniffing the music as opposed to listening to it, is Jodie Brown, giving ear to Gilley's songs a second time. After the first run through all she said was "Play it again, Sam." Gilley seems tense, awaiting her verdict.

Jodie's walls are decorated with gold records, some of them Gilley's. Her office is up on Mason Street, Nob Hill. Oliver spent a fearful half-hour maneuvering his car up and down the roller coaster streets in a fog, seeking a parking place.

What to do about Jamey? Oliver will have to confront Sybil McGuid, and tell her Jamey can survive on his own. If she wants, let a panel of shrinks prove otherwise under the *Probate Act*, a conservatorship application.

After the last cut ends, "Don't Wake Up," Gilley can't endure the pause. "Well, do you dig them or think they're ground meat or what?" Jodie silently looks at Gilley, and scratches her thigh. "Got some dynamite hooks, right?" Gilley urges.

Jodie's tape machine clicks off and she takes a little Dutch cigarillo from a box on her desk and lights it. Jamey remains smiling, confident.

"He actually lasted two months without a drink?" she says to Oliver.

"Just."

"I had a relapse but I'm goin' strong again."

Jodie grunts in disbelief. "You can get the band together? Winston Ogumbo?"

"How about you go down to that monastery and exchange notes with him. He'll keep his vow of silence, but that don't extend to sax and rhythm guitar. What do you think of the songs?"

"Still need a bass player."

"Forget Blinkie, I got a sub, Jamey here, I discovered him. He's a genius."

"That's me," Jamey says.

Jodie scans Jamey skeptically.

"Stop horsing me around, Jodie, what's the verdict?"

"Let's put number one aside, 'Small-Town Girl.' Two, four,

five, and ten are all better than any songs in your last two albums, although that ain't hard. Three, seven, eight, and eleven are two grades up, they're killers. I'd drop six and nine and go with four a side, you still got a record so deep we can pull singles out of it all year."

"I think she likes it," Gilley says to Oliver. He leans across the desk to Jodie. "Hey, man, if I wasn't afraid of whisker burn I'd kiss your face. But we ain't gonna put number one aside. 'Small-Town Girl in the City,' that's going out as the first single."

"Gilley," she says, "Royalty Distillers has a hu-*mungus* campaign going with that tune, it's a heavy breaker, it's Gavin's pick of the week, they're gonna announce it number seven on the Tuesday report. The video's number one. There's gonna be a fifty-foot Times Square billboard, Tom Slider knockin' back a glass of Tinglewine Cooler. It's big, big bucks. There's no record company is gonna want to get into a courtroom bloodbath with Royalty Distillers over this song."

"Well, my lawyer ain't afraid. It's *my* fucking song!"

"They'll say you heard it on the radio. You copied it."

"I wrote it over two months ago. I got an army of honest witnesses."

"I can sell the album without it."

"You ain't gonna. Oliver's got plans. We're gonna blast these weasels outa the sky."

He sweeps his arm around, introducing his lawyer to the crowd. Oliver feels uncomfortable, he doesn't like the way Gilley is counting on him.

"You could cover it."

"I ain't gonna pay royalties on *my own song!*"

"Then no one's gonna record it for you. Unless you can prove it was ripped off."

"Oliver'll do it."

"Yeah, he'll *really* do it," Jamey says.

"The best theory," says Oliver, "is Splint and Garson, who are kind of street musicians, turned on the tape machine in

Gilley's car, realized they had Gilley's new song and they hawked it to an agent for Oriole Records. Gilley thinks they're professional music pirates, but I doubt it."

Jodie muses. "Maybe they *are* pros. The word is Oriole Records were desperate for a hit for this album. They did all the publishing houses, hired a few name writers, but nothing good came out. They claim this goof Tom Slider, their lead singer, showed up at a recording session with it at the last minute."

"Well, that sounds pretty weak, don't it, eh?" Gilley says.

"Oriole came out with that song only a couple of weeks after Splint and Garson stole the car," Oliver says. "Is that possible?"

"I think so," says Jodie. "Two weeks to record it, do the mixdown, cut a lacquer and metal stampers, do the artwork. Yeah, it's possible, especially if they had to meet a deadline for launching their wine cooler. Garson and Splint, huh? Anyone talk to them two?"

"She said they were going to San Francisco," Oliver says.

"That's all she said?"

Oliver feels himself reddening. "We had a little conversation . . . " He's blocked that disturbing scene. *Do you want to fuck me in the tent for fifty dollars?* Her sticky body against him, in Sybil's headlights. A prostitute, and now he remembers her seeking advice.

"Yeah?"

"It's funny, I forgot. She said she skipped out of a prostitution beef in Vancouver, she was worried about being deported." He thinks. "There'll be a sheet on her. There'll be mug shots and prints."

He'll call Jesse Gonzales about that.

CHAPTER

11

After interminable hours of sweaty boredom on the endless I-5, Oliver yearns to wash up, but in Kelly Lagrange's cottage in Venice there is no bathtub, and the shower stall is full of wet babies' clothes. The little house, in fact, is full of wet babies, aged six months, eighteen months, and two and a half years. Kelly Lagrange's wife or whatever, Skylark, is pregnant with number four. She wanders about the house with a joint between her lips, doing aimless chores while Oliver dandles the kids, and Gilley, Kelly, and Jamey play music.

Kelly Lagrange is Gilley's former keyboard player, and he's learning the new songs. Jamey is right in there, a world of total ecstasy.

But this isn't Oliver's scene, outside or in. He had gone for a walk. Venice seemed an eerie place, full of strange beings. On Washington Boulevard, the street was ruled by tall, muscled men on skateboards. More muscles on display in an outdoor, fenced-in playpen on the beach, guys lifting weights, pretending to be oblivious to the people staring. Near the boardwalk, he encountered a freak under an awning offering Jungian therapy sessions at twenty dollars an hour. A pretty girl in a bikini had worked Oliver, a rube in a straight suit, for five dollars for cab fare.

Now he is back, sitting on his bed, which is to say sitting on a three-inch foamie with baby-handfuls of the fluff ripped out, it will be like sleeping on Swiss cheese. On the foamie is a sheet with some suspicious stains.

Oliver scrambles forward to pick up the year-and-a-half crawler, who is making a beeline for a cockroach.

In the corner of this hectic little living room is a color TV. The sound is off, but music video images appear on it. When do these people hit the sack, they've got to put the kids down soon.

Kelly Lagrange is a little mole, a few mustache hairs under a pointed snout. As he plays his electric keyboards, he can't stop staring at Jamey, who is smiling like a saint, his eyes closed, keeping up a driving tempo on his bass guitar. Oliver worries: what must Sybil be thinking? Jamey phoned her tonight and said he's okay, told her not to worry and then just hung up like that. Oliver feels guilty, then he sees Jamey's smiling face and realizes the fellow is free and happy, and what does Oliver owe Sybil?

Gilley is reassembling his band. They're going to rehearse, get down the new songs while their manager does a record deal. Buddie-Joe Boogie Bronson, Gilley's drummer, had been here earlier for dinner, which consisted of a family-size Kentucky Fried Chicken pail being passed around.

Tomorrow, while Oliver is sneaking off to Tommy Klein's law office, Gilley will track down his ex-bassman Blinkie Smith to pump him about the stolen song. Gilley has already tried phoning Blinkie, but no answer.

Skylark comes from the bathroom carrying a load of wet clothing, and Oliver escapes from the babies, gets his towel and bathrobe, and goes in to take his shower. He wonders if it's dangerous to shower in L.A. water. He looked kind of stupid bringing his own bottle of purified water from the store.

Cold water comes from the hot and cold water comes from the cold. If he could find an excuse that wouldn't offend his hosts, he'd spring for one of those cheap hotels nearby. He gathers strength, then stands benumbed in the shower for two minutes.

When he returns to the living room, everyone is watching an interview on one of the music channels.

"Dig this," Gilley says.

Long Tom Slider with a pretty interviewer. A glittering, silvery bead-studded vest drapes a bare chest. He's handsome and rangy, relaxed in front of a camera, although there's something slightly crazed about his eyes. Maybe it's the mascara. Or he could be on dope.

"I want to ask you about the title song of your album, it could be a monster, 'Goin' Down for the Last Time.'"

"Yeah, babe, I put input into a buncha the songs on the album."

Gilley snarls, "I'll give him input. A rod up his ass."

"How did you come to write 'Goin' Down,' Long Tom?"

He takes a drag from a cigaret, then leans toward her. She smiles cozily.

"If I tell you, you'll think I left my brains on the pavement."

"Who is this phony slice of fruitcake?" says Gilley.

"Like I hope my manager ain't watchin'. He says, talk about the weather, talk about the national debt, don't talk about how you wrote this song, everyone'll think you're jerkin' 'em."

"I'm interested."

"So okay, one afternoon I plugged in and I was just, you know, scrabblin' around, thinkin' of clever riffs, and I had this psychic experience."

"Psychic exp – " Gilley blathers. "Who gave birth to this guy, an inflatable woman?"

"Shut up, Gilley," Oliver says.

" . . . mystic, man, like I was transported," Slider is saying. "I mean I went through some changes. This is kinda heavy, but I'm layin' it out like it is 'cause people are always askin', right? And I heard this melody, this hook catchin' at me over and over again, and I realized, hey, man, bitchin' mondo, I just minted some gold, this could be a hit. Kinda worked up the lyrics later, the rest is in the press releases."

A manic grin. How had Jodie Brown described this fellow? A space cowboy, Oliver recalls.

"How's it feel to be a sudden success?"

"Hey, I'm spinnin'. I mean, ten years in the trenches, man, playin' jobs in all the juke joints. I feel like - what's that old flick? - Judy Garland, *A Star is Born*."

"This guy gets up your nose worse than McCartney," Gilley roars.

"What about the criticism that you're tied in with a liquor company, your tour's being sponsored by one."

Slider withdraws slightly, as if being delivered an unexpected hit. "Sure, Royalty Distillers, they're backin' us. Schlitz did The Who, I'm gonna argue with that? Z.Z. Top, Phil Collins, everybody's doin' it. It's like, industry supports the arts, right?"

"Whip off, you fascist fairy princess," Gilley barks. "You capitalist pig-sucking whore. Fag! Fudgepacker!"

Oliver tries to shush the furious Gilley, but the interview has ended.

Oliver wonders what this Looney Tunes will say about the song if he's under oath, giving depositions. A psychic experience: they could have thought of something more credible than that.

This could be an interesting case. Why is he giving it up to someone else? He's not such a coward in his dreams.

*   *   *

The verdant offices of Klein, Ingle are in one of the Century City towers. You need a machete to chop through the jungle here, some plants go right to the ceiling. The lawyers are dressed like they're in Waikiki - jeans, flowered shirts, there's one guy running around in here with a Panama hat. Oliver, in his suit, sees through all these not so laid-back lawyers, men and women hiding their big-city angst behind masks of L.A. cool, wondering if they should bother trying to save their latest marriage.

Tommy Klein has a good spot, a massive corner office from whose windows you can see the smog stretch for miles, east and south. Klein doesn't have a desk in here, what does he work off of? Jimmy Buffett or something coming from behind some palm fronds. Oliver sits on a high-backed art deco arm-chair sipping a capuccino Klein's manservant brought in.

Klein is supposed to be some kind of Southern California personality, you hear him guesting on open-line shows. Big, bushy 'stache and burns, a flouncy-sleeved peasant shirt open three buttons down a hairy chest. A gold chain with a peace pendant around his neck, a professional liberal. He's got slippers on, for God's sake, his feet up on the coffee table as he finishes reading Oliver's memorandum of facts. He's suffering from a runny nose, and sneezes occasionally. Must be from the air pollution.

Klein shakes his head. "C.C. Gilley has a reputation as a prank artist, old boy. They'll use that. They'll claim he stole the tune from Slider."

"That's impossible. We have witnesses."

"They'll buy better ones. And they'll hire half a dozen experts to say the songs aren't the same. They'll bury your Aloysius Rigby."

Tommy Klein flips the papers onto the table, and stretches and yawns.

"It'll be expensive, let's get that out of the way right now, old boy." *Old boy*, where does he come by this English affectation? "How is Gilley fixed?"

"He's flat broke."

"Let me background you. Two years ago Royalty Distillers was looking to go the way of the dinosaurs, it was diversify or die. Five months ago they bought Oriole Records and hired some bright boys from Madison Avenue to figure out how to work a record company to sell booze."

He wipes his nose with a big silk hanky, then lounges back again, yawns, his hands clasped behind his neck.

"They tried for some established bands, but stars like Huey Lewis or Van Halen would've eaten up half the advertising pie. So they decided to *make* a superstar, got this klutz Long Tom Slider out of Paducah or somewhere who never took home more than five hundred a night in his life but does great cock rock on the video, pretty good actor, they backed him with some major talent, and turned on the star-making machinery. That machinery only works if you've got a hit song."

He pauses for emphasis. "A thousand records a week are dumped on the market in this country and there are only two rules in moving ahead of the herd. One, get on the radio. Two, stay on the radio. Airplay is all, old boy. So you need a top forty breaker and 'Goin' Down' is it, it's hot, it's a moonshot. We're talking a fifteen-million-dollar ad campaign riding on that song. The profits from twenty million albums."

"Adds up to a big damage claim, Mr. Klein."

"We're also talking a two-month trial and sixty-thousand dollars in expert witness and investigator fees. That has to be paid out of somebody's pocket. In advance."

"The song was stolen, Mr. Klein. If the justice system works, we'll win."

Klein smiles a sunny smile. "Call me Tommy. They call you Ollie?"

"No. Oliver."

"What kind of practice have you got up there in Humboldt County, Oliver?"

"A little bit of everything. You get the odd big case." Why'd he add that?

"That's always been my dream, get off the fast lane, take off to some little place, surround myself with ordinary, loving Americans, not grasping thieves." He yawns again. "How do you prove access by Oriole, Oliver?"

"I'm thinking maybe evidence that the car and tape were stolen is enough. We've got Hein versus Universal Pictures – 'a striking similarity proves copying.' Inferred access. A federal court held George Harrison unconsciously plagiarized 'My Sweet Lord' even though he denied copying it."

Oliver has studied the law.

"Oliver, in 1977, three brothers by the name of Barry, Robin and Maurice Gibb, better known as the Bee Gees, were hiding out at an estate in France composing music for *Saturday Night*

Fever. They came up with a hit called 'How Deep Is Your Love,' and the album sold twenty-five million copies."

Oliver guesses Klein is trying to sell himself.

"Along came a guy, some antique dealer in Chicago, claimed to have written the song a few years earlier, said he sent it off to a bunch of record companies. He sued for twenty-five million dollars. The plaintiff's expert said in court, and I quote, 'The two songs have such striking similarities they could not have been written independent of each other.' Same as your expert. The judge found for the Bee Gees."

"No, a jury found for the antique dealer. Judge Leighton of the Federal Court in Chicago overturned the jury's verdict." Oliver sneaks a look at Klein, enjoys seeing the plastic smile stiffen.

"Whatever. It went to the U.S. Court of Appeals." He stands up, strolls to a computer on a table and types out some commands. "Selle versus Gibbs," he reads. " 'Proof of copying is crucial because no matter how similar the two works may be, even to the point of identity, if the defendant did not copy the accused work, there is no infringement.' That's what the judges said."

"They also said access can be proved on a reasonable possibility. By circumstantial evidence. Each case must be decided on its own facts, that's what they said. I know what the law is. I also know Oriole Records stole that song somehow."

Klein sips his coffee a while before saying, "You know, if I could clear the decks . . . yeah, I wouldn't mind taking this on, sounds like a break from the tedium. I know a damn good firm of investigators, we can probably get them for about five hundred a day. I'll tell you what, old boy, if you can come up with thirty grand for disbursements, I'll match you, and I'll gamble on a contingency fee."

Thirty grand. Oliver flinches.

"What kind of contingency fee do you think would be acceptable to Gilley?" Klein says.

"I was thinking of suggesting ten per cent for myself."

Klein looks shocked.

"Oliver, I charge out at seven hundred dollars an hour. I'm risking major dollar loss if we don't win this action. I'm in for fifty per cent or I'm in for nothing. And you should take twenty."

"What will that leave for our client?"

"What risk is he running? He obtains our services for nothing. He's probably more interested in vengeance than money."

"Fifty per cent seems pretty stiff, Mr. Klein, Gilley won't go for it. In fact, he doesn't go for retaining another lawyer. He wants me to handle it on my own."

Klein's expression combines astonishment and amusement. He sits there as if waiting for a punch line. "And what did you tell him about the wisdom of that?"

"If I have to do it on my own, I'll just do it the best way I know." He hears his own hot air. How many points can he shave from this grasping lawyer's fifty per cent?

"And what would be your first step?" Klein says.

"Apply for a preliminary injunction."

"In Los Angeles? Over a megadollar song?" He laughs. "Not the chance of a snowstorm in Singapore."

"I wouldn't file in the Southern District," says Oliver. "I'd file in San Francisco, it's less hostile territory, a jury there would give us more bucks." With more emphasis than he intends, he adds, "Up north everyone kind of despises L.A."

"The defendants are in Los Angeles, the questioned song was recorded here, this can't be heard in the Northern District."

"The song was stolen there. We have *locus*, I've looked it up."

Klein doesn't sound as if he's on top of his stuff. Maybe too many late nights.

"Ever done any plagiarism cases, Oliver?"

"No."

"Ever done any entertainment law?"

"Not really."

"A preliminary injunction?"

"A couple. A tree license trespass, and I defended one, people blocking some train tracks."

"Ever done any trials in Federal Court?"

"Can't be much different from the superior courts."

"Wait 'til you see the judges. Some of them are out of the Twilight Zone. Hell, I like your spunk. I can work with you. Look, I'll go in for thirty-five per cent, and you fifteen."

Oliver gets up. "I'll think about it. I'll maybe call you."

"Listen, maybe we can scare them into a quick settlement."

"Well, I'll have to take instructions."

The smile shuts off. "This isn't slow pitch, Oliver, it's big league. You have to know your way around, and you have to know your judges."

As Oliver walks from the office, he feels a tickle of relief. Tommy Klein is more bluff than stuff. Imagine working in court with that guy, he'd treat you like a lackey. While he gets all the glory in the press.

There must be better guns for hire. What a coward, why doesn't he strap on his own?

CHAPTER

12

Oliver Gulliver stares down from the swimming pool patio at the ocean far below and at an ocean to his left, Los Angeles ablaze at midnight. He is somewhere up in the Santa Monica Hills, above Topanga Canyon, in a mansion that rises from the chaparral forest, showplace of Sandor Schmidt, the head of Eulogy Films, one of Royalty Distillers' family of companies. Three hundred people are here, mostly media, a promotion party to push Long Tom Slider and his album. Byron Jones is here. Byron Jones, Oliver's idol. Byron Jones, who actually shook his hand fifteen minutes ago.

Gilley sneaked Oliver into the grounds in a rented limousine. Security at the gate didn't ask for their invitations. "In L.A. if you're in a limmie you can be Mickey Mouse and you're waved to the front door," Gilley said. He's staying sober.

They came here to try to bump into Blinkie Smith, and the two of them have him surrounded now, out by the swimming pool. Blinkie looks part black, part native Indian, he's tall and evil and pockfaced and has a tic in his right eye.

Gilley barely keeps his voice down. "Slider says God sung it in his ear, or something, some psychic fuckin' sci-fi trip. Anyone actually *believe* that?"

"Listen, I can't talk to you guys, there's too many people," Blinkie says.

"Come on," says Gilley, "you ain't been answering my calls, what's going on?"

"The cat came into the studio at the last minute with this song, okay? It astral-traveled into his fuckin' head, I don't know. He came in with this Jesus *song* – what else can I say? Oriole hired a ghost to write the lyrics, and we recorded it." Blinkie gives Oliver a look of disapproval. "I don't like lawyers around."

A little exasperated, Gilley turns to Oliver. "Okay, enjoy the sights, Oliver, Blinkie's gotten a little shy."

Oliver wanders off, worrying at the hostile attitude of this man.

The Joy Flakes just arrived – they'll be setting up later to entertain – but Gilley and Oliver have been here a while, and Oliver, not exactly nursing his bourbon, has gotten a little light of head. He's a moderate when it comes to alcohol, but the drinks are free, and he's ready tonight to release some tension.

Mixed with the alcohol is the adrenalin of inner debate, which has been bubbling since he left Tommy Klein's office. The guy was a blustering lightweight, scheming for the bucks, is that the best L.A. has to offer? If Oriole puts a sleaze like that against him in court, Oliver could finish the ten rounds and maybe win the fight.

He looked up the names of a few other entertainment law specialists, but some little stubborn man within him kept pulling his hand away from the phone.

He's good in court, everybody likes his feisty style. As a G.P. he's done a little of everything, he's elastic. But it's all been small stuff. How do you know you can stand in there with the best until your balls are on the line?

He's dreamed of it so many times in so many ways. The big trial.

Fifty years old. He'll never get another chance before senility sets in. He'll go into a penurious retirement, unremembered for any single lifetime feat except for becoming mayor of Foolsgold by acclamation four times running, plus going bankrupt.

He has the time. He's got no other clients. No excuses but cowardice.

Be serious, Gulliver. You'll make a fool of yourself, the world will be laughing at you, you'll lose the verdict, you'll have given up months and months for nothing, a time when you should have been rebuilding your practice.

I'm like you, Dad, I don't take chances. Real conservative.

He could prove something to his daughters. What would Madelaine have advised?

It's a major life dilemma, a career crisis, another dimension to his mid-life woes. Will he be remembered as a coward, a fool, or a hero?

Oliver seeks diversion for his troubled mind. Clutching his J.D. on the rocks, he strolls around the swimming pool and sneaks a look at the starlets in the water, panties but no bras. Bimbos. This is your basic Hollywood, it's just like he'd imagined. Some naked couples crawling into a big whirlpool built into the natural rock. People probably fuck in there, he wonders if the AIDS virus lives in the warm water.

He goes back into the house. It's a Mexican courtyard effect, with tables at the center piled with shrimp and caviar. The bar offers Tinglewine, but most people are into champagne. Oliver knows he looks square in here with his old-fashioned suit but he'd feel more uncomfortable without it. Flash and punk seem to be what's in. So many faces seem familiar, it's eerie.

And there's Byron Jones, himself, the great Welsh actor and bon vivant. Surrounded by sycophants under a potted palm. But who is Oliver Gulliver to talk about sycophants? Hadn't he, just half an hour ago, spoken about trout fishing with Byron Jones? Trout fishing. He relishes the encounter. "In *Never Look Back* there was a scene where you were fly casting, you had the right action, looked like you knew what you were doing." That was his opening, rehearsed for twenty minutes while he waited to make his move. It turns out Byron Jones owns his own trout stream in Wales.

Long Tom Slider is surrounded by a gaggle of hangers-on, mostly girls. He moves with the fluid grace of a cat, sexual,

powerful. Flashbulbs pop as he strikes a pose with two bim-
boettes. Those guys near him with plastic smiles, they're probably Oriole brass, the enemy.

A slight, pot-bellied man with horn-rimmed glasses, about
thirty-five, detaches himself from the group around Slider and
comes up to Oliver, who is trying to hide in the shadows
near a vine-covered arch. "Turning on the star-making machinery to make kids into winos, it's a new low," he says to
Oliver. "They even flew a PD from New York out here, coked
him out and fucked him blind for airplay." An Eastern rapid-
fire voice.

Oliver wonders who this man is, the local cynic. He asks,
"Which one is the president of Oriole Records?"

"Little balding guy there? Bennie Ford, looks like Bugs
Bunny, except without the carrot. Crooked as a climbing
mountain road."

Oliver spots him. Early forties, all ears and eagerness, the
mouth going.

"Peter Principled his way to the top, used to be their head
counsel, can't tell a flat from a sharp. What you got is lawyers
and accountants running the music business for distilleries.
This Tinglewine tie-in is Bennie's big push, and he's under the
gun to produce."

"Who's the guy with Long Tom Slider?" A hairy barrel of a
man with a stomach that slops out over his belt, a stub of a
cigar in his mouth.

"That's Louis LeGoff, Slider's manager, a real crass act from
Kentucky, I mean a *real* crass act, he mooned the Grammies in
'83, just missed national coverage. Real sleazoid, he'll sell you a
pig's asshole for a wedding ring. He picked up Slider out of a
nut farm far as I can figure, he used to call himself Flush
Gordon. Jeffrey Elphinstone's the guy's real name. Can't sing
worth shit, but video's the game now, cock rock on the screen,
music doesn't matter."

Oliver recognizes a movie face, but can't pin her down.
Talking with Byron Jones. What's her name? Played the girl
with spinal meningitis in *Don't Cry 'Til I'm Gone*. He remem-

bers he had tears in his eyes at the Opera House, tears he manfully strove to hide from his daughters.

"That fascinating-looking fawn you're staring at is Crescent Wells, she's staying as a guest here. She played the sister in *Don't Cry 'Til I'm Gone*, remember, the cheerleader who became like a cripple?"

Yes, that's who she is, Crescent Wells, incredible, so shy, so gentle, he loved her.

"She's a mattress."

"A what?"

"She'd screw a rockpile if she thought there was a snake under it."

Oliver stares at her wide-eyed. His mouth is dry. "Do you actually know her?"

"I know everyone and everything here. Except you. And your thing."

"I'm Oliver Gulliver." He extends his hand.

The man takes it. "I'm Charles Loobie. I work the entertainment beat for the *L.A. Times*. I saw you come in with C.C. Gilley."

Oliver wants to be careful with what he says. "I'm his lawyer."

"What's he doing here with his lawyer? You got a story? I don't want any 'Gilley Makes a Comeback,' I'm talking story."

Oliver gives him a card from his wallet. "Call me here next week."

"Foolsgold? This is a story?"

"I think so. I can't talk about it, yet, I'm sorry."

Crescent Wells gives the fat producer a little Hollywood kiss and makes her way in their direction. She looks older than the movie, twenty-five. Not as frail.

"You promise me a beat on it?" says Loobie.

"Okay."

He steps across the tile and fetches Crescent Wells, who has a sad, faraway smile on ghostly light-pink painted lips. "Crescent Wells," says Loobie, "this is Oliver Gulliver, he's a great fan of yours."

Oliver sticks his hand stupidly out, but she brushes past it and kisses him softly on the mouth, she seems a little drunk. He comes up with, "The last time I saw you, you had me pretty choked up."

"That silly movie?" she says. "Oh, you're sweet."

"I'm going to steal some food for my dog," Loobie says, and walks off.

"Do you smoke?" she asks Oliver.

"Twenty years I've been off them."

"I mean do you smoke *smoke*?"

He melts in her smile. She produces a cigaret from her bag, it's rolled neatly but twisted at the end. A joint. Oliver finds himself scrambling through pockets looking for a match. As he lights it, she touches his hand and takes a great pull on it, her tits rising under her dress top. Oliver feels horny, nervous. A mattress, the reporter said.

She passes it to Oliver. "Yeah, sure," he says, AIDS doesn't transmit through saliva, right? This won't do anything, a little puff, the two times he's tried it, he never felt anything. He inhales, holding it between middle finger and thumb, the way he's seen it done. He's Mr. Cool.

He is afraid he'll cough, but this is like syrup, sweet. Holding his breath he squeaks, "This local shit?" Oliver has defended some grass cases, he knows the language.

"One-toke Thai stick," she says. "I think they must have laced it with junk, it really levels you out."

Oliver exhales, what is he doing, marijuana laced with heroin, it's how they get you.

"You're cute," she says. He blushes. "What's your name again?"

"Oliver V. Gulliver. I'm a lawyer."

"Oh, how exciting."

She takes another toke, swaying as she does. He wants to touch her. He doesn't feel stoned at all, in fact everything seems incredibly clear.

"Where're you from?"

Is she coming on to him? What's the protocol here? "Foolsgold, it's called. I'm the mayor." That's ludicrous, he shouldn't have added that.

But she laughs. "That's neat. And you have a law office there and everything?"

"And a house and garage and a car and a trailer."

"And a cat?"

"A dog."

"That's absolutely, incredibly delicious," she says.

"I guess you know Byron Jones. I'm his greatest fan."

"We've done some things together." She smiles.

He's starting to feel relaxed, okay. It's not the marijuana.

"You're a wonderful actress, Miss Wells, and very attractive."

"*Thank* you." A phrase that tinkles out like birdsong. She tamps the joint and puts the roach in her bag. "I better watch it." She giggles. "This makes me nuts."

As she staggers, her hand goes out to Oliver's chest, and he catches her and puts her upright.

"*Thank* you." She steadies herself and peers at him. Then she puts her lips close to his ear, hot breath pouring into his brain. "I like you. What are you doing later?"

She giggles and weaves away. The mayor of Foolsgold stands by the vine-covered arch, his heart pounding, his juices boiling.

Maybe there will be an assignation here. She practically invited him to her bed. He's not back in stuffy Foolsgold where everybody and their dog knows his business, why not take advantage? What about disease, is she safe? Why are all women he lusts for young, girls as old as his daughters, explain that, Freud. Did someone put some colored lights on here? Why is his brain bouncing around from one thought to another? Maybe it's the grass.

He suddenly realizes, it's like a thunderclap: he's stoned. This is what it's like. Will he float if he moves? Will he be able to walk? He takes a step forward, and it works. Another step. It's not hard, it's not like being drunk.

Looking around, Oliver finds magic here, it's beautiful, he

feels a humanity with these people of Tinseltown, he's caught up in their liquid sexual dance.

Oliver finds himself chuckling as he watches Loobie unfold a bag and scoop a platter of Danish ham into it. And speaking of scoops, Charles Loobie will have his, the *L.A. Times* reporter who introduced him to Crescent Wells.

What are you doing later?

Everyone does it, you wouldn't believe what goes on in Foolsgold, especially in the rainy season. Madelaine will never find out . . . Oliver stops in his mental tracks. Suddenly he's awash in guilt and depression as he remembers her.

He looks for Crescent Wells, and sees her talking to Byron Jones and to . . . what the hell is he doing here, that snotty counsel to the stars, Tommy Klein.

They're all gesturing and laughing, something very funny, obviously an in-joke.

Oliver suddenly sees them all turn around. Klein points at him. They're still laughing.

Byron Jones standing there with a martini in his hand, laughing at his best fan. Oliver's eyes make painful connection with theirs, and they all turn away in embarrassment.

Oliver is mortified, it's major paranoia, he's a yokel from the North Coast. *There was a scene where you were fly casting, you had the right action.* How awful. *Do you smoke? Twenty years I been off them.*

He feels ill, he shouldn't have done that dope. He bumps heavily out the door, looking for Gilley, finding him still by the swimming pool with Blinkie Smith, at whom Gilley seems extremely pissed.

"I wrote that song, Blinkie," he says angrily.

"Yeah, well, I'm gonna tell you somethin', man. I happen to think Long Tom wrote that song." He turns to see Oliver behind him. "That's all I'm gonna say."

"You're a slimy Judas," Gilley shouts. "You're gonna desert me for this hokey glitter band?"

"I can't work with you no more. You're a drunk."

Gilley shoves Blinkie hard, backwards into the swimming

pool amid screaming starlets. "Let's split," he says to Oliver, who groggily follows him.

"Why is he covering up?" Gilley says viciously. "The asshole, he's a part of the conspiracy."

Oliver is groggy, hurt, he's suffered major self-esteem damage. But these feelings are already starting to be consumed by a slow fire building in his gut.

CHAPTER

13

Oliver pauses for a few minutes from the labors of his desk to slash Byron Jones into confetti on the witness stand. Eighteen counts of buggering young boys.

"Oliver," Mrs. Plymm says, "are you going to finish that affidavit?"

He opens his eyes to find her there, in front of him. He picks up his dictaphone. "I was planning strategy."

Mrs. Plymm hands him some rough copies and changes his tape. "I hope *this* isn't a daydream, suing for fifty million dollars. Isn't that a little steep?"

He pencils corrections. "Yeah, but it'll look good in the headlines. I think I'll stiffen this up, ask the judge to impound all the records in all the stores in all fifty states and the possessions." His application will be heard by a Federal Court judge whose writ extends to every little dark corner of the country. Oliver intends to get some respect.

Two nights in L.A. have aged and toughened him. He is going forward on his own, preparing a civil complaint for plagiarism under the Copyright Act. The claim for relief, in addition to real and punitive damages, includes a preliminary injunction, *pendente lite*, as they say, pending trial. Shut the song down, the album, it's the only fast way to force Oriole to its corporate knees. A trial will take a year to get under way, so he'll try to short cut through the clogged court calendars. He will seek his injunction immediately, this week, in San Francisco.

He has to file today, Monday. He must get a judge to give him short notice, this as an exigent matter, delay defeats the unaggressive plaintiff.

Oliver will throw everything he has into this injunction, but it's a long chance, injunctions aren't given out like lollipops. Your case has to be almost ironclad, which Oliver's isn't close to. But an early skirmish is sure to get publicity, start people wondering. He'll use that reporter somehow, Charles Loobie, who despises the music industry, the cynic.

"If you intend to have it served tomorrow, stop dreaming and get cracking. Honestly." Mrs. Plymm leaves.

Oliver speaks into his machine. "Attached hereto as Exhibits G through double-K and made a part hereof are the statements of twenty-six persons who attended at the aforesaid party on the thirty-first of July." Elora and Lindy helped him, went around to everyone they could find during the weekend. Lots of kids remembered Gilley singing "Small-Town Girl" two weeks before the album was released.

That evidence, and the annexed report of Dr. Aloysius Rigby, would get him a foot in the door. Oliver's allegations focus on the theft of car and tape by Garson and Splint. If Jesse Gonzales can get a line on Splint through the police in Vancouver, where she skipped bail on that prostitution misdemeanor, maybe they'll get the evidence to actually win the injunction, to shut down everything, records, tapes, video, the whole Royalty Distillers ad campaign for Tinglewine Coolers. Keep dreaming.

Jesse Gonzales paddles into his office with a file.

"I just got through a hairy session with Sybil McGuid. She thinks I should be proffering a kidnap charge against you."

"Come on, Jesse."

"I ain't gonna, but she's on my butt about it, and she's got a point, Jamey ain't helpless, but he's an official retardant." He

98

picks up the latest *California Reports*, and starts perusing it, he likes to keep up with the law.

"I'll produce Jamey if she wants him tested by a board of psychiatrists. That's my position. He's capable on his own, I've seen him. Nobody realized that because Sybil kept the leash so tight. She was afraid he'd lose his dependence on her." He sounds like Gilley. "He's a lot smarter than everyone thinks."

Oliver and Gilley had left Jamey behind in Los Angeles. He wants to stay in Venice, and Kelly and Skylark say he loves the kids, he's a perfect babysitter. Oliver isn't going to squeal on him.

"Here's a case, a rubber full of heroin up the defendant's reproductive orifice, she gets off because nobody read her rights. Jeez, gimme a break." Jesse paws through some of Mrs. Plymm's rough drafts on his desk. "Taking on the L.A. record nabobs, huh? Gettin' to be a real interesting case. Whyn't you tell me sooner about that girl being charged up in Canada?"

"You got something?" Oliver senses his friend indeed has, he's acting too blasé.

"Well, yes, maybe I do." A happy wheeze of satisfaction. "Maybe this is the end of my summer of advertency." Oliver reads adversity. Jesse pulls some mug shots from a file. "These just came in."

It's Garson and Splint, fronts and sides, Garson looking bored, the girl defiant.

"Splint a.k.a. Sonya Boychuk, born 1970, Red Deer, Alberta, three juvenile convictions up in Canada for bad checks and theft. She's also wanted on that prostitution warrant."

He points at Garson's picture.

"Garson Schuter, born 1960, Winnipeg. Arrested with his girlfriend in Vancouver, but charges were dropped."

"Procuring?"

"That, however, ain't his main notoriety. He's an arsonist. There's a juvenile record, he has two adult convictions and is suspect in four other fires, mostly buildings, one boat. His M.O. is regular gasoline. Arson Garson. Two recorded convictions for car theft, as well, by the way, so there's your proof about Gilley's Mercedes. He's a kind of satanist, gives homage to the god of fire or whatever." Home-idge, Jesse pronounces.

Oliver remembers Arson Garson standing on the driveway, looking down at the carnage of that beautiful building. *It's spiritual, man. I love it when things burn.*

"This is the guy who burned down the Opera House," Oliver says.

"And people say you're feebleminded."

"He must've broken into it that day."

"That night," says Jesse. "Arson Garson probably figured he could use the party as his alibi and he absented himself for half an hour."

"What about all those oil cans that were in there, where'd he get those? And why would he choose the Foolsgold Opera House?"

"He heard the kids complaining, plus he wants to destroy the centers of Western religion. I don't know where he got the gasoline. Anyway, I'm gonna disseminate a statewide warrant on the teletype."

"Well, great, but you solved the wrong crime as far as I'm concerned."

"So sue me. If you'd of cooperated with the authorities earlier we'd have this wrapped up by now."

Mrs. Plymm pokes her head around. "Well, are you finished?"

"I just got some new stuff from Jesse I'm going to throw in." Street musicians and professional thieves – even if they're not arrested, their background will raise some questions, and the judge will want the answers from the defendant company. Oriole will have to file affidavits, and Oliver will gain quick discovery of their defense.

After Jesse leaves, Oliver and his secretary finish quickly, and, armed with plaint and affidavits and motion for injunction and memorandum of points and argument and affidavits and exhibits and thirty dollars in Xeroxing, Oliver steps boldly out the front door of his little office building, and can't avoid The

Competition, coming out of the Savings and Loan, stuffing money into his wallet.

"Hey, I got to talk to you, Oliver."

"I'm on my way to the airport." He tosses his briefcase into his car. "If it's about Sybil, she knows what she can do."

"We'll apply for a conservatorship," Bolestero says. "It's not about that. Look, Oliver, this is hard."

Oliver wonders, now what?

"Gus and Harry some of those guys at the Lions have approached me. Also Wilf from the Legion."

Oliver says nothing. What has Ernie been cooking up now?

"Anyway, what's happening, some people're thinking maybe I should run for mayor."

"What are *you* thinking?"

"Listen, I'm not the kind of man does things behind people's backs, and frankly I believe you're the best guy for the job, but I have to tell you, as friends, maybe there's been some confidence lost. I don't know, they think you've become too liberal, you know where the people of this town are at, seventeenth century." A pause. "No one is even sure you're going to run this November."

Here's a guy ripped off most of Oliver's business, and now he's trying to steal his self-respect. "You know, Ernie, you've only been up here in Foolsgold for five years, suddenly you want to be mayor. It's no big deal, believe me. You don't get paid. Your voters expect you to give them free legal advice as part of their taxes. People phone you all day with complaints. You deserve the job, Ernie. But you're going to have to wrestle me for it."

Bolestero looks startled, but recovers, slapping Oliver's back as he gets into the car. "Hey, okay, the best man'll win."

Oliver would love, one day, to get this schmuck.

CHAPTER

14

Oliver steps off the elevator onto the seventh floor of the Oriole Building in North Hollywood. He is about to face the enemy, stare him unblinkingly in the eye. Benjamin Ford, president of Oriole Records. He could serve the papers on some lowlier boss, but having traveled all this way, he'll go to where the buck stops. Ford is up in promotions, his secretary told Oliver. Promotions is entered from the elevator corridor and consists of one big open-space office, and right now it's as busy as a rush-hour bus.

"I've got some papers that have to be delivered personally to Mr. Ford."

The receptionist is all paint and peroxide. She looks at middle-aged Oliver, his conservative blue suit. He doesn't look dangerous. She shrugs.

"Help yourself."

"What's going on?"

"It's bedlam in here, the trades are just phoning the weekly figures in. Sweep week Tuesday."

"Where's 'Goin' Down for the Last Time'?"

"Coming in around three or four."

Oliver is holding two large manila envelopes, documents sealed this morning by a clerk of the Federal Court, Northern District. They include a complaint, summons, supporting depositions, and an order appointing this Friday, three days from now, for hearing of the injunction application in San Francisco.

He will be ready to go on Friday, he will oppose any motions for adjournment. Plaintiff's counsel intends to strike while the song is hot and rising up the charts.

The federal courthouse in San Francisco was a forbidding, dark tower spilling gloom to the street below, Golden Gate Avenue, near the Civic Center. Before leaving the building, Oliver dropped into one of the courtrooms, so sterile and menacing. The lawyers seemed eloquent and sure.

The clerk warned him the papers had to be served today to give the defendants two clear days' notice. Oliver took a shuttle to Los Angeles International, and a cab to the Oriole Building.

Someone yells, "We're number one in Denver."

People cheer.

Oliver pokes his way into the milling throng in the office area. At a table, a man with a jackhammer voice is on the phone, a dozen people surrounding him. That must be Bennie Ford from behind, his bald top staring back at Oliver. At the far end of the office area is a bar, and Oliver's in luck – Long Tom Slider is standing there, hoisting a beer with his manager, the allegedly scrofulous Louis LeGoff. Oliver has named Slider as a defendant, he has papers to serve on him, too.

The man at the phone sounds like a bookie, shouting out numbers to a client on the line. "Why ain't you got any jumps for me? It's a jack rabbit in Atlanta, twelve thousand units moved there in two days. We got twenty-eight points in Cincinnati, twenty in Seattle, eighteen in Montreal, I got a hundred CHR stations, I got heavy rotation, I got crossover, the song is blasting out of every fifth radio station in North America fifteen times a day, and you can't budge it in New York? Make it move, Sammy. Bring me Z-100 or bring me your head."

Oliver feels invisible here, an anonymous man in a blue suit. The only person to notice him is a young woman near the bar, olive-skinned and just five feet, jeans and no makeup, who gives him a long, curious once-over. Then her eyes dart away abruptly. She seems to have a permanently startled expression, as if she finds life amazing.

She looks again at Oliver, smiles at him, her eyes sparkle like agate, Latin eyes, playful, vampish. He smiles back shyly.

Oliver works his way toward Ford, who is loudly announcing to the world at large, "We flew this New York program director out to a party Nero would be ashamed to attend. He still insists he doesn't like the sound." He takes the phone from the promotions man. "Tell the PD we're putting up a Times Square billboard. Tell him a wooden mock-up of Tom Slider will rise fifty feet above it, fifty feet, tell him."

"Mr. Ford?" says Oliver. "I've got some papers for you."

Ford looks at him, blinks. "Who are you?"

"An attorney."

"You're from McRae, Tchobanian? These are the contracts for the tour?"

Oliver smiles innocently, and extends one of the manila envelopes. Just put it in his hands, that's what the rules of personal service require. If a party refuses to accept service, touch him with the documents and let them drop to the floor.

Benjamin Ford takes the envelope and looks at his name typed on it, and sets it down on the desk.

"I'm putting a hold on them for a few days," he says. "The price may be going up. The product is hotter than we expected, we're moving a hundred thousand pieces a day."

And that is that. Oliver turns into a piece of furniture as Ford goes back to the phone whence issues the plaintive voice of their New York promoter. "I busted my gut. I was all over him as hard as I could, but he says it ain't a New York sound, and personally I think he's reacting to the hype."

"Charlie, do what you gotta do, help the Peruvian economy."

A sudden hush around the phone. Not so smart, Oliver thinks: the president of Oriole Records speaks too openly. Drugola. Gilley told him about this, most program directors on what they call Contemporary Hit Radio have plastic noses and carry a suitcase full of blow. Oliver's reassured, the enemy is corrupt – bribery, trafficking, and theft are office routines.

He drifts away from there toward the bar, toward Slider, but as he reaches the young woman with the sparkling eyes, she asks, "Who the heck are you?"

"I'm an attorney."

"And what are you doing here?" She isn't challenging him, she's smiling. She is striking, jet black hair with an off-center pony-tail, wispy bangs in front. Someone should feed her a few meals. Hard to tell her age. Mid-thirties.

"I'm starting a suit."

"But I like the one you're wearing."

"One of these days it'll come back in style."

They both laugh, and their laughter is drowned by Louis LeGoff, down the bar, raising his voice hoarsely into a phone, a loud Kentucky growl.

"Whatta ya mean, y'all can't get the Spectrum either. I got me a fuckin' star, he's hotter than a grunt, they'd rather have fourteen hundred out to see a fuckin' bunch of niggers throw a fuckin' ball around or twenty thousand to see a fuckin' spectacle? Tell them we're thinking of Soldier Field, our guy'll be like Springsteen, play the fuckin' ballparks."

"Loathsome," she murmurs, then holds out her hand. "My name's Tricia. I'm having an n.b."

"Oliver." Her handshake is tight, forceful. She has those quick little smiles she snaps at him. She's strange, maybe she's on something. "What's an n.b.?"

"You're not from here, are you? It's Hollywoodese for nervous breakdown."

Oliver nods. Interesting little conversation. "And why are you having this breakdown?"

She shrugs. "Everyone else talks about their breakdowns, I want to have one of my own. Who are you suing?"

LeGoff's big bass intrudes, "Tell them we want a forty-five-foot semi for the T-shirts and stuff, and don't give 'em dishrags, give 'em some fuckin' class, folks got a right to somethin' nice when they pay twenty-four bucks for a T-shirt."

Slider ducks under his manager's telephone cord and starts

to move to their end of the bar. Tricia says, "I'm strong, I can handle him." He's immensely tall, loose, lithe, you think of a basketball player moving down the court intent on scoring. With Tricia?

Slider has a big, dozy smile. His eyes don't glint of overpowering intelligence. Like almost everyone else around here, he acts as if Oliver doesn't exist. He easily squeezes him out of the play with an illegal block, his arm stretching out past Oliver's nose, leaving him to sniff a left armpit. Slider has to lean way down to the little-over-five-foot Tricia.

Slider says to her, "Yeah, as my daddy used to say, if you got jack you got slack, if you got zip take a trip. Wanna come up to my place tonight and watch my video while we fuck and talk about existential philosophy?"

"Sorry, Lesbian Alliance meets Tuesdays."

"I like short chicks, I don't know what it is, a fetish."

Oliver taps a finger on the back of Slider's shoulder. He turns and glares down at him. "What's the matter, I'm stepping on your foot?"

"This is for you, Mr. Slider." He hands him the second manila envelope.

"What's this?" Slider says.

"It's about a song, I'm a lawyer – "

Slider interrupts, calling over to his manager, "Louis, here's some yobbo with a hassle."

LeGoff tosses down the phone and comes barreling over, yelling, "Nobody bothers my client!" The man grabs the envelope from Slider in one huge, angry fist, and with the other wrenches a startled Oliver Gulliver by the lapels of his suit jacket and marches him to the door.

Oliver is at first too astonished to resist, his legs are scrambling, barely keeping up.

"Nobody but *nobody* comes near my property! Where's the fuckin' security here? How do they let creeps come in here and bug my client? One day it'll be a guy with a fuckin' gun."

In the elevator hall now, Oliver can hear loud laughter back in the office, everyone having enjoyed this piece of live theater.

"Get your hand off me or I'll sue it off," he says.

Tricia's voice from behind, she has followed them out here. "Louis, he's a lawyer."

Oliver wrenches free, his suit jacket tearing. LeGoff punches the elevator down button. "Yeah, here they come. Every time you get a hit song, a buncha Norberts come crawlin' outa the fuckin' woodwork claimin' it's theirs. You wanna bet I'm wrong?"

The paper he pulls from the manila envelope is a letter, on Oliver's stationery. He starts reading: "Oliver Gulliver, Attorney-at-Law, Number Thirty-One Madrona Street, Foolsgold, California. Re: 'Goin' Down for the Last Time.' Dear sir, please be advised that the undersigned has been instructed to commence proceedings in damages under the Copyright Act. . ."

He crumples the letter, then pulls out the legal documents and crumples them, too, into a big paper ball. "This is what I think of lawyers." He unbuckles his belt and drops his pants and before Oliver's horrified eyes he bends over and wipes his naked hind quarters with the legal documents.

"Louis!" Tricia screams.

He drops the papers on the floor, buckles up, and marches back to the offices. "Y'all get outa this building. Dumb fuckin' hick."

After he closes the door there is a moment of silence as Oliver looks down at the crumpled documents, looks at the door behind which LeGoff disappeared, looks at her.

"I'm sorry, he's an animal," she says.

"What species?" Oliver says. He feels totally demeaned, the anger hasn't set in yet.

"About your song. I'm afraid Oriole doesn't accept unsolicited material. For just this reason, plagiarism suits. So it's unlikely. . . ." She pauses, then says, "Or is it?" The elevator door opens. "Who's your client?"

"C.C. Gilley."

She apparently finds this funny. She starts to laugh.

Oliver enters the elevator. She's still laughing as the door starts to slide closed. Oliver can't tell if she's having fun at his expense or is drugged out or really is having that breakdown. Oliver always feels lonely in the city, why can't he meet anyone normal and nice?

"Wait," she says.

*   *   *

"The n.b. has made me a little hysterical, but I wasn't laughing at you. I just suddenly felt light headed when the truth hit me."

Tricia seems to know quite a few people in here, Le Dome on Sunset, where apparently the music and recording industries meet. They are at a quiet table. The restaurant is dark and glitzy, the luncheon menu rich and expensive.

Her name is Tricia Santarossa and she's New York Italian. Been out West fifteen years, he'll call her thirty-five. No wedding ring. She talks like a New Yorker, rapidly, efficiently, she's Julliard-trained and she's the head scout for Artists and Repertoire at Oriole Records. She reluctantly helped sign Long Tom Slider – for peanuts – then put the back-up band together.

All this Oliver has learned over lobster bisque. Sitting there with his torn lapel. He's going to get that guy, LeGoff.

"I've been wondering what happened to Gilley. Last I heard he was in some scruffy hotel in the Tenderloin in Frisco. He was the worst I ever worked with, as bad as Sly Stone in his prime. But great when he was on."

She talks breathlessly, looking directly at him, her eyes emitting those dark sparks.

"So it turns out I'm a hustler for a six-and-a-half-foot male member and his stolen song. Three months ago he was a cheap act around the Ohio River Valley. Sign him, they said, he looks good on the tube. Boy, if rock and roll isn't dead, it's sure begun to smell a little off."

She had picked up the scent from the time Slider walked zombie-eyed into the studio and played some chords. Everyone else was content to believe the song had somehow sprung from Slider's inner musical soul, but Tricia's nose is good and her ears are better.

"I knew I recognized another voice in that song. I didn't think Gilley. But it's Gilley."

"How can you be sure and I haven't told you the whole story?"

"I have ears that earn me a hundred thousand dollars a year. My ears say Gilley." She darts one of her edgy little smiles at him. "It's a love song."

"To my daughter."

She pulls some loose hairs from in front of her eyes and gives him the full wide-eyed astonished look. He feels embarrassed.

"I'm going to powder my nose." She gets up and goes.

She's off to powder her nose. What brand of powder is this, South American? Does it account for that brightness in the eyes, the laughing fits, the rapid speech?

Druggie or not, here is Oliver's inside source, this little energetic oddball. Or is she playing a clever game, seeking to find out what he knows before reporting back to Bennie Ford? Oliver has nothing to hide, it's all in the affidavits. No, she's too genuine to be conning him. Sometimes you get honest people.

She returns, and she's even peppier.

"Bennie Ford, with his phony front, he's in on it up to his little bunny ears. Boy, haven't I been the good company girl? The loyal Oriole, the company's little team-playing spark plug. Fine. I've been looking for an excuse to give them my notice. Ever since the music mobsters took over Oriole Records with their sex and Tinglewine show I've been feeling like a regular old whore."

"You're going to quit?"

"Yeah, I just decided, and you know what, Oliver? I don't feel like I'm having that n.b. any more. I feel terrific. Like a rat that's found its way out of the maze."

With hardly a pause, "I'll tell you what I know. They had a song. 'Comin' Up for Air,' Morrie Walters wrote it and he's had five hits in a row. They worked it up and recorded it, but it wasn't in the grooves. You can hype a lot of chaff into the charts, but they needed a bullet single for the ad campaign, and this wasn't anywhere near it. They didn't believe me, and they

109

ran a market test, and it got the same kind of response mud on the carpet gets. They axed it and sent a cattle call out to the music publishing houses."

"What day did they axe it?"

"Late July. The twenty-sixth, I think, the Tinglewine campaign was on line for launch in a week. They had to have a fast song or the campaign would go under, fifteen million dollars out the window. Bennie had a career to save. I wonder how many others are in on it. Louis LeGoff, that was a strange reaction, maybe he's scared, bluffing."

She pauses to fiddle with her salad. Oliver isn't eating his chicken either, his stomach is burbling with the acid of the Louis LeGoff encounter. But not a bad trade-off for the insult: inside the defendants' camp, he has a friendly.

"Six days later, one day before deadline, Slider walked into Studio c on the third floor, looking like he truly *had* seen God, and he tuned his guitar and played. It was good. It *is* good. What does Gilley call it?"

" 'Small-Town Girl in the City.' "

She smiles. "What's your daughter's name?"

"Elora. She's eighteen. There's also Lindy, and she's fifteen."

"And who else is there?"

"No one now."

She doesn't ask him to expand on that, just that quick flare of an inquiring smile.

"Tell me the story of the song, Oliver."

He gives her his whole side of it, the arrival of Gilley in Foolsgold, the Last Friday in July Day, the search for Splint and Garson. She keeps popping that little smile, her dark eyes burning him. The story is entertaining the way he tells it, there are anecdotes about Gilley and Jamey and Mrs. McGuid. He even tells her about Tommy Klein and Crescent Wells and Byron Jones laughing at him. He tells her how he saw red and decided on a sudden, first-strike war strategy.

He can tell she is starting to like him, the way he tells stories on himself.

110

She laughs a lot, it's a big laugh from a small person. Oliver can be a charmer when he wants, he's just not had the opportunity. Those brilliant eyes, it's not cocaine, she's just that way, electric.

He can't stop talking, his dam is bursting on sympathetic ears. He tells her about the law, his problems of proof, and she looks thoughtful.

After a while she says, "What can I do for you?"

"You could talk to Slider."

"He's too much of a poophead."

"I saw him coming on to you."

"Someone told him I was easy." The smile.

Oliver waits for her to amplify, she doesn't.

"I don't like the idea of being a tattle. Goes against the grain. But I hate them for the corruption." She muses, there's a sadness. "Rock and roll was virtuous once, in the beginning, innocently born of revolution."

She extends him a warm, conspiratorial smile. "Okay, Oliver, I'll be your mole. Nothing I say gets repeated?"

He nods.

"I'll never get another job in the industry, so please, give me your word."

"On my honor."

"What's your number in Foolsgold?"

CHAPTER

15

Oliver, in his pyjamas, tosses between the sheets in his room on the Van Ness motel strip, staring into the dark, feeling bubbles of panic pop in his stomach. He has accepted that two hours' sleep will be his allotment for the night. He tries to escape with daydreams, one of them a short, hot fantasy starring Tricia Santarossa instead of Raquel for a change, but he can't keep her, she withdraws from him, he lays abed unsatisfied, confronted with the looming reality of the mayor of Foolsgold walking alone into a courtroom against the world's number eighteen corporation. This morning.

It's Friday, September second, the day before the Labor Day weekend. Oliver has earned his holiday weekend, he needs it to recover. His eyes are shot, he sees headnotes and footnotes swimming in front of them, thirty hours in the Berkeley law school library. Presumptive ownership from registration, piracy *pro tanto*, substantial similarity versus striking similarity. Arnstein versus Cole Porter, "Night and Day," "My Heart Belongs to Daddy" – Cole Porter seemed to spend a lot of time in court – Jewel Music versus Feist, Hein versus Harris. Then finally a case in which the plaintiff wins, Judge Learned Hand enjoining the publication of a song believe it or not called "I Think I Hear a Woodpecker Knocking at My Family Tree."

The defendants, the thieves of songs, win nine out of ten of the reported decisions, that has become cruelly obvious.

In many of the precedents the "accused" song, as the jargon has it, and the complaining work were discovered to have been, unconsciously or otherwise, borrowed from a common prior source. Could that be the case with Gilley and Slider? If so, there's no triable wrong.

He'll need a lot less law if he can gather more facts. Proof of access is still the key. But Garson and Splint elude their seekers. Tricia Santarossa, his spy – was she serious? – hasn't reported in with anything.

He looks at his watch. Five o'clock in the morning, five hours before show time. U.S. District Court judges are said to be impatient, conservative guys who like to take all their tribulations out on you. The defendants' lawyers will be rapier-witted and silver of tongue. Oliver's tongue will feel like a lead weight in his mouth.

Over and over he has rehearsed a speech for the judge. "We are not dealing with theft of a mere material thing, but of a man's intellectual and emotional creation, a theft of his art that can never be restored. A popular song by its nature has a short life span. The defendants must not be allowed to bleed all the profit from it in the several months this case will take to get to trial."

Straightforward and not flowery. Somehow he has to get it out. It probably won't be like his daydreams, where he's eloquent and *ex tempore*, where judges grovel and opposing counsel slink off like whipped dogs.

As long as he doesn't get patronized. That's what Oliver can't stand, it's worse than them laughing at you. *What kind of a practice you got up there in Humboldt County, Oliver?*

The phone rings. His wake-up call. But it's Gilley, in Foolsgold.

"Oliver, I phoned to tell you me and the fiancée are driving down to San Frank today, a'right if we take the truck? You can get us through Jodie Brown, we'll be rehearsing up at her place in the Castro. How's it goin', eh?"

"Fine."

113

"Break a leg."

*   *   *

Over breakfast at a Market Street café, Charles Loobie lets his eggs cool as he reads Oliver's documents. "How come this hasn't broken? Not one reporter has looked at this court file? I like it, this story's got sex and larceny, it's got names. It'll sell papers and make the publisher happy, won't that be nice?"

They walk down Polk to the Federal Court Building. Inside the front entrance, Loobie looks about suspiciously for other reporters. "Pass me the Tinglewine," he sings softly, " 'cause I'm goin' down for the last time."

Ten minutes before the opening of the courts, the federal building is churning with impeccably dressed men and women who make Oliver's old three-piece suit look like it used to hold potatoes. All these briefcases and worried smiles, which ones are the thousand-a-day hit men for Oriole Records?

In the crowded elevator, Oliver can't breathe, the intense city energy of the lawyers around him burns all the oxygen.

"I hear Mathilda the Hun is in motions court," one lawyer says.

"Why do I always draw that stone-hearted antediluvian bitch?" complains another.

Oliver feels sudden slack in his anal muscles, he clenches them.

On the eighteenth floor, he wobbles along behind Loobie and the lawyers to motions court. Injunctions have precedence in order of call, he'll be on right away.

Oliver takes a back bench, and Loobie sits beside him.

The clerk calls out, "All rise." Bang goes his gavel. "U.S. District Court for Northern District of California, Judge Mathilda Atleigh presiding." Bang, bang.

Forty lawyers stand for the entrance of the judge, a woman whose glowing countenance marks her as a likely candidate for apoplexy.

After everyone is again seated, the clerk calls, "Polk versus

114

Mainland Motors." Five lawyers scramble forward.

"What is this?" Judge Atleigh studies the court file.

"Class action injunction," says one of the lawyers. "False warranties by car dealerships."

"*Allegedly* false," another lawyer says.

"How long?" she asks.

"Agreed estimate two hours," comes the answer.

"Call that other injunction, the copyright," she says to the clerk.

"Gilley versus Oriole Records," the clerk says.

Oliver jerks to his feet as if popped from a gun. "For the plaintiff," he croaks.

"I can't see you let alone hear you. Get up here."

Oliver comes numbly forward. "Oliver Gulliver for the plaintiff, your honor."

"Who's for the defendants?" the judge says.

Oliver takes a peek around. No one is forthcoming. "I guess they're late," he says.

Oliver watches Judge Atleigh prowl through the file looking for proof of service upon the defendants. Oliver filed it yesterday, the affidavit is in detail, down to the insulting behavior of Louis LeGoff.

She grunts with displeasure. "What is this mess, a three-page affidavit of service?"

"There was a lot of circumstances to explain." There *were* a lot, plural.

"No answer filed by the defendants." She looks down at Oliver. "Late. I don't like late. Particularly today when I have thirty applications in front of me. Why does everyone bring their motions on just before the long weekend?"

Oliver hopes this is rhetorical, not directed at him.

"Should the defendants deign to wander in, Mr. Gulliver, how long will this take?"

"Cutting it to the bone, I'll be half an hour myself."

"Is Judge Sherman coming in or not?" Atleigh snaps to the clerk.

"He's on his way, your honor."

"All right," says the judge, "Mainland Motors, I'll take it first. Gilley and Oriole, I'm sending that down to Court Eleven, Judge Sherman."

It is with relief that Oliver walks back down the aisle. No judge could be grumpier than Mathilda the Hun.

Court Eleven is one floor up. The door is unlocked, but no one is inside. Oliver and Loobie sit down, and fifteen quiet minutes pass while Loobie scribbles in his pad, every once in a while looking anxiously at his watch. "I've got a deadline in an hour, they better get the show on the road. Where are the defendants?"

Good question, Oliver thinks. Maybe Bennie Ford didn't pay attention to the date. Maybe he never read the legal papers, he thought they were contracts from some booking agency. But in a case like this the judge will insist on their being phoned.

He has got his first words out in a federal courtroom. He has survived Mathilda the Hun. He feels a little confidence, just a little.

A black man about Oliver's age strides abruptly out of the judge's door of the courtroom. He's wearing jeans and a wind-breaker and a slouch hat. He doesn't look awfully happy.

"I'm Judge Sherman. I wasn't expecting to be called in. I had plans to get out early this weekend." He's tall and big-boned, looks like he used to get his way on the playground.

"I'm Oliver Gulliver, your honor." He stands. "I feel real bad about your ruined day, I know what it's like when I set one aside. This matter is emergent." He means urgent. Get it together.

"The clerk said it's about a song."

"Piracy of a song, your honor. Really interesting case." Oliver studies that colorful little hand-tied fishing fly pinned to the side of his hat.

"You claiming irreparable harm? You're saying this can't be made up in damages at trial?"

Oliver starts talking rapidly, he can't get the words out fast enough. "Well, your honor, it's a popular song, and you know

116

they have short life spans. A trial will take at least eight months to get going, I checked with the clerk's office. By then, all the profit from the song will be sucked dry by the defendants."

The judge looks long at him, frowning.

"It's something perishable, your honor. Treat it like a truckload of peaches on a barricaded highway."

Sherman allows half a smile. "Okay, I won't wait for the clerk to get the file to me. Give me your copy and I'll read the material while we wait for the defendants to show up. I know it's not your fault, Mr. Gulliver, but it just cheeses me off having to change my plans. I had an extra day owing."

"No one feels worse about a delayed fishing trip than me, your honor." He gives Sherman the file.

"You do some fishing?" the judge says.

"I've got a little place back up the Foolsgold River, north of Eureka." Which he may have to sell, he wants to say, if he doesn't win this injunction.

"Sure, I know the Foolsgold. Good mess of sea-run cutthroats go through there, I was up there once."

"We got cuts running there now, and steelhead."

"I'm up at Engle Lake," Sherman says, "I've a little cottage there."

"I've been over to Engle a few times, got a few twelve-inchers, rainbows."

"Oh, they go a lot bigger if you know some of the holes. There's a brown trout there, Grandpa Moses, he'll go fifteen pounds if we ever get to finally doing business."

"What do you use?"

"Mepps spinner, Nobby Wobbler, casting from the boat, just drift-fishing. I like the peace."

"I'm with you there. Dissolves all the burdens, doesn't it?"

Sherman looks through the file. "Humboldt County. You came a ways for this."

"Two hundred and fifty miles by road, basically. Well, I'm just over the Salmon Range from your cabin, so I know you got a long ways to go, too. I'm real sorry."

"No problem, I'll read this." Sherman starts to stroll away. "You phone Oriole Records, Mr. Gulliver. Give them my compliments and tell them if they don't have a lawyer here in forty-five minutes we'll proceed without them." He goes.

Loobie, through all of this, has been like a fly on the wall. He says, "Why don't you just *say* you phoned them?"

But Oliver leaves the courtroom and finds a lawyer's interview room with a phone in it. He won't do anything to lose the favor of this judge. Oliver's gained a lot of composure, he handled himself pretty damn good.

He asks the woman at the Oriole switchboard for the president's office.

"I'll put you through to his secretary." Several rings. "I'm sorry, she's not at her desk."

"Take this message. Tell Mr. Ford it's Oliver Gulliver, and I'm a lawyer and I'm in Court Eleven of the U.S. District Court in San Francisco, and what he better do is get a local attorney into court here right away or the judge says we'll start without him in forty minutes. Got that?"

After a repeat, she has it. She doesn't seem too bright.

This is good, thinks Oliver. Some lawyer will come racing in here wild-eyed and unprepared, pleading for delay, infuriating Judge Sherman, who has his weekend plans. Maybe Oliver has a little edge.

Loobie is outside the courtroom, pacing furiously. "I got a deadline, I'm going to phone some copy in, they'll hold the lead."

Loobie is on the hallway pay phone for half an hour. No one appears for the defendant. No one. Oliver can't believe it. What's their problem? Some of these corporations are like the government, they're so swallowed up in the fat of their own bureaucracy, they move with the speed of a walrus on a rock. He has to be back in front of the judge in a few minutes. He wants to look good with this judge, and will bend over backwards.

He phones Oriole again. This time he gets, "I'm sorry, Mr. Ford's in conference and says he can't be bothered."

"Okay." Oliver hangs up and returns to the courtroom and waits until a clerk arrives to announce Judge Sherman, who, suited up now, steps up to the bench. The clerk calls the case. "Gilley and Oriole."

"Any word?" says Sherman.

"I phoned twice, left a clear message. I was told the president of Oriole Records can't be bothered."

"Can't be . . . " Sherman seems astounded. He shakes his head, but somewhat ruefully. "Mr. Gulliver, you're entitled to your costs and your attorney's fees on this, but I don't like to make an *ex parte* order on a matter of such gravity. It really should go over to Monday."

"That's a holiday," says his clerk, a young pipsqueek guy.

"Tuesday, then."

"Your honor, why should they enjoy the luxury of a delay they haven't even shown up to argue for? Delay only benefits the defendants, and it causes real harm to the plaintiff."

"Yes, I take your point." Sherman riffles through the file, musing. "You do have strong evidence of a tape being stolen here. And you've an expert's report that says pretty emphatically the two songs are the same."

"The defendants can always move to set an order aside," Oliver urges. "Myself, I don't think they're paying due attention to the U.S. Federal Court. Did you read in the affidavit of service, how they treated the matter?"

"No, no, I didn't look at that." Sherman finds Oliver's sworn account of the serving of the papers. An incredulous look takes over his face. Sternly, "Somebody who wipes himself with formal pleadings isn't asking for much sympathy from this court. Or calling a member of the bar a dumb hick."

After another moment's thought, he says, "All right. I won't give you a formal injunction, but I will grant a temporary restraining order under Rule 65, I think it's paragraph b, and it'll run to Tuesday, and I'll hear then the full argument from both sides. I'll either dissolve the t.r.o. then or grant you your injunction until trial. Under the circumstances, I won't order the plaintiff to post surety."

A temporary restraining order, thinks Oliver, it's good, it's excellent, same thing as a preliminary injunction, just runs for a shorter time period. "So what I'm asking is that the court impound all recordings made of the questioned song, and Oriole Records be enjoined to withdraw them from sale."

"You may have your order, Mr. Gulliver."

Oliver produces a draft prepared for the judge's signature. "I just have to make a few changes so you can sign it, your honor. I'll just cross out where it says injunction and put in the t.r.o." He makes the changes in pen. "I hope that's not too messy, but I don't want to hold you up, I guess it's about a five-hour drive up to Engle Lake." He's ebullient, he's talking too much.

"This is a mess," says the clerk. "I'll type up a new one. You'll have to serve it, you know, for it to have effect."

As the clerk leaves by a side door to do repairs, Loobie sidles out the front door, and Oliver and Judge Sherman talk trout and salmon. Oliver's trying to be cool, all in a day's work, he's just nailed the defendants to the cross.

The clerk returns with a clean copy of the order, the judge reads it over and signs it, and hands it back to the clerk to be sealed and stamped, made an official proceeding.

"Give my regards to Grandpa Moses," says Oliver. "Ever want to do some fast-water fishing, I got some spots."

Court is recessed and Oliver bolts out of there, past Loobie who is dialing at the coin telephone. "I like it," he says.

Oliver, numb with triumph, follows the clerk to his office and gets his stamped copies of the restraining order, then rejoins Loobie, still on the phone.

"Yeah, I'll get him on the same plane, we've got to get the order served this afternoon at Oriole Records. Check the photo library, there must be some old shot of Gilley looking triumphant. Elora, the girlfriend, you better get a camera on her, too, I'll find out where she is. Naw, I won't let him out of my sight."

In a few minutes they step out into a suddenly brilliant San Francisco day.

"Look important," Loobie says, stepping aside for his photographer. Oliver is blinded by a flashbulb.

▶ ▶ ▶

"Did you find any history of past mental problems suffered by the defendant?"

"None whatsoever. I found that odd."

"Why so?"

"One would have expected a history of previous breakdown, a pattern exhibiting increasing tempo. A psychosis such as claimed for by the defendant rarely in medical history comes unannounced, out of the blue."

"What about these appearances of mental disorder, this Sergeant Pepper code name, the quasi military-intelligence organization that he says controls him?"

"In my opinion it's all an affectation of a clever man acting out schizophrenic delusions to convince me he believes he was mentally disordered. For the purposes of this trial, I would describe him as a mental malingerer. I believe he is as sane and intelligent as you and me."

"And what are the other bases of your opinion the defendant is faking mental illness?"

"Objection. Not so characterized by the witness."

"Overruled."

"One tries to put this in a factual, historical context. You have obvious motive. He held toward both victims an anger he couldn't still. He was purposeful in obtaining a handgun from a locked drawer. Then on top of that you add the results of the psychological testing, and I can go into some detail there."

"We'll take the recess."

"All rise."

■ ■ ■

CHAPTER

16

At two-thirty in the afternoon, Oliver has more reporters around him than the Ayatollah on a visit to Disneyland. The story made the midday edition of the *Times*, complete with a front-page photo of a smiling Gulliver, and a mob was waiting for him inside the lobby of the Oriole Records building. They followed him up to the eighth and topmost floor, where Bennie Ford's office is, where two heavy, smiling men stand in front of the inner sanctum door in T-shirts saying "Long Tom Slider. The Tour." Nobody is to pass by them.

A clutch of microphones are under Oliver's chin as he asks Ford's secretary nicely if he could serve some papers on her boss. His request is recorded for all of history by the major networks. The secretary is one Phoebe Lane, according to the name-strip on her desk. She's nervous about the cameras, maybe it's the attention they're paying to her boobs, braless behind something see-through.

"I'll speak to Mr. Ford," she says.

Oliver sees, as the inner door opens and closes for her, a pall of cigar smoke, and brooding, hostile faces around a boardroom table. Oliver waits happily, chatting up the reporters, riffling through the messages on her in-tray.

His constant shadow is Charles Loobie, who has vigorously overseen his triumphant return to Los Angeles, hustling him from airport to airport, giving advice. Try to avoid the TV guys, they can kill you with that camera, look what they did to Jimmy Carter. Don't let some smiling chick with perfect tits get you alone for any so-called exclusive, they lodge you in a spot where they can write anything and you can't deny. Stick with Loobie who has contacts, who knows people in the entertainment industry, Loobie who can assist in the righting of this evil wrong.

Oliver has disappointed Loobie, however, being open and talkative to the other reporters, he's charming, ebullient, all countryside. Oliver's run a few political campaigns. He knows what the public likes.

"Mr. Gulliver, what are you going to say when you serve the restraining order on them?" A woman with her radio mike.

"Well, I'm going to tell them it's about time they hired a lawyer."

O wondrous miracle that Oriole fouled up and failed to show in court. Whose heads will roll?

A blond preppie in a hand-painted tie exits the big room wherein the Oriole brass smoke and fume. Oliver guesses he's public relations.

"It was just yanked from the KISS-FM playlist, Mr. Moquely," a reporter says. "That's the fourth major market station that's gone off it in the last hour. What's your comment on that?"

"I have a four-point statement. Number one, the accusations are lies. Number two, they constitute a slander. Third, we're going to have this restraining order set aside immediately. And fourth, that's all we're going to say until we find out what kind of publicity stunt this is." He fixes on Oliver. "I guess you're Mr. Gulliver." To his T-shirted bouncers: "Nobody else comes in but Mr. LeGoff."

He gestures to Oliver, who follows him in. Loobie attempts to come, too, but is immediately muscled back out the door by the guards.

Oliver looks around, a dozen men and women, looking like they're waiting out a firestorm in a bomb shelter. Himself, he's feeling pretty good, he's struck first blood. Tricia Santarossa, she's here, a barely perceptible nod from her. His spy, they have to make contact.

"I'm Oliver Gulliver."

"I'm Bennie Ford." He rises from his chair with a strained smile, makes a show of coming around and grasping Oliver's hand. "Sit down."

"No thanks. I don't want to interrupt your meeting, I'm sure you've got important things." Oliver figures the way to treat them is with dignified contempt, which is how he feels, it's honest.

"Do I call you Oliver?" Bennie says.

"That's what my friends call me. You've probably been calling me lots of other things."

Nervous chuckles. Oliver notices several copies of the *L.A. Times* and *Herald-Examiner* draping the table. "C.C. Gilley Sues for his Love Song." "Judge Orders Hit Record off Racks."

"I just came here to serve you with the court order." He opens his briefcase.

"Mr. Gulliver, I want to explain a few things to you," Ford says. He doesn't return to his chair, but tries to hold middle ground in the room, punching a cigaret out of a pack, lighting it.

"C.C. Gilley has threatened to get Oriole Records. Out loud and often. When that fact's pressed home to a jury, his credibility as a witness will be minus zero. You'll look like the winner of the 1988 Klutz Award. In the meantime, each day our records remain off the shelves we lose hundreds of thousands of dollars. We're going to get it back by suing you for malicious prosecution and slander. We'll break you if we have to, Mr. Gulliver."

"I'm broke already. I've been paying for this case out of my pocket, I had to explain that to the press."

Ford is thrown off his speech, takes a second. "Mr. Gulliver, when you came in here the other day to serve those documents, you lied to me, you said you were with McRae, Tchobanian, a firm of attorneys we deal with."

"All I said was, quote, 'I'm a lawyer.'"

"As a result, I only just now looked at the papers which you said were contracts for a tour."

"What about the phone calls?" Oliver says. "I called for you twice personally this morning."

Ford takes an impatient hit from his cigaret. "That's an absolute lie."

"The messages are out there on your telephone in-tray."

Everyone else is silent, but they're looking a little relieved – it's Bennie Ford's can that is on the line over this, they're probably safe. Tricia has put her sunglasses on. She's as deadpan as the Sphinx.

Ford's voice is like a clenched fist. "Service on me was fraud-ulent, the facts will be set out in an affidavit and your order will be set aside. Tomorrow."

"Tomorrow's Saturday," Oliver says. "The courts are closed."

"We'll open them. I don't care if we have to drag this Judge Sherman out of his swimming pool to hear us." Ford reins in, starts talking with slow emphasis. "After we set the restraining order aside, you may want to consider dropping your action. In that case, we could agree not to sue you. If you insist on going to trial, the proceedings are going to be long, costly, and dirty. You've put yourself in the spotlight." Ford stabs a finger at Oliver's picture in the newspaper. "Where reputations are lit up."

"The only stain I got is on my tie, Mr. Ford. It's last Sun-day's gravy." He extends to Ford the restraining order and Ford hesitates, takes it, looking like he's gone off stride again.

Louis LeGoff comes wheeling in, red-faced, towing Tom Slider, whose face is white and tight. The door swings closed against the jostling, shouting media.

"It's extortion, and I say fuck them." LeGoff seems in a reasonably sour mood. Oliver takes pleasure. LeGoff ignores him, and almost jams himself up against Ford, backing him against the table, hunching down over the smaller man. "You couldn't put a finger up your ass without poking yourself in the eye, Ford, how'd y'all manage to screw up so bad, you're a lawyer, y'all don't know enough to oppose a fuckin' injunction?"

Ford's voice is soft and controlled. "Louis, the story has you wiping your butt on the court documents. Didn't you read them first?"

LeGoff gestures at Oliver. "This guy came in with some papers, I told him he could stick them up his butt, and I showed him how. He didn't say nothin' about a court date."

Oliver speaks pleasantly, offering a copy of the restraining order. "Where do you want to stick this?"

He rolls up a copy of the court order and places it in LeGoff's jacket pocket. LeGoff looks like he's about to take a swing but Slider comes between them, two cold, pained eyes staring down at Oliver.

"Mr. Gulliver, I'll take a hundred lie detector tests. I can *prove* I wrote that song."

"How?"

Ford interrupts. "It will be in the affidavits." He points to a door. "A few private minutes, Mr. Gulliver."

Oliver thinks about this. Okay. He follows him to a small side office, really a lounge. There's a small bar and a long couch, mussed, its pillows awry.

"Scotch? V.O.? Sit down, for God's sake, I'm not going to pull a knife. Relax."

Oliver, standing stiffly there. Yes, relax. You're a lawyer, a professional man, not a cop on a bust. He sits on the couch. "You got fresh orange juice?"

"I don't like the folderol," Ford says, behind him, pouring drinks. "I don't like the dance. A lot of attorneys negotiate like Bedouins, two hours of tea and figs before work. We haven't got that much time."

He brings the drinks, a scotch for himself, and pulls up a chair beside the couch. "Problems," he says. "Radio stations going off the song all weekend, record shipments being held." He shakes his head. "I'm not going to underestimate you. No, you're not a dumb hick. Real smart."

Oliver just nods.

"This is going to cost us a fair buck. I don't know what Melvin Belli charges on a per diem, but it's probably flagrant. Plus our expert witnesses, Mancini, Previn, they won't be cheap. You lose even when you win in court. It goes against my instincts - frankly, I'd like to see Gilley ground into the court-room floor - but I've got to be a businessman and try to save the company money."

"And?"

"So what do you want for your song?"

"It's not for sale."

"I told you we don't have time to play the game, Mr. Gulliver. We'll have to swallow three million to do a trial. Let's say instead we buy your copyright for a million bucks."

Oliver waits, says nothing.

"You weren't expecting it to be so easy. Grab it and run with it. A nice fee there for you. But please understand. This is the final round of negotiations. Tomorrow if we have to set aside the restraining order, the offer goes to zero. No, zero minus, you pay us, because we'll be flying at you with complaints and summonses. We'll bury you alive, Mr. Gulliver."

"You think about it a little more, Mr. Ford. I'm not saying we can't come to terms on damages, but you're not getting our song."

As he stands up, he brushes a cushion to the floor, revealing part of a brassiere. Oliver knows why Ford wasn't answering the phone.

Oliver exits smiling, past the curious faces in the boardroom, into the welcoming arms of the press. He has the ball, he's running with it. The other team is missing tackles. He's never felt better in his life.

*   *   *

Tricia Santarossa looks too much into the role in her dark sunglasses. She wears a man's white shirt, it blankets her, she's thin.

"The board of directors will think bad of Bennie, their presi-

127

dent, who eats his secretary on company time." Tricia's smile flickers on and off. "Why am I being so snobby? Three years of my life lost to a married man. It's fundamental, it's in all the teachings, you don't fall in love with a married man."

Oliver has questions but doesn't ask them.

She says, "A million dollars, that's pretty high for starters, don't you think? Like an admission of guilt."

"That's how it struck me."

Their rendezvous is a bar near her apartment building, up toward the Hollywood Hills in the trendy part of East Hollywood. El Cerro, it's called, nachos and Corona beers. It's on a high switchback, and he can see the night dazzle, Hollywood at Oliver Gulliver's feet. At the end of his press conference by the little pool of the Capri Motel on Airport Boulevard, Mayor Gulliver thanked them all, and told them they should come up for a little North Coast hospitality. Foolsgold will be hosting the Fall Fishin' Fair in a couple of weeks.

Later someone called his room from "Entertainment Tonight" wanting to do just that, come up to Foolsgold and sketch a Gulliver family portrait. He should hold out for "60 Minutes." After that he called Tricia at home, and they arranged a meet over a beer.

"This is tricky work, playing Mata Hari," Tricia says. "Had Slider up at my apartment the other night. Beautiful to look at it but what a prong. Smoked reefer 'til it was coming from his ears, the stuff went to his tongue. The first part of the evening was Everything You Want to Know about Tom Slider and More. With the complete Dreams and Ambitions. Too weird. The last part of the evening was gropesville."

"Gee, I'm sorry for all the trouble. Did you get anything?" He wonders if gropesville led to bedsville.

"Tom Slider was tripping when he, as it were, wrote that song."

"Tripping."

" 'I finally knew who I was, man,' " she mimics. " 'I saw inside myself.' I think he liked what he saw, he's developing this starfucker attitude."

"What do you mean, tripping, falling down?"

She grins. "Oliver, you're sort of a Fifties person, aren't you? That must have been a great time." She says this kindly. "'Shrooms. Psylocibe."

"Magic mushrooms."

"That's what he says. Silly 'cibes, grown on Texas dung, total organic voyage, man, like who needs chemicals, this stuff makes an acid trip like poppin' downs. He's going to import his own Texas shit and grow psylocibin in his basement. He figures if he can come up with a hit song every time he consumes some 'shrooms the world will forget Mick Jagger."

"A magic mushroom trip. From this came his psychic experience?"

"Transported to the land of song."

"Along with who else?"

"I surmised he wasn't alone. I don't know who and I don't know where. He stiffened up when I started asking questions. He's been told not to talk about it."

"By whom?"

"Bennie. Looks bad in the press, rock star inspired by mind-altering substance. Tom doesn't agree with that, wants to share his formula for genius with the world. After he's made it to the top he's going to write a book."

"You said Bennie. Ford."

She shakes those stray waifs from in front of her eyes. "Yep. Bennie. You can't tell anyone I told you that."

"He and Bennie Ford have some game going, I wonder what it is."

"I don't know, Oliver, he seemed kind of sincere."

"Sincere?"

"He's too dumb to lie well. He was quite hurt that he's been accused of plagiarism and he's going to take a polygraph test. Pretty confident about it."

"Gee, you couldn't have worked him a little more?"

"He was getting a little physical. I had to threaten to call the doorman."

Oliver and Tricia find another spot for a late-night bite and a

129

bottle of wine, a kind of cellar, candle-lit and gentle. Tricia knows her Los Angeles, she loves it here. Oliver tries to argue with her about that, but apparently L.A. does a slow grow on you. She hated it, too, when she first arrived. You have to get to know the town a few layers down.

The city works for her, but the music industry doesn't. Not at this level, the bureaucracy, finding talent, coddling it, shucking around with the promoters. Everything is up for sale to Madison Avenue to move beer and running shoes, the purity of rock has died, corruption has set in like a cancer.

The industry has done her in. Sometimes she'd just like to run away to a cabin with a piano and play Liszt and dream. Her drug turns out to be cocaine, there's no real habit, she says, it's no big deal. Two failed marriages and a failed affair with a married man, a film editor who made the choice of wife and kids last year after months of anguish, dragging it out until Tricia nearly went out of her mind. Suddenly Tricia became a figure of tragic abandon, her affairs were notorious. Her therapist tells her she did this to hurt the married guy.

"I walked into a cocktail party last New Year's Eve and looked around and saw four men who had woken up beside me one time or another during the last eight months, all looking guilty. I went straight home, and made a resolution. I've been a nun for the last eight months."

Her openness seduces Oliver into the telling of his own loneliness, his great love for Madelaine, his disintegration at her death, how he pulled it together so fast he never found time to mourn, and she's still with him, and there hasn't been any other women except once, the druggist's wife at the Christmas party, Mrs. Harvey Sweet, in the back of that van. He was so ashamed. He thinks the girls found out.

He talks on, it's a dam breaking, he's never opened up to anyone like this. He speaks of his daughters, tells the stories of their growing up, and suddenly in the midst of this, it's wildly embarrassing, horrible, he starts to cry.

Tricia takes his hand. She has her sunglasses off and her eyes aren't sparkling now. They seem soft in the candlelight.

"I guess it's the wine," Oliver says.

*   *   *

When Tricia drops him on the grounds of the Capri Motel he leans over the leather of her classy Jaguar XKE and lightly kisses her on the lips, he's bold with wine. Should he ask her in for a nightcap? - Oliver's got a few Miller Light in there. She's a practising celibate, he should respect that.

She finally interrupts his thoughts and he's aware she's staring at him, smiling. "I better go."

An hour later he is still awake, tingling, sitting up in bed in his pyjamas watching James Stewart in a gunfight and sipping a beer from the can, relishing his day.

There's a light knock on his door and he thinks it's her, Tricia, she couldn't stay away. He gets up, goes to the door, but is careful, this is the city.

"Who is it?"

"Bennie Ford. I have some documents."

Oliver unlocks and opens but doesn't invite him in, stands there in his pyjamas as Ford, here by himself, brings a large binder from his briefcase and hands it to Oliver.

Ford's voice is too businesslike. "It's an application to Judge Sherman to reopen his order and to set it aside and to fix a new date for both sides to be heard. Bunch of affidavits."

"You have one from Tom Slider?"

"Naturally. The application is set for tomorrow morning. The judge's clerk says he's up at some lake in Trinity County, fishing. We're flying out at six AM by executive jet to Redding, and we have a floatplane rental from there. Please be our guest. There'll be you, our chief counsel and Tommy Klein."

"Tommy Klein?"

"We've retained him as trial counsel."

Oliver is about to blurt a protest. It's unethical, Oliver consulted Tommy Klein. But then he thinks, Klein, the aging hipster and posturing fop, not the quickest draw in the O.K. Corral.

131

"Or we can agree to reverse the order by consent, set a full hearing on your injunction application for next week, and we'll of course pay your costs to date. I don't doubt they're up around a hundred grand."

Oliver shakes his head.

Bennie sighs deeply. "All right, you win. I can get authorization to buy you out for two million dollars. Certified check on Tuesday."

"We're not selling out for, you'll excuse the expression, a song."

"Damn it, what's your figure, let's see if there's talking ground."

"I think I'll enjoy the trip to the lake."

"You know what? I'm coming to the not-so-reluctant conclusion that you do have a scam going here, Gulliver. You're real brave holding that gun." Lower still, "We're coming after you, pal. You're going to come out looking like you just walked into the 5:10 to Union Station. I don't think you want to do that to yourself."

Oliver is reassured by the threatening tone. This guy's scared. Oliver figures there's a reward for living a boring, blameless life. There's no way they can do a Gary Hart on the pure of heart.

CHAPTER

17

At a non-commercial hangar at the Burbank airport. Oliver greets Ford and Oriole's veep for legal, a Mr. McRae, and a relaxed and hearty Tommy Klein, all suited up for court. Oliver's in jeans.

Klein quickly draws him aside. "Play it cool, old boy."

"Why?"

"We'll have a chance to talk." He gives Oliver heavy eye intensity, he's got an important confidence to share.

"Why is he here?" Klein indicates Charles Loobie, who is shaking hands with an irked-looking Ford.

"I want someone along who makes accurate notes."

"Here's the thing, we couldn't get anything bigger in a float-plane than a Cessna 185. With the weight, we can squeeze one more guy in the back, but that has to be Judge Sherman's clerk, that's five, maximum crew including me as pilot."

"You as pilot."

"I've flown hundreds of these suckers. Own my own."

"Oh, yeah, I read in *Trial Lawyer*, Vietnam ace, too."

"The thing is we don't have room for Loobie."

"Kick out Mr. McRae."

*   *   *

On the first leg of the trip, aboard Oriole's Lear, Bennie Ford morosely watches Loobie pour paragraph after paragraph into his writing pad. Klein is up beside the pilot, he's flown a lot more complicated machines than this. Opposing counsel has The Right Stuff. *We'll have a chance to talk*. He wishes Klein would stop treating him like a fool.

Over a cup of coffee, Oliver rereads their two experts' opinions. Persuasive enough, if you don't dig into them, but phrased too coyly, relying on what Dr. Aloysius Frisby described as "colorable variations." Colorable, said Oliver's expert, in the sense that alterations to the plaintiff's song – some notes and bars here and there – seemed unnatural and purposeful, intended to deceive, to make the unauthentic seem original.

Rigby's report is full of muscle. These two hasty studies by company stooges are all skin and bones.

The affidavits are of more interest. Ford's says Arson Garson and Splint are "not known" to Oriole Records. His company is grossly insulted that it could be accused of dealing with song pirates. Tom Slider brought the song into the recording studio on Wednesday, August third. It is true he had some assistance with the lyrics, but Oriole Records has every confidence he is the composer. The plaintiff Gilley is known to have strong negative feelings about Oriole Records. Attached hereto as exhibits are newspaper clippings quoting the plaintiff as saying such and such.

Oliver looks at one of them from *Variety*. "Label Sucks, Says Singer."

Slider swears he wrote the song unassisted, no mention of the magic 'shrooms, let alone of the fact Bennie Ford told him to say nothing about said 'shrooms. So Oliver has evidence of deceit here, deceit by omission.

"I was at the aforesaid time staying at an apartment on Wilshire Boulevard. On the third of August while practising my guitar I began to meditate and had what for lack of better words I have publicly described as a psychic experience. That was a metaphor to describe the strong creative feeling I was enjoying as I was in the process of composing 'Goin' Down for the Last Time.' "

What copy writer fed him this?

The reader is given no further insight into Slider's creative processes. Five paragraphs, two pages, the lack of detail speaks volumes.

But flying colors on the polygraph test, which was run by a professor with pages of credentials. Maybe Slider's a skilled psychopath, able to beat the machine. Somehow that doesn't quite work for Oliver. Is Long Tom dumb enough to have been persuaded he wrote the song? While hallucinating?

After a while, Klein slides into the chair next to him. The chance to talk.

He says, "I told you they'd find experts. They picked out some pretty significant differences between the songs."

"One of these guys works for Oriole Records, the other used to. They were honest enough to admit that in their credentials."

"They're a holding pattern until we can get the top-shelf guys."

"No explanation about how my phone calls got ignored." Instead, much groveling, even a florid apologia from LeGoff.

"You tell anyone you tried to retain me?" Klein leans close. He wears a yellow, tarty three-piece suit.

"No."

"Good. Leave it that way." He comes within inches, Oliver's nostrils fill with aftershave. "I told you already I think your case has some serious holes, but I've given Bennie a different story and I've got him running a little scared. Between you and me, I think I can work him over and jack him up."

"What's the offer?"

"I wouldn't be surprised we can ding him for around four million."

Oliver takes a few seconds.

"Tell him no."

*   *   *

Judge Sherman's clerk is waiting at the airport at Redding, near the little floatplane Oriole rented. It's a weathered veteran, and Loobie, a poor flier, asks for Klein's credentials as a pilot. He doesn't want to hear how many combat sorties he went on in Vietnam, he wants to know if Klein has flown little planes with floats on.

Klein offers to leave him behind. Loobie gets on the plane.

Getting up beside Klein to navigate, the clerk explains he isn't sure if the radiophone message was delivered to Judge Sherman's cabin, which has no phone. The clerk says he doesn't like this at all.

The plane climbs into the mountains under a glimmering September sun, and after a while there's the lake, its long fingers crooking up the valleys, a wilderness forest enclosing it. They're up in northern California in the Trinity Alps, home is over the range. Oliver's been on a whistling boil for the last several days, and he misses home, the girls. He wonders what they'd think of Tricia Santarossa.

Was his rejection of that four million deal too quick and too cocky? He prays his instincts about this case are correct. Ford is guilty of a tort, if not an outright crime. Oliver intends to keep him on the run. What a gamble – if Sherman reverses himself, Oliver loses all momentum. But if he can convince the judge to continue the temporary restraining order until Tuesday, he can squeeze Oriole tighter. And maybe on Tuesday he'll somehow have his evidence and be granted a full preliminary injunction.

They've been groaning slowly in and out of inlets, working too close to the treetops for comfort, Klein probably doing it for Loobie's benefit.

Finally the clerk points out the cabin, a station wagon out front, but no sign of life. "The boat's gone from the dock. I don't like this."

Oliver remembers, the judge has a favorite fishing hole. He's not going to help, let them find him if they can.

The water's a soft blue-green, lots of biochemical processes going on in the life-giving heat of late summer. A boat putts through a channel, a line following. Oliver knows it's not Sherman, who doesn't troll. They startle the fisherman, Oliver can see him open-mouthed, then the plane moves on toward a little bay into which a high-mountain stream empties. A cabin cruiser there, twenty-foot. As they do a pass, Oliver sees it's a black man. He recognizes Judge Sherman's headgear, that slouch hat.

The judge doesn't even turn to look at the plane. He's fighting a fish.

Oliver holds in his stomach one more time as Klein skids the plane into a sharp turn, wing tip nearly skimming water, and straightens, the pontoons planing the waves, sending up a skirl of spray aft of Sherman's boat. Oliver sees from his window a brown trout rise to the surface, showing the lure, and it thrashes and falls. If it's not Grandpa Moses, it's his brother.

The pontoons tangle and cut Judge Sherman's line.

Oliver closes his eyes.

After the aircraft's engine stills, an eerie silence comes over the cabin. It is made the more awful by the muffled sound from outside. "Gaw-*damn!*"

Klein unbuckles from his seat. He has a nervous smile. Oliver can't tell if he realizes what has happened.

"You better announce us, old boy," Klein tells the clerk.

"You announce yourself." The clerk is looking numbly out the window. Oliver turns and sees the judge standing there with a limp line, his boat slopping quietly in the waves about thirty feet from them. Sherman is staring at the plane with a look that could fry rocks.

It doesn't seem as if the clerk is going to unhook his safety belt. Loobie plays working reporter. Bennie looks bewildered. "Well, do it," he says.

Klein climbs out a door and onto a float.

"Sir, my name is Klein and I appear for the defendants in this action, Gilley versus Oriole."

"What do you want?"

"This is an application to reopen the temporary restraining order you granted, sir."

"Were you at the controls of this plane, Mr. Klein?"

"Yes, I'm extremely sorry about the inconvenience – "

"Get your mother-fucking ass out of here."

"I'm sorry, your honor?"

"If that plane doesn't take off in the next thirty seconds, I'm going to demand you show cause why you should not be cited for contempt and I'm going to have you arrested on that charge. All of you."

Klein's face, ghost-like, comes into view in the doorway. "Oliver, say something."

Oliver leans toward the open door. "I've been hijacked, your honor. I had nothing to do with this."

"Let's go," says Bennie.

*   *   *

On arrival at Redding, Oliver finds there's a flight to the McKinleyville Airport north of Eureka. Loobie, chortling, "I like it," races off to a phone, working to one of his own paper's illimitable deadlines. Oliver wants to sneak back to Foolsgold undisturbed, relax in the womb of his hilltop home. He calls Lindy to ask if any reporters are hanging around. No, just Pastor Blythe.

"Pastor Blythe?"

"He's sitting in the living room. He won't say why."

Saturday afternoon. He should be practising his sermon in front of the mirror.

*   *   *

Oliver's taxi speeds him up the 101 and he's buoyed by the closeness of home. Once more he enjoys the scene back at Engle Lake, it's like light cider, he's tipsy with it. Now he has breathing room to Tuesday, two more days to find Garson and Splint. He'll call Jesse Gonzales about how that's going.

Garson and Splint, their names have been delivered into the

homes of every newspaper reader, radio listener, and TV watcher in Canada and the U.S. Someone's got to tip off a cop somewhere.

As Oliver pays off the driver at the back door of his house, Tennyson, who must have got into the vitamins, bounds up from under his favorite shade tree and greets him with a slurp to the hand, thus acknowledging his master's fame. Lindy quickly pulls him into the house.

"I told everyone, no interviews. I'm taking the phone off the hook. Heroes are entitled to their rest. Oh, Dad, I'm proud of you." She hugs him. On the stove he sees pots of garden vegetables simmering. The oven sends secret, meaty scents. Through a doorway, Oliver observes the pink cherubic figure of the Reverend Wilfrid Blythe parked on a favorite chair, sipping a Seven Up.

"I'll get rid of him. Maybe he thinks I'm suddenly rich, he wants to hit me up."

He takes a can of Budweiser from the fridge and pops the tab open and goes into the living room. Blythe gets up.

"Oliver. Bless you." He shakes Oliver's hand eagerly. Maybe he's a fan, watches Oliver on TV. "So good of you to see me on your day off."

"I'm going to be watching the Southern Cal-Oregon game in half an hour, I've got a little time."

Oliver switches on the TV set, but slides the sound off. The set is in front of Oliver's chair, an old white rattan whose cushions have molded to his personal body shape over the years. Pastor Blythe lowers both cheeks onto those cushions and his elbows onto the armrests and his fingers make a little church roof.

"I wish to talk in confidence, minister to lawyer."

"Minister to lawyer." Is he in some kind of trouble? "You don't mean client to lawyer? If this is advice, I have to send you a bill." Oliver's smile does nothing to dispel the chill in his voice. Maybe the fellow has diddled one of the girls after Sunday School. And she's blackmailing him. Oliver's fee will be large, Blythe's been a major parasite worm, bleeding poor Sybil McGuid. Along with that other famous leech, Ernie Bolestero. Maybe there's a conspiracy. We get her out of Gulliver's clutches and divide her fifty-fifty.

Oliver sits on the stool he normally rests his feet up on. He pulls a couple of throatfuls of beer from the can.

Blythe takes time to measure his words. "Ah yes, yes indeed, I'm calling on your services. It's, ah, about another in your profession, and it's best that we retain absolute confidence. Client to attorney, yes."

Oliver waits, wondering.

"Ernie Bolestero."

"Go on."

"Apparently he's persuaded dear Sybil to reduce her contributions to my, ah, ministry. Rather severely."

"And you're thinking she's not of sound mind."

"Ernie has her ear. He's with her every waking moment. And, ah, she's very, how shall I put it, trusting. Ernie is, ah . . . I don't like to think evil of people."

"Of course not." Especially after Bolestero axed the gravy line.

"But while I was visiting Sister Sybil yesterday – she had to take her maid home, she was ill, the poor dear – I happened to be standing by her writing desk, and her checkbook was out."

"And as you were looking through it, what did you see?"

"Well, staring me in the face was a check stub for twelve thousand dollars. It was made out to a Prestige Investments Corporation. I found several others, smaller amounts, all to the same firm."

"Over what period of time?"

"The last month. Do you know anything about that company?"

"Never heard of it. I can't find out until Tuesday."

"She told me yesterday he's advised her to invest in semiconductors."

"Maybe that's what she's doing."

140

"I think Bolestero is milking her."

"What proof do you have of that?"

"I suspect you'll find it to be the case."

Oliver reads the proof in his face. Maybe he snooped around more than he's admitted.

CHAPTER

18

After a lazy Sunday breakfast with Lindy, Oliver's *omelette de bon surpris*, the phone goes back on the hook and the calls begin. Oliver praises his opponents, saying their move to ambush Judge Sherman took great courage in view of their prior neglect to answer a federal court summons. He regrets that so much in shareholders' profits has to be wasted in this court case.

A camera pursues him to his car. Here's Attorney Gulliver leaving his house, folks, look at that jaunty step, the bold way he victory-fingers you. Maybe Oliver will run for the state senate, he should test the waters.

Of course the air could go fast from his bubble if he loses that restraining order, a weapon of improving potency, it's been producing an effect akin to that of a terrorist's grenade in an airplane. That is the leveler, maybe his edge.

Four million dollars. Tricia Santarossa said one million was an admission of guilt.

Oliver has arranged for Mrs. Plymm to come in, although it's Sunday and the long weekend and all. "I hope you know what you're doing, Oliver," she says as he closes and locks the front door. Mrs. Plymm is why he's never made it big, she infects him with self-doubt.

"No calls, please."

Jesse is standing by Oliver's desk reading through a copy of the *California Reports*.

"Here's a guy got charged for publishing an obscenity - to wit, 'Fuck the Pentagon' on a T-shirt - court held it was protected under the First Amendment. The abominations people get away with."

Oliver sits at his desk and opens the thick file Jesse has put there.

"Garson and Splint must've submersed somewhere once their names hit the news," he says.

Their mug shots also went out. The only information Jesse has suppressed is his suspicion Garson torched the Opera House.

"We're getting reports in, but only a few of them tenable. A good one had them in a communal house in L.A. two weeks ago, they were thinking of going back to Vancouver. A pawnbroker, also L.A., comes up with Garson pawning his guitar last month, says he was in a high dungeon about some money owing him. If he's sore at Oriole Records, could be to our advantage once we find him."

You've got to give the chief credit. He's amassed, in the last few days, most of the police reports and some of the court documents relating to Garson Schuter's eleven previous convictions and aquittals, most of them in Canada. Oliver figures Jesse, with all the TV cameras on him, is burning to solve this case, but of course he has to be cool, act unfazed, it's the chief's way.

Oliver does an overview, flipping from file to file.

Jesse is still reading the *California Reports*. "Here's a drunk driver, blows a nineteen, walks because they forgot to date the breathalyzer certificate. This is called justice."

"Arson of a sixty-foot cabin cruiser," Oliver says. "Owned by a Seattle stockbroker. Doesn't say if he was a broke stockbroker."

"So what's on your mind?"

"One of them's a definite." Oliver has the report in front of him. "Warehouse full of old trucks, a transport business that was going bankrupt. The owners were apparently under suspicion of conspiring with Garson, but no proof."

"I read it."

"Notice there was an insurance claim in every one of these? Maybe he's not just some weird religioso who burns buildings for God. Maybe he burns for a less worthy motive."

"I hear you and I've thought about it. But who would hire him to torch the Opera House? It's a theory, Oliver, but it don't stand under analysis. No motive. Who would gain by that antique building burning down?"

"Ernie Bolestero," Mrs. Plymm says from the outer office.

Oliver feels a click in his brain, like the tumblers of a lock turning.

"He doesn't want to interrupt, he says just fifteen seconds."

Oliver shivers off a little aftershock. Is it thus that enlightenment descends, from the voice of Mrs. Plymm? He picks up the phone. "Hi, Ernie."

"How do I run for mayor against a campaign like this?" Bolestero says. "Listen, why don't you take on the presidential primaries instead, give me a chance. How're you doing, Oliver, nailing any good stuff down there in Hollywood? They say you got your own fan club complete with groupies hanging all over you."

Ernie spent a few years in the Public Defenders' office in Orange County before moving up to the North Coast. Why, Oliver has often wondered, why Foolsgold?

"It's been a real trip, Ernie." This man, a reliable informant says, is siphoning the accounts of a lonely old millionairess. At the end he'll tell her the semiconductor industry has collapsed. "For what can I do you?"

"I've been retained by Oriole Records, they like my courtroom style. Hey, truly, I'm their guy. Okay, it's only to serve some documents on you. They found I'm the only other lawyer in Foolsgold, and I told them I'm cheap. Motion and supporting affidavits to bring the injunction before the ninth circuit, Federal Court of Appeal in San Francisco, day after tomorrow, Tuesday, September sixth. Courier's delivering them to me about four o'clock and I'll get them right over."

Oliver feared something like this. Oriole knows Judge Sherman will be waiting for them, salivating, in Court Eleven of the Federal Building in San Francisco. This motion to bypass him will come before a three-member division of the appeal court.

Oliver doesn't ask Ernie about the Prestige Electronics Investments Corporation. After he hangs up, he looks at Jesse, who reads his mind.

"Ernie Bolestero?" Jesse says. "Okay, he's a sleeze. But counseling arson?"

"Why does a guy like that come up from where the money is to poor little old Foolsgold? Maybe he's targeted a not-too-bright rich lady and figured out a way to give the competition the shove."

"I know you don't like Ernie, but I hear you saying he hired Garson to burn down the Opera House."

As Oliver tells him about Pastor Blythe's visit, he remembers something.

"In his datebook, he had 'E.B.' written a few days before the fire."

"Who?"

"Clarence. Maybe he wasn't able to talk to me, I'm family, maybe he unloaded on Ernie, told him he'd stolen the premiums. Ernie knew Sybil would fire me if Clarence screwed up, she said as much to the whole wide world. And he also knew Sybil would have to get another lawyer, I couldn't act for her against my brother-in-law."

"He's an attorney, Oliver, he . . . ." Then he says, "Maybe you got a point."

"Did you ever talk to Ernie about why he left the L.A. burbs for the woods?"

"He said when he was a student he worked up here a couple of summers. Fell in love with the North Coast. Maybe it's bullshit, maybe he's running from something."

"Who'd he work for those couple of summers?"

145

"He was working at a tree nursery."

"Who'd he work for?"

"Sybil McGuid."

The last file abruptly knits things together. People versus Garson. July 12, 1984, Anaheim. In Orange County. Attempted arson of a tavern. Winning defense counsel, Mr. E. Bolestero.

"We must talk to Ernie," Oliver says.

*   *   *

Oliver does the NBC show in the afternoon, an hour and a half of camera for what they say will be a three-minute segment. Lindy tries to shoo every one else away after that, she can see her father's busy thinking. Brooding is the word, preparing himself for Bolestero, who cannibalized Oliver's practice. Succulent thoughts of revenge dance through his head, all ending with Ernie being led away in handcuffs.

Shoved from center stage but still back there niggling is the forthcoming joust with Oriole in the federal court of appeal. Foreign waters to Oliver, perhaps shark-infested.

Jesse Gonzales shows up before Ernie, and Oliver takes him to his private, quiet den and seats him.

The plan is Oliver will play the wheeling-dealing D.A. to Jesse's hard-nosed dick. The chief has reservations.

"We're giving away the store."

"You can't make Ernie on the Opera House, we're giving away nothing."

"Oliver, ain't you becoming a little possessed about winning this civil case of yours? I'm noticing changes. You're acting more like a lawyer."

"I *am* a lawyer."

"A real lawyer, I mean. A shyster."

"I'm playing with the big boys now, Jesse. Law is about tactics, not legalities. Just think, you can be the guy who charges Oriole Records with conspiracy to defraud C.C. Gilley, you'll be famous like me."

."Events have gone to your head."

But Oliver's intuition is right - the chief quietly hungers to solve the case of the stolen song, this week's number one hit crime across America. The president of Oriole Records would be a bigger collar than crooked little Ernie Bolestero. Jesse doesn't need much persuading.

They play a couple of hands of cribbage while they wait.

When Ernie arrives, he sits him in a chair beside Jesse's, a softer chair, they want him to be comfortable.

Ernie asks Jesse, "Not interrupting your game, I hope."

"Nope."

Oliver goes to the kitchen and returns with some cold beers.

Ernie has about a hundred-page document in his hand. "I do hereby serve thee."

Oliver takes it, copies of all the court documents, affidavits, arguments on law, a fancy job of binding. Oliver will have to prepare something in reply tomorrow. What's it called - an appellee's answer in opposition.

"Hell of a legal machine they operate, Klein, Ingle," Ernie says. "They can really get into war gear. Even on holidays."

There are three applications. One, as expected, is to overturn Judge Sherman's t.r.o. The other comes as a jolt - they're seeking prohibition against Oliver's favorite judge, applying to prevent him from presiding further over the case. Oriole has pleaded anticipated bias. This worries Oliver a lot. Sherman is his not-so-secret weapon.

The third application is for a change of venue to Los Angeles.

"You been following Oliver's case here," Jesse says.

"Can't escape from it. I told Oliver, I said, how do I run for mayor against that?" A chuckle. "Hell, I'm going to have to withdraw my name - "

"What's your hypothesis about these people Garson and Splint?" Jesse asks.

"The people that took the car? Oliver's song thieves?"

"You've seen their pictures in the paper and TV," says Jesse.

"Well, what about them?" Ernie is showing some ill at ease over the icy climate in here.

"Ever met them? This guy Garson Schuter?"

"Why would I? I wasn't at Oliver's party."

"Never before?"

Ernie hesitates. "I don't think so."

"Ever defend him, Arson Garson?"

Ernie thinks. "Let me see that picture again, have you got a copy?" The Arson Garson file is right on the desk, and here is the firemaker's sneering portrait. "Isn't that funny, in a way, he *does* look like a guy I - "

"I think you knew he was a professional torch," says Jesse. "I think you knew he'd been in town the night the Opera House burned down. Why didn't you confer with me about these things?"

"Garson Schuter," Ernie says, eyes staying on the photo. "Yeah, this is the guy. I think I defended him. On an attempt arson. Got him off, but he was guilty as shit."

"Always wondered where he got all those gas cans from," Jesse says.

"Hey, just a minute." As if it's just dawning. "What're you guys cooking up here? This is starting to be unfriendly."

"We may have some evidence we don't want to manifest at this time," says Jesse. "Maybe it's a little short of proving a circumstantial case of counseling arson, maybe it's not."

Oliver comes in. "Quite honestly, Ernie, I don't think there's enough to stick. Unless Garson talks. God knows what will pour out if he finally surfaces."

Ernie is white, expressionless. He's an ex-criminal lawyer, he'll know, as Oliver conceded, there's no case against him without a confession from Schuter. Still, their proposal may be too good to refuse.

"I could arrest you, and maybe I could decide not to," says Jesse.

Bolestero looks tightly from face to face.

"I'm the aggrieved party," says Oliver. "I don't really have to issue a formal complaint. But I could."

"I'm dreaming," Ernie says. "It's three o'clock in the morning, and if I open my eyes it'll be dark out, and I'll have a good laugh and go back to sleep."

"The thing is to get to Garson before someone else does," Oliver says. "And someone will, he's very prominent these days. He's the kind of guy might even see his way to telling his story to *People Magazine* for a fee. But if we get to him fast, and he cooperates, Jesse may be willing to trade. The Opera House for Oriole Records. He gives us a statement against Oriole, no charges would be laid against him for theft or arson."

"And the kicker is, Ernie, no charges will be proffered against you, neither," Jesse adds. "You can't ask better than that."

"All we might request is you pack your bags and head for sunnier climes. And give up your law ticket. Otherwise, my guess is twelve to eighteen."

"This is crazy. Why the hell would you even think I know how to reach this Schuter guy?" Ernie's smile is so inappropriate and so taut it shouts guilt.

"You did it before," says Oliver. "Last July, when you got him to come up here, suggested he pretend to be hitchhiking through. And hasn't he been phoning you, something to do with money?"

Ernie takes a swig of beer, and wipes his lips, seems to calm a bit. "I get it. Oliver, I knew you were pissed at losing some files to me, but isn't this going a little too far? Goosing up your buddy here to threaten me with phony charges?"

"Then there's the matter of Prestige Electronics," Oliver says.

Ernie's animated. "Now just a minute, where did that come from? Let me guess, His Eminence Wilbur Cardinal Blythe, he's a part of the plot to tar-and-gravel me out of town, yeah, you bet. I told him, and the facts are, those are speculative issues, Sybil's aware of that, she can quintuple her money in two months or lose a few bucks, no more than she was throwing away to the pastor with *no* hope of a return."

He gets up. "I notice no one's reading my rights, so I guess I'll go."

"We're making an offer," Jesse says. "You can accept it or we can read you your rights."

Bolestero leans fiercely toward them. "You charge me with something you can't prove, Chief, I'll sue your fat ass from here to kingdom come, along with the aggrieved mayor here. Damages for conspiracy to maliciously prosecute, except maybe it's a dry judgment against Oliver, he can't afford a pot to piss in. I'm calling your bluff, bud, charge me and take your chances."

Things seem to be backfiring here. Bolestero has sensed weakness in the enemy, appears willing to take a brave but calculated stand.

Jesse gets up wearily. "Tomorrow morning, ten o'clock, I want you to come by my office. I'll have one of the county sheriffs in to witness. I want a full statement about your dealings with Schuter. Then I'll be filing a report with the D.A. and he'll decide on what charges."

Ernie hears this serious tone, pauses at the door. "Are we off the record?"

Jesse says, "Okay."

"For the sake of argument," Ernie says, "let's assume – and Garson is a former client – I can get some lines out to this guy. I mean we don't have to go through all this bullshit, maybe he'll be *happy* to cooperate. About the song. Assuming he's not going to be charged over this Opera House thing. Then maybe the dust can settle and we can all be pals again."

"How quickly can you reach him?" Oliver asks.

"I might not. It's a grasping-at-straws situation, but give me a day or two."

"I need him Tuesday, day after tomorrow."

"Oliver, I want to help. I wish you guys had just asked me nicely instead of all the empty threats."

CHAPTER

19

On Labor Day, Oliver goes up early to the courthouse library in Eureka to get straight what he has to do in a federal court of appeal and to look up some law on reversing injunctions, and on prohibition. The defendants' affidavits describe in honest, saddening detail the dialogue between Judge Sherman on his boat and poor Tommy Klein on the float of the plane. They aver they can never hope for a fair hearing in front of this judge.

Oliver intends to argue that a judge has a right to hate someone's guts for cutting his fishing line, but we appoint intelligent people to these high courts who are capable of being impartial in the end. The appeal is vexatious, insulting to the judge below.

As he works, Oliver endures a feeling vaguely like a wad of cotton is stuck in his throat. The Federal Court of Appeal. Judges so high up they're lost in the clouds. Razor-sharp minds and withering tongues elegant of phrase, theirs is the realm of pure law, unleavened by passion or feelings. They aren't going to be seduced by the country lawyer schtick.

Oliver is going to make the best legal argument he can. They've got to be nearly human, these judges. They'll see what's right and what's wrong.

But they'll not see evidence of access. Oliver and Jesse really Keystone Kopped that back-room deal with Bolestero. Surely the man will immediately contact the arsonist and his hustler ladyfriend to tell them a pair of one-way tickets to Tahiti are in the mail. The bungling twosome opened their books to this crooked lawyer, showed him their weak case, gave him sound legal advice.

What you should do, Ernie, is get a hold of Garson right away and bribe him to clam up so we can't charge you, and so you can stay in Foolsgold a few more years until you finish milking the town dry.

But does one write off the chance that Ernie, at the end, was on the level? Might he really intend to persuade Garson to cooperate? Ernie doubtless doesn't want an ambitious D.A. looking into his private drawers.

If Ernie does come through, delivering him Garson and Oriole Records, has not too perverse a bargain been struck? Bolestero's and Garson's freedom for a song? Maybe Jesse's right, Oliver is developing an unhealthy obsession about this case, tunnel vision.

As of Monday evening, no word from Bolestero.

Tricia Santarossa calls, nothing to report, just wants to know how things are going. Is he coming down to L.A. soon? Be nice to get together. Oliver thinks: she likes me, this hip little lady out of L.A.'s musical smart set actually digs shy old Oliver.

Gilley reports in, burbling and excited, just before Oliver leaves for the airport, with the news that some big independent labels are suddenly very serious. A&M and Argonaut and maybe Polydor. Jodie's phone has been jingling day and night. Protected by that restraining order, "Small-Town Girl" has become an item with alluring market potential.

"We got a song that's every night on the news, eh? Oriole and Royalty Tobacco have launched a fifteen-million-buck campaign to sell it. So a record company's advertising will be paid for - paid for, hell, comin' at the public so hard there ain't time to swallow. Oliver, if you can hang on to that preliminary restraint order or whatever it is you've got, we're talking five, ten million with the successful bidder. So what's goin' down at your end?"

*   *   *

It's ten to ten. Oliver sits in the attorneys' lounge rereading his argument. Presently he will walk into what is basically the second-highest court in the country. Above this, there's only the Supreme Brethren. Oh, to be able to announce to these three learned gentlemen that Garson Schuter has just confessed, he's named names.

But Ernie Bolestero remains unheard from. Nor could he be raised last night or this morning. He's a bachelor, no answer at home. His secretary thinks he's out of town. Maybe he'll abandon his practice, and never return.

Oliver's armpits are clammy. A clerk told him his three Ninth Circuit judges have been sitting nine days on a complex corporate tax issue. That they have agreed to set aside time for this interloping application means they think it's important, the clerk said. Also, they want to get some ink, she added. Oliver figures it will be best to shut up unless called upon, keep those feet out of the mouth.

Tommy Klein enters the lounge, behind him a trail of subordinates and their briefcases. Here comes Bennie Ford, with him a couple of Oriole's own legal beagles. An army against Oliver.

Klein doesn't talk to him, he's still crabbed about the calamity on the lake. Oliver looks over at him once and gets a vengeful glare back. Counsel for the plaintiff has a feeling nothing will come easy this first Tuesday of September.

*   *   *

Appeal judges Ames, Ormond, and Prosnikoff look like the kind of anonymous men you see at service club lunches, well-barbered polished apple faces. The Chief, Ames, hasn't uttered a peep. The wing men, Ormond and Prosnikoff, however, are

153

particularly active, hitting Tommy Klein with everything but their paperweights, scaring Oliver half to death - what are they saving for him?

Judge Ormond has a squeaky voice like a dentist's high-pitched drill. "But the plaintiff alleges in his secondary affidavit that Oriole Records faced a deadline to find a saleable song, and along comes this itinerant street singer with a criminal record, and steals the plaintiff's car, and a tape with the song, and a week later, it's being recorded by the same company that needed that saleable song. What do you say to that, Mr. Klein?"

"I say that those aren't the facts. But they're the only allegations Judge Sherman heard - one side of the story. He refused to hear the other side. That's not one's traditional perception of how justice is done in America."

Klein isn't bad, Oliver dare not underestimate him.

"Well, he's waiting to hear the other side right now, why aren't you in his court, and why are you in ours?" says Prosnikoff, who has shown himself blunt and quick of temper. "There are too many facts to weigh. This is a court of law."

"It's also a court of justice." Opposing counsel isn't afraid to give lip.

Oliver sits as still as a prairie dog. Maybe they won't notice him here. Maybe they won't call on him. Maybe he will hear those magic words, "We do not need to hear from you, Mr. Gulliver."

Prosnikoff says, "It is by dint of the wanton negligence of your clients, in failing to answer to the complaint in timely fashion, that they find themselves looking at the business end of a restraining order, and frankly I don't feel like bailing them out. I'm not made more sympathetic to your cause by the disgusting use to which court documents were put to by Mr., ah, this Mr. LeGoff."

"Your honor," says Klein, "I was made sick when I heard about that. And plaintiff should be entitled to all costs and attorneys' fees, maybe even double fees. But I plead with the court, when all the ugly little side issues are set aside, this remains a plagiarism case without the smallest iota of a scrap of evidence of access on the part of Oriole Records or Tom Slider. Access, may it please the court, is the *sine qua* . . . "

Judge Ormond interrupts. "The point is, we're being asked to weigh evidence. That's for a District Court judge. The only thing I'm not sure of is whether that judge should be Judge Sherman. What do you say to that, Mr., ah, Gulliver?"

Oliver takes a second to rise, as if not at first aware that the shot that just rang out was being fired at him. "Your honor, it would be insulting to suggest a member of the federal judiciary could be prejudiced because of losing a fish."

Prosnikoff utters a hoot of pleasure. "That sums it up," he says, sitting back. Oliver's got him all the way.

"On the other hand," says Klein, "a judge who has ordered the defendants to get their mother-fucking asses off his lake might be seen by the public at large not to be the fairest choice to hear their cause."

Oliver can feel the sands shifting and opening up beneath him. Even stolid Chief Judge Ames smiles. Klein, with that one good punchline, has got back in the fight.

Judge Ormond, Oliver's sometime friend, is now full gallop behind Klein. " 'Justice must not only seem to be done but must manifestly and undoubtedly be seen to be done.' " Oliver remembers the quote from law school, an old English case. "We may know Judge Sherman is incapable of bias, but does the public know that?"

Judge Prosnikoff leans almost over Chief Judge Ames' lap. He intends to be *sotto voce* but he's not *sotto* enough, and Oliver can just hear, in the good acoustics, "Christ, Frank, that's just a pile of crap."

But Ormond ignores his brother judge, and addresses Oliver, "Mr. Gulliver, you're not suggesting another trial judge couldn't be just as fair as Judge Sherman. Are you?"

"Well, your honor, I think I join in whatever Judge Prosnikoff just said to you."

There is silence. Oliver has made too bold. Then Prosnikoff starts to chuckle and then so do the other two, and at the table beside him, Klein and Bennie Ford are laughing, too, but dutifully, uncomfortably, they don't like Oliver stealing the show.

When it comes Oliver's turn to argue, he gets a respectful hearing. They don't jump on him as they did his opponent. Oliver speaks to them directly, not using notes, tries to rein in his run-on sentences and not garble too many phrases. What he loses in elocution he makes up for in eagerness. They can see he believes in his cause.

He's clearly lost Judge Ormond on the issue of whether Oliver's favorite trout fisherman will continue to be seized of the case, but he has Prosnikoff in his pocket. Chief Judge Ames asks no questions, remains poker-faced, unreadable.

They don't break to make their decision, but go into a huddle. Intense low-voiced murmurs that Oliver can't hear.

One of Tommy Klein's coolies enters from a side door and places a notepad in front of Klein and Ford, who hunch over it, and they're joined by McRae, head of Oriole's legal department, another huddle.

Oliver has a sense of tension from the adjoining table, a fluttery excitement. It makes his own nerves tingle, his warning system's going off. What do they have?

Oliver feels his aloneness. It would be nice for him, too, to have someone to huddle with. Tricia Santarossa comes to mind, a quick mental snapshot, and he feels a twinge, something pleasant. Why do they get along? She's not his type. They're worlds different.

In the first row behind him, reserved for the press, is Charles Loobie, whose weekend special on Gilley versus Oriole and Slider earned the reporter a little picture beside his byline. Oliver came out quite well on the printed page, a clean-living American hero, a lawyer you can like. Lindy, like Chief Gonzales, warned him not to let all this go to his head.

But this is image-conscious America. Oliver is proud to have staked out his claim to being Saint George, the white knight from the boonies taking on the corporate dragon.

Oliver jolts back to reality as Chief Judge Ames finally

speaks. "As to the temporary restraining order, we will not allow the appeal. The order stands."

Oliver wants to jump, but stills himself.

"The prohibition succeeds, with great respect to the judge below."

"I dissent most strongly," says Prosnikoff.

Elation wilts. A victory much watered down. Oliver keeps his restraining order but he's lost Judge Sherman, a most important ally. Who will he get instead? He prays not Mathilda the Hun. He still holds the whip, how long can he stall things?

Ames continues, "As to the application for a change of venue to Los Angeles, we think the balance of convenience favors the defendants. They will, however, pay the entire costs of the plaintiff in having the matter transferred to the California Southern District. The clerk will examine the rosters of trial judges to see who is available there."

Oliver is stunned. He had passed lightly over this motion, not thinking it had a chance of a snowflake. Now he must fight the war on the enemy's battleground.

Chief Judge Ames asks Klein: "When would you like to start?"

"It's only eleven o'clock," says Klein. "I'd like to get going this afternoon."

"This *afternoon?*" the clerk blurts.

"There's no reason we can't conclude this today."

"I'm sure there's paperwork," says Judge Ames. "The clerk will give you every assistance."

"All rise," calls the clerk, grumpily.

As the judges shuffle out, Klein steps over to Oliver's table and says in a low voice, "All offers are withdrawn, old boy."

*   *   *

The mills of justice, oiled by the vast sums of mazuma Oriole is spending to get the t.r.o. reversed, have begun to grind exceeding quickly. Oliver hadn't expected they could strike tents and move this traveling legal circus so quickly to Los Angeles, but here they are, three in the afternoon and everyone has just been jetted and helicoptered to the downtown L.A. Federal Building, and Oliver's waiting for court to assemble, wandering around the seventeenth floor of this great, squat structure looking for a free phone.

Earlier, strapped into his seat in a Royalty Distillers' executive jet, Oliver assessed this unsettling news: the judge appointed to hear the case is one Hollander Bainsley Willabee, who happens to be one of the president's recent appointments, they should be called disappointments.

But Oliver thinks: what's wrong with conservative? He's the little guy battling the establishment, Oliver represents local business, small-town America. Maybe he can use to advantage Willabee's reputed lack of a blazing intellect. During congressional hearings, they found he was next-to-last in his graduating class at a non-prestigious law school.

Where's an attorneys' lounge? He doesn't, like, dig the intense vibes in this busy, milling place. San Francisco was easier, here he's in the heartland of America's music industry, an interloper, a raider.

All offers withdrawn, it's a bluff, he thinks, else why haven't they amplified? After court, Tommy Klein was smiling, suddenly courteous. He was sorry he couldn't explain what's up, he's under instructions. He congratulated Oliver upon his able address to the court and hurried off to join his confreres.

What are they cooking up?

Oliver, with a few minutes before Court Seventeen assembles, gets one of the clerks to let him use a phone in their office. Maybe Jesse heard from Ernie Bolestero.

"Oliver, how's it going?"

"I'm jumping from foxhole to foxhole, guns firing, they're still coming. Anything?"

"Okay, Ernie called. Sounded real staged, as if he was with a witness, maybe a lawyer. He wanted to reiterate he had absolutely nothing to do with the fire at the Opera House, had no idea his former client Garson Schuter was in the area that night and has agreed to try to locate Schuter because he, Schuter, might want some legal services from Ernie."

"Sounds like it was written out. Why do you think . . . . Hang on."

He looks across a couple of desks to the counter, where Tommy Klein is setting a file. The man beside him Oliver immediately recognizes but he isn't sure why, and for a second can't put a name to him.

It's Ernie Bolestero out of context.

And he is ushering forward a neatly groomed young man whom Oliver also knows. *It's spiritual, man. I love it when things burn.* Arson Garon in a casual new sports jacket.

"You better get down here," Oliver tells Jesse.

CHAPTER

20

Oliver watches, feeling a little dizzy, as an affidavit is thrust in front of Garson Schuter. A clerk asks him if he's read it and he nods.

Oliver lets the receiver settle back into its cradle and takes strength for a few minutes, watching them.

"Do you solemnly swear the contents of this affidavit to be the truth, the whole truth, and nothing but the truth?"

"Yeah, I do."

The clerk takes up pen and signs it.

Oliver finds his calm center and stands up and walks over. "What are you getting paid for this, Ernie?"

Bolestero just winks.

Klein says, "Hi, Oliver, didn't see you there. Goddamnedest coincidence, you two practising in the same little town."

"Yeah, it was Oliver gave me the idea to hunt my old client down," Ernie says.

Oliver wants to smash his grinning teeth in.

He asks Garson, "So what have they got boned up for you to say?"

"I don't know nothin' about . . ." Garson begins.

"Shut up," says Ernie.

"He don't know nothing about no stolen tape," says Klein.

"It's all in here." He hands him a stamped copy of Garson's affidavit.

"And I didn't rip off nobody's wheels up at your – "

Ernie says impatiently, "Schuter, you ever wonder why people call lawyers mouthpieces? So you don't have to open your own. Zip up."

"We're late," says Klein.

In the corridor, Charles Loobie looks at Oliver with concern. "Hey, you're all white."

"They've bought Garson Schuter."

In Court Seventeen Bennie Ford smiles contentedly at Oliver from the next table, and says, "Last round."

Oliver forces himself to read Garson's deposition. It appears that the deponent was just passing through Foolsgold, hitchhiking down Highway 101 with his girlfriend, one Sonya Boychuk. They were offered a ride by the plaintiff. He does not recall what song was playing on Gilley's cassette player, and moreover does not recall hearing at any time that day or at the party that night a song called "Small-Town Girl in the City," or anything that sounded in any manner or form like a song he is currently familiar with, "Goin' Down for the Last Time."

When he and the said Sonya Boychuk left the premises of the said Oliver V. Gulliver, counsel for the plaintiff, shortly after dawn by foot, the aforesaid 1965 Mercedes sedan was no longer in the yard. They were given a ride by a trucker on his way to Oakland. They have never in any manner or form been connected to the music industry. They never sold any song to any representative, real or held out as such, of Oriole Records Inc.

"All rise."

Enter Judge Hollander Bainsley Willabee, whose small twirled-up moustache makes him look like a French gigolo. A serious, unsmiling one. His hair is dyed, maybe it's a black wig. Vanity fair.

"Your honor," says Oliver, "I have just been handed a false affidavit. I would like the rest of the day to study it."

"It's only three pages – " Klein begins.

"That's the problem. There's an absence of detail. Like the fact he's been paid a lot of money to swear this affidavit. Like the fact he's a human crime wave. He has a lengthy criminal record, your honor."

Willabee looks puzzled. "Will someone tell me what's going on? I have different applications here. What's yours, Mr. Klein?"

"To set aside a temporary restraining order given *ex parte*."

"I'm applying for an injunction until trial," says Oliver.

"I read the file but I haven't totally absorbed it," Willabee says. "They just threw this at me. Don't expect miracles right away."

Oliver says, "Your honor, in fairness there's some new evidence which I have a right to rebut."

"Before you decide on that issue," says Klein, "let me acquaint your honor with the story behind the newspaper headlines."

Oliver doesn't get another word in as his opponent begins a masterful synopsis of the facts in issue, summarizing the evidence on both sides but with a gentle bias toward the defense. Willabee listens and nods as Klein cries the monetary blues, beguiling the judge with stories of his client's dire straits, hundreds of thousands of dollars lost a day, a fifteen-million-dollar advertising vessel about to be thrown against the rocks, massive layoffs, court cases threatening, the t.r.o. is a monster eating up not just Oriole Records but the whole music industry, the judge must end its life.

Oliver worries: are Judge Willabee's eyes becoming misty with sympathy? Or is that the glaze of the wandering mind?

During a pause, Willabee says, "Well, who filed for copyright first? Doesn't that end the matter?"

Klein looks a little depressed upon hearing this question. "I wish that were the case, your honor. No, it's a question of who first created the intellectual property in issue."

"I see." A pause. "Okay, you're saying your client didn't copy the plaintiff's song." Willabee turns to Oliver. "And you're saying he did. Well, how am I supposed to solve that?" He holds out a fistful of paper. "With these affidavits?"

"And with the assistance of the law I am about to quote," Klein says, gesturing to one of his assistants, who hands up to the bench a fat binder of photocopied cases. He opens his own copy to the first case and slips on his reading glasses. "Without proof of access by the defendants to the plaintiff's song no suit may lie and no injunction succeed: Gibb versus Selle in the Seventh Circuit U.S. Court of Appeals, 741 Federal Reporter, Second Series . . ."

"Approach the bench, please." Judge Willabee is beckoning counsel to come forward.

Oliver straightens his tie as he gets up. He fears this isn't going too well, Klein's very smooth. He should have interrupted, what about his application for a delay? He needs overnight at least, to give Jesse Gonzales a chance to get down here and arrest Garson and question the truth out of him.

The three heads come together. "There's no chance of this getting settled, is there?" Willabee says.

"No," they chime, but Oliver gets his in a little first.

"Okay, just a thought."

The two counsel return to their tables, Klein to his authorities, but the complexities seem to make the judge restless.

After a while, "Who am I to believe, Mr. Klein? Plaintiff alleges this Mr. Schuter stole the song. Schuter claims he didn't. I mean, the way I see it, the issue revolves around access, isn't it as simple as that?"

"That's what I've been – "

Oliver has got up to interrupt. "I couldn't have said it better, your honor. You put your finger on it. Access is the key. Garson Schuter, who as mentioned happens to have a long criminal record, stole Gilley's car and his tape and sold the latter to the defendant company, that's what I say. He's right here in the courthouse, I saw him. The best way to tell if he's lying or not is put him on the witness stand. What possible harm is there in me asking a few questions?"

"Time is critical," says Klein. "That's why these cases are

decided on affidavits. That's a preposterous idea, this isn't a trial."

"Your honor can have him called to be cross-examined on his affidavit. It's in the rules. I say I can prove he's a liar."

"Mr. Gulliver has thrown the gauntlet, Mr. Klein."

Klein turns to Oliver. "I hope you'll hurry it along. I'd like to call this a wrap by dinner."

Klein's quick consent rattles Oliver a little, the fellow must assume Oliver to be a clumsy cross-examiner.

Klein turns to the judge. "I'd like it on record we'll oppose vehemently any further exceptions to the practice against *viva voce* evidence. I don't mind bending over backward once for Mr. Gulliver, but I don't want to be stuck in that position."

"Under these unusual circumstances, I rule we can hear from this one witness. We won't make a habit of this." Willabee says to Oliver: "You're sure you want this man called?"

Oliver has jumped, all he can hope is the parachute opens. *Goin' down for the last time, don't pull the ripcord.* To the judge, confidently, "By all means."

Stall things, get information. The chief will be down here soon. Oliver will get at Schuter before they can prepare him any more. It's better than adjourning for the day, and it's nearly four anyway, the court won't sit after five at the latest.

"Bring in Mr. Garson Schuter, please," Klein says to one of his minions.

Oliver watches them escort the punk into court, watches him take the stand and swear on the Bible. He's pouting and his eyes are downcast. Oliver tries to remember back to *The Art of Cross-Examination* by Wellman, the many entertaining examples there.

Oliver first defines the territory for the judge, keep things simple for him.

"Now I'm going to suggest you and your girlfriend stole my client's car and everything in it."

"Yeah?" He clears his throat. He won't look Oliver in the eye.

"Yeah."

"Well, we didn't." He sneaks a sideways look at all the people making notes back there.

Now stiff-arm him. "How much did Oriole Records pay you for this affidavit?"

"Expenses and a reward for information."

"What does that all come to?"

"Maybe over thirty thousand, somewhere there."

Oliver lets the whispering settle. Himself, he's not surprised. Bolestero probably got even more.

Garson says, "That's what they negotiated. The lawyers."

"Mr. Bolestero, he's acting for you."

"Yeah, like he . . . yeah."

"Defended you on an arson case some years back, didn't he?"

"Well, yeah."

"Where'd he find you?"

"Vancouver, B.C. Live with a girl there, it's in my affidavit."

"Oh, yeah, Splint - how'd her prostitution charge work out?"

"Okay."

"You're her pimp, right?"

"Now *just* a minute," Bolestero says from behind Oliver.

"Who are you?" Willabee says.

"I'm his attorney."

"Well, sit down, you don't have standing here."

Oliver likes this judge's attitude. A don't-coddle-crooks kind of guy.

Willabee lets Oliver lead the witness through a résumé that is not exactly calculated to find him a position as a Brinks guard. Garson admits to a life of antisocial behavior with a resigned unease, agrees stoically that twelve jurors once refused to believe his sworn denials as to stealing a car in Canada, and shrugs off the, "And why should we believe you now?"

Oliver takes his time, painting a picture of a career thief, procurer, and firebug, one who loves his work, even injects a little spiritualism into it, worshipping as he does at the throne of Shiva, the god of destruction. The judge is looking aghast at the witness, and gives Oliver free rein.

It's five o'clock, no one is talking adjournment, as Oliver says, "On July twenty-ninth you weren't just hitchhiking amiably down the highway, you were coming to Foolsgold to burn and pillage."

"I don't know where you got that."

"You burned the Foolsgold Opera House down, didn't you?"

Garson, after glancing back at Bolestero, says, "I want to plead the First Amendment."

"That's freedom of speech, religion, and assembly. Which do you choose?"

"Whatever the amendment is."

Ernie's told him not to answer questions about the fire. But it's as good as an admission. Oliver has him by the old cojones, time to bring the matter home. "And I suggest you also stole Gilley's car."

"We wouldn't of ripped off C.C Gilley's wheels, he's, like, a hero." Oliver hears an uncomfortable note of sincerity.

"You claim you woke up in my back yard and Gilley's car was gone. You were in a tent nearby. Are you saying someone came up there at night and drove off without you waking up?"

"I ain't sayin' that."

"What are you saying?"

"I'm sayin' someone did come up there and wake me up."

Oliver has a disorienting sensation, one that comes when you've asked that one question too many.

"Who?" he asks.

Oliver looks over at Klein, his expression says he's sizing Oliver up for his trophy case.

"Some geek stole the car."

"What do you mean?"

"I heard some shufflin' in the grass outside, and I looked out, and there was this guy, like drunk. He went up to the back door of your house there, like he wanted to knock or whatever, and then just stood there, like he was gonna knock and didn't. He was kind of like crying. Drunk, like staggering. I guess Gilley left the keys in the Mercedes and he just got in and drove off."

166

"Describe this geek." Oliver assumes Bolestero wrote the script. He's unnerved, though, Garson's voice has taken on a different tone, unguarded, frank.

"Sort of tall and flabby, and like not in good shape, walked like a chicken. He had a big, red bow tie."

Oliver intends not to say the name, but his vocal cords form it up and send it out of their own accord.

"Clarence."

"Will my learned friend be much longer?" Klein asks. "I have some photographs of Mr. Boggs I want to show the witness in re-examination."

Clarence? They have pictures of him . . . . What kind of zinger is being pulled here? Ernie coached him well. Clarence was nowhere near . . . . Impossible.

But as Oliver probes for error, his own doubts make him awkward, fumble-mouthed, while the witness seems more relaxed and candid. The deeper Oliver digs for details, the more accurate they sound from Garson's lips. His description of Clarence's movements has an unrehearsed ring of truth that begins to sound as clear as churchbells to Oliver's horrified ears. His account of being picked up by a friendly transport driver is detailed enough, although he didn't get the driver's name or the company name on the truck. A load of machine tools from Seattle.

It meshes too satisfactorily: Clarence, panicking over the Opera House fire, his own car battery-dead, could have walked up the hill and tried to summon the courage to call on Oliver. He couldn't find the courage so he took Gilley's car. Bolestero found this out from Schuter and called Klein.

No, Ernie made this up, Oliver's being taken in by a practised courtroom liar.

What is Judge Willabee thinking? Only once does he interrupt, when Oliver asks Garson if he was using drugs on the night of the twenty-ninth.

"I smoked some pot."

"Narcotics," says Willabee.

"Yeah, like that."

167

"You were under the influence of narcotics that night?"

"I guess. You could say."

It's five-thirty, and surely they'll have to adjourn overnight. As Oliver's engine dries up and he slowly subsides to his chair, Klein stands. "This is the gentleman you referred to, Mr. Clarence Boggs?"

Oliver recognizes it as a picture from an ad in the *Foolsgold Weekly Inquirer*. From when Clarence started his doomed insurance business.

"Yeah," says Garson.

"May the photograph be the next exhibit." He hands to the clerk and to Oliver copies of some new depositions. "These affidavits, your honor, disclose Mr. Boggs fled rather quickly from Foolsgold because of his fraudulent conversion of thirty-five thousand dollars in insurance premiums. Plaintiff's evidence of access has failed him, and I suggest the case must be resolved in favor of the defendants."

"But that's assuming I believe this witness. And if no one's producing this mysterious Mr. Boggs, I'm not sure that I should. The story sounds pretty incredible to my ears. He admits to a long criminal record and he was using narcotics, dangerous drugs, that night. Mr. Gulliver will argue the witness shouldn't be believed. Won't you?"

Oliver sees there's more than a ray of hope. "Of course," he says, raising himself from his chair.

"Witness," the judge says sharply, "you're through, I'd ask you to leave the courtroom."

Garson retreats stony-faced under the judge's glare. Willabee had mouthed the word "narcotics" with a singular abhorrence. Had not Oliver heard somewhere he's a vicious sentencer in drug cases, some controversy over whacking a small-time L.A. celeb with a jail term over interstate transport of a bag of cocaine?

"So where does that leave us?" Willabee asks.

Klein sighs impatiently. "To complete argument."

Oliver rises, once more to the breach. "Before we get to that, your honor, I have one more application to make, to cross-examine Tom Slider. I have information that says he was using a dangerous drug with an unnamed friend when he claimed to write that song and was ordered by Oriole Records not to mention it."

A last chance to storm their fortress. If the back door to access is swinging shut, he'll try the front. Through Tricia Santarossa, Oliver could prove evidence of conspiracy: Bennie Ford ordered Slider to keep silent about the magic mushrooms, a hallucinogen this judge will readily agree is of dark and suspect record.

"A drug?" says the judge.

"Psylocibin. It's like LSD, the same thing Charles Manson used."

Oliver expects the allusion will bring a stinging rebuff from Klein, but he has returned to his seat and is as still as everyone else. Willabee sniffs.

"He doesn't mention the narcotic in his affidavit," Oliver says. "I think I should have a chance to test his story on how he claimed to write that song." It's a flier, perhaps Long Tom is off center enough to spill the beans.

He sees the reporters are scribbling away.

Klein says, "Your honor, Mr. Gulliver's a practised fly caster, he knows fishing expeditions are carried out on rivers and lakes, not in courtrooms. I object. Your honor ruled there are to be no further witnesses."

"Will counsel approach the bench?"

When they get there, the judge says to Oliver: "You're saying you can prove the defendant was using this, ah, stuff?"

"I can have an affidavit in the morning." Oliver wishes he were certain of that. Tricia said she'd never get another job in the record industry.

Willabee turns to Klein, "If he comes up with that, I'm going to look bad if I don't let him have a run at your client."

"You'll look worse if you keep changing your mind," says Klein, blunt but with a smile. "It will look particularly bad in the court of appeal."

Oliver knows most trial judges dread their decisions being

mauled by appeal courts. Willabee turns to him. "Maybe Mr. Klein's right, I've made a ruling, I have to stick to it."

"What are the defendants afraid of?" Oliver says.

"Well, Mr. Gulliver, I've made a decision – "

"I'll offer a deal," Oliver interrupts. "If I don't get anything from Slider, I'll pack it in, you won't have to listen to argument. Darn it, your honor, Slider was brainwashed under drugs to believe he wrote that song, let's find out how they did it."

Maybe the judge is hooked by the intrigue Oliver offers up so temptingly. "I'll reserve until tomorrow morning at nine-thirty when I can look at Mr. Gulliver's affidavit."

"Your honor – " Klein begins.

"No, I've made up my mind, that's what we'll do. Come on, gentlemen, give me a break, it's been a long day."

"Your honor may wish to read some of my cases this evening," Klein says acidly.

Oliver has bought another night, gambling everything to get Slider to the witness stand.

As the two lawyers return to their places for adjournment, Klein mumbles, "This guy's got the backbone of an amoeba."

"That was a dirty play, Klein."

"Trap play, old boy."

"Didn't quite work out as you hoped, buddy."

"But you know the little prick is telling the truth, don't you?"

"I doubt it," Oliver says insincerely.

"All rise."

Bolestero scampers out quickly to see to his client. Oliver sits and breathes slowly for several seconds, then exits into the corridor just as a woman rushes up to Klein, she's from his office. "We've got him. Blane Uppledick, driver, Puget Machine Tools, Seattle."

She sees Oliver behind Klein.

"Whoops."

Klein turns around. "That's the icing on the cake, Oliver. Have a good night."

As Oliver walks out the Spring Street entrance of the court-house, Bennie Ford is talking loudly to reporters: "You can bet there's something fishy. This Clarence Boggs who went on the lam is Gilley's girlfriend's uncle, brother-in-law to Mr. Gulliver there. I'd call that a tight little circle."

21

The room offers one of those help-yourself-and-pay-later bars. Jesse has retrieved a can of Beck's from it and is looking at Beverly Hills out the window.

"So it's gotta be Clarence." Jesse and Oliver earlier watched the news, the ABC interview with Blane Uppledick, who remembers driving Garson and Splint to Oakland. He's shy and friendly, five kids, twenty years with the same company.

"It's Clarence." Oliver, freshly returned from the shower, plucks a fat grape from the cluster in the fruit bowl and feels it slide gooily down his throat. "I sunk all my arrows into the wrong target."

Sly Clarence, he thinks, Madelaine's bad-ass brother, the Foolsgold fraud artist and porn flick king. Yes, this is his brother-in-law's kind of gig. But if he is in bed with Oriole Records, surely the defendants wouldn't have so gaily trumpeted his name, passed out his picture to the press.

Although the emergence of Clarence into the tableau asks as many questions as it answers, it's clear that Oliver has tripped over his own feet and fallen flat on his face. Bennie Ford was quick to put the boot to his downed adversary with that quickie press conference, accusing him of everything from the standard delaying tactics and fishing expeditions to the more exotic sins of seeking personal aggrandizement, not to mention attempted extortion.

After court, Oliver skulked back to the Beverly Wilshire Hotel to wallow in a room that must be costing Oriole a few shekels, it's where they put him. To keep the bottom from falling out of the Foolsgold police budget, Oliver has invited Jesse Gonzales to sleep in the other bed.

Jesse arrived in L.A. to find that Ernie Bolestero counseled Garson to refuse to answer any questions about the Opera House. Bolestero took similar counsel for himself, even dared the chief to implicate him, sassy and scornful of Jesse's off-the-wall theories.

"I'll get them."

"Forget those guys. Clarence is here, Jesse. Find him."

The chief turns, watches Oliver slap Mennen on his cheeks. He takes a gulp of beer from the can. "You want me to go outside and look for him?"

"I feel his presence," Oliver says gloomily. "Clarence, you slack-ass, you're near, speak to me. He told me, 'L.A., the movie business, that's where the boola boola is.'"

"Well, I guess I'll just amble right on over to Universal Studios and no doubt bump into him. This is a city of eight million people, all of who work in the movie business." He lays down on the bed and opens a new book from his Literary Masterpieces Club. "Best place to seek him out is right here, by the phone. When he sees his picture on the TV news, he may want to track us down."

Oliver suspects the chief is depressed, too, affecting nonchalance. He'd come down to L.A. seeking to bust someone for something.

Oliver straightens his tie in front of the mirror. Suck in the gut. Chin up. Look like a man confident of his cause.

"Where you going?"

"I'm going off to celebrate this joyous day, to dance and drink the night away."

"How come you're dressed up?"

173

"I have business."

"What kind of business? You put after-shave on, I never known you to want to smell good. Of what sexual persuasion is this business?"

"As it happens she is of the opposite sexual persuasion. She's a witness who swore me to secrecy. I'll phone in to pick up any calls."

There have already been many of these, mostly from a harrassing press. What about Ford's allegations of an attempted blackmail sting? What about Gilley's threats to get his old record company? Only faithful Charles Loobie remains on his side, Loobie who phoned to warn him that Oriole may be planning scummier smears yet, and to be careful.

"You got a clandestine affair going here, Oliver?" Jesse says, as the mayor of Foolsgold rubs a shine onto his shoes.

*   *   *

El Cerro hosts many merry, chattering Angelenos. Oliver feels like he's souring the good mood walking in here, like a ghoul might, fresh from the grave. At the bar he orders a J.D. on the rocks. No sign of Tricia. He wants maybe more from her than her affidavit, her soft shoulder to cry on.

An obviously gay guy takes the next stool and orders a Cinzano and something. He seems to be sniffing at Oliver. Maybe it's the Mennen, he used too much.

"Don't we look a little dejected," his neighbor says. "Death in the family?"

"There may well be."

"Oh, my, I think he means it."

From behind him, "Agent Santarossa reporting in," and he turns and she's there, taking in the measure of Oliver's new friend. "Would you mind shifting stools? How sweet." The gay guy scrambles over couple of places with his drink.

Tricia sits on the vacated stool. "Who was my competition?"

"I thought he was real nice. I wanted to tell him my problems."

"I heard on the news."

"Yeah."

"Aw, hey," she says, and takes his arm. "Oliver, when you look sad like that, you know what?"

"What?"

"You remind me of my old dear-departed teddy bear."

Oliver smiles. "What did he die of?"

"I hugged him to death."

"I'll apply for the job. I'm looking for a new one, lawyering isn't my line."

He decides he likes the way she never makes herself up, more honest than these painted masks you see all over. Jeans and an oversize man's white shirt is what she likes, easy and unaffected.

"I'm resigning from Oriole tomorrow. I'll give you your affidavit."

She has that cocky way of shaking back her hair, it's reassuring to find her chipper, a comrade in bad times.

"Thanks, it's my only hope, I've got to get to Slider."

"Going back to what I like best anyway. Freelance production."

She picks up Oliver's whiskey tumbler and salutes him with it, and takes the last sip, her eyes never leaving his, sparklers on the Fourth of July. "Small-town lawyer in the city. It's still a big hit, Oliver, especially with me. Don't give up on it. Let's go up to my place and conspire. I have wine."

"I guess I could use your phone. I've got to bring my client up to date. He'll be frantic." He gets up. "And we can work on the wording of the affidavit, maybe we can do something a little theatrical in court." He's feeling better. A little wine and conspiring might get his juices up for the fight again.

Tricia slides from her stool and grabs his sleeve and looks up at him. "Oliver Gulliver," she says, that's all. She shakes her head and takes his arm and they go out into the night, with Tricia laughing to herself.

*   *   *

Her apartment is in a posh, five-storey building cake-layered up the hill. She's on the penthouse floor, with a stairway from her balcony down to a large swimming pool. The view is to the east, the Hollywood Hills.

Her interior décor is bamboo and glass and plants and stereo speakers. In the living room a baby grand piano, several framed gold and silver albums on the walls. The bedroom, from its open door, looks equally as inviting as intimidating. A woman asks you up for wine and conversation, it's unliberated to assume she means more than that, this is the modern age. He'll establish trust, he'll keep his paws off her in her own home. Maybe something could happen here, though, in the long term. She likes him, apparently not just in an avuncular sort of way.

But she's not his type. This is just a novelty item for her, the Mayor of Foolsgold to add to her collection.

"Where can we do this?" Oliver asks, looking around.

"Do what?" The snap of her smile. She's a bird. Flicking a look, flicking her bangs, flicking the eyes.

"The affidavit. Do you have a typewriter?"

She takes him into an office with a word processor and printer and says, "Okay, business before conspiracy." She sits down and pulls out a diskette. "You dictate."

"Tricia, what's your best theory?"

"Simple Slider met a spider going to the fair. I think the spider is Louis LeGoff. I heard he got into show business dealing acid at Ozzy Ozbourne concerts."

"Yeah?"

"Okay, a theory. Tom does 'shrooms with his manager. While he's in the rush, in total, ecstatic communion with God, Louis plays Gilley's song over and over again from hidden speakers. Louis gives him the old Timothy Leary and convinces him he's written it. That explains the lie detector test."

Oliver squats beside her. "Ever take any hallucinogens, Tricia?"

"Long time ago."

"Is it true what they say, for instance those CIA experiments,

176

brain-washing people, could you do that under heavy doses of that stuff?"

"As long as your victim has a willing mind. And a reasonable empty one. Dictate to me, Oliver, put some words in my mouth."

The way she says this last sentence comes out kind of erotic. Oliver senses some ill-defined but prickly energy in this apartment as he works out the affidavit with her, trying to keep his mind off possibilities. She's been a nun, she said. Oliver's been a monk. But mainly he's a lawyer and she's his witness, it's not ethical to think such thoughts.

He doesn't want to let her know what's on his mind, it would make her think he finds her cheap. Which he doesn't, no way, she's a really nice woman, a lot different from Madelaine, mind you. Even more straightforward, he appreciates the no bullshit.

If he tries to do anything, maybe she'll think *he* is cheap.

They're too different, nothing in common.

As the printer chatters out the final version of his affidavit, Tricia fetches him an immense helping of white wine, seven ounces in a tall cold glass. "Come out and look at the stars," she says. "You can actually see them tonight."

"Sure, just two seconds."

From her desk phone he tries to raise Lindy, and there's no answer, or she's unplugged the phone. He doesn't at all like leaving his nervy fifteen-year-old for days at home alone.

"Couple of seconds more."

Tricia leans against wall, sipping her wine, watching him. He phones Jodie Brown's house in the Castro, where Gilley and Elora and Jamey are staying, where the band is rehearsing in the basement. Jodie tells him an A. and R. man from Argonaut Records is listening in but refuses to talk contract until the court situation clarifies. Jodie heard about the hitch today, the probable collapse of the Arson Garson theory. "Gilley don't seem too concerned." She asks for his number and says Gilley will call when he finishes the set.

Elora tells him, "Hang in there, Dad. We all love you. Where are you now?"

"At a friend's."

"What friend?"

"Oh, sort of someone helping me with the case."

"Good. Relax. Have a couple of beers with him. You're doing great, Dad."

As he hangs up, Tricia says, "Couldn't tell your daughter you were in a woman's apartment, huh?"

Oliver takes a slug of wine, and follows her to her living room. She pauses at a bank of stereo equipment. "What would you like to hear?"

"What are all those gold records there?"

"Okay. This went flat on its ass here, but won awards in Germany, Jules Zoltan on synthesizer." She plugs a disk into a CD machine. "The electric cello was my idea."

She flicks a few switches, then downs her wine awfully quickly, and picks up the bottle and gives Oliver a come-hither, and he follows her out into the warm Southern California night. Low, sweet moans of cellos swirl from speakers under the eaves. Oliver looks at this city's sorry excuse for a sky.

"You call those stars? Up the North Coast, on a cloudless winter night, the stars will blind you."

"I'll keep L.A. I had visions of running off with you to Foolsgold, but the thought of those cold winter nights makes me shiver."

Oliver's confused, skittish, he's not sure what's expected of him, or how to go about it. She walks to the railing and spins on a heel, and holds the bottle out toward him.

"There's supposed to be a moon out tonight. I'm sure it won't be your typically glorious Foolsgold moon, but it'll have a certain ravaged beauty about it." She pours into the two glasses. Oliver replays in his mind the plots of those erotic fantasies in which he's sure and bold, whips off women's clothes. A languorous melody comes up over the cellos, Zoltan's synthesizer.

Tricia looks at him over the brim of her wineglass, and

laughs softly, as if to herself. She turns away from him and looks east toward Hollywood Mountain, which is rimmed with a pale light. She laughs again, and shakes her head.

Oliver stands there uneasily, unsure. He listens to an insistent bongo from the left speaker, it's telling him something.

"I've been thinking a hell of a lot about you," she says, speaking to the empty void. "Since that evening we talked so much." She turns to face him, leaning back, setting the bottle of wine on the ledge. She stares at him as he stands there ten feet away, hearing cellos and distant street noises, immobile, frozen in his shyness.

She says, "Oliver."

"Yes?"

"Aren't you going to make any kind of move?"

"Well, I've thought about it."

She bursts into laughter, and smothers her mouth with her hand. "Oh, goodness," she says.

Oliver takes a couple of steps toward her, his knees shaking, he's escaped from Judge Willabee and Clarence Boggs and temporary restraining orders, they're as far away as those distant, blinking stars.

She holds out her hand, telling him to halt.

"Listen, Oliver," she warns.

Five feet from her, he stops advancing, he's gone too far. He's misread the messages, hers is a subtle L.A. humor, he feels awkward, a yokel.

"Can I tell you something?"

"What?"

"I *honestly* don't do this all the time. Chase men." She drains her wine and closes her eyes for a few seconds, then opens them, and smiles at him. "This is ridiculous," she says.

Then they meet halfway across that five feet of no man's land, Oliver isn't sure what vehicle he uses to get there, his feet have gone numb. His upper lip catches her right nostril, his bottom teeth click with her top, it's a disaster.

She bends her head back with a burst of laughter. She's small and soft against him, wiggly like a kitten. Their next coming together is 2001, Oliver's somersaulting out into space toward a moon of Jupiter.

After a while one of her lips peels away like adhesive tape from one of his. He observes that a moon of planet Earth, the color of baked tile, has just climbed over Hollywood Mountain.

Tricia buries her head into his shoulder, and repeats, "This is ridiculous."

They kiss again, voluptuously, and Oliver's cock in straining for freedom muscles up painfully through the fly of his boxer shorts, bunching his trousers at a point just above her pressing pelvis, and as she gets up on her toes, climbing him, he feels her softness rising to reach his hardness, moving, wriggling, Zoltan wailing in the copper moonlight as if from a jungle, behind him the urgent thrumming of bass and cellos and drums. Oliver has endured several years of want, whole armies of repressed hormones are awakening and answering the battle cry. He gasps, the world opens up beneath him and out flows Oliver Gulliver, shuddering, prematurely climaxing with a flow rivaling Mona Kea's.

They stand glued in the moonlight.

Oliver is disgraced, mortified, racked with shame.

The phone rings, shrill and derisive.

"Maybe you better answer it," Oliver says.

"Oh, dear, I'm sorry."

"This is ridiculous."

As he peels from her, he notices the wet splotch on her blue jeans near the right hip. His cock retreats like a guilty, spanked puppy, leaving his loins syrupy and sticky. The phone rings, please somebody answer it.

"Where's the bathroom?"

He can't look at her, studies the floor.

"First left. Oh, God." She starts to giggle. "I don't mean that, I'm not laughing at you." She tries to suppress it, and it comes out as a snort, a kind of pig's oink, and that causes her to laugh out of control, gasping between bursts, as he retreats to repair himself, "Oh, Oliver, I don't mean . . . it's the *situation* . . . it's not . . . Dear God."

Taking off his pants beside her round, enormous whirlpool bath, he hears her finally answer the phone. "Hello," and she laughs again. "Yes, yes, he's here. Sorry, just a case of giggles."

She discreetly passes the phone in through the barely opened bathroom doorway.

He takes it. "Who is this?"

"Who was *that?*" Gilley asks him. "At eleven at night."

"It's nobody." That's not what he meant, he hopes she's not there listening. "I mean, look, just don't say anything to Elora, okay, I'll explain later."

"Why you old stallion, Oliver. '*Course* I wouldn't breathe a word." An evil chuckle. "Well, goddamn. Oliver, I know you're doin' a great job in court despite everything, and I apologize for this coitus interruptus or whatever, but this may be helpful."

"Pass me out your pants," says Tricia.

Comes Gilley: "Don't I recognize that voice?"

"No, I'll look after – "

"Just give them to me, I know what works."

"Oliver, who *is* that? What does she want with your pants?"

Oliver gives them to her. "Never mind. What've you got?"

"Mail. Mail from my old address here in San Frank. On goin' over it, I see there's a parking summons, a no-parking zone. For my car. In L.A., August third, four days after it was stolen."

Oliver pauses while soaping the area where the bomb went off.

"It charges me that I, to wit, C.C. Gilley, own a vehicle, to wit, a Mercedes sedan, to wit my license number, which was parked on the 2500 Brooklyn Avenue, contrary to, blah, blah."

Oliver calls to Tricia, "Twenty-five hundred Brooklyn, would that be a residential street?"

"Boyle Heights. Little Mexico. It's old L.A."

"Oliver, this ain't your hotel, where are you staying?"

"Gilley, hold onto that summons. Maybe I can use it to buy time. I'll call you later."

He emerges in a few minutes wearing a big beach towel around his waist. In the kitchen, Tricia has soaked out the stain

181

and is preparing to iron his pants dry. Efficient, serious, the laughing jag licked.

She says, "I've been thinking. Twenty-five hundred Brooklyn, there's a club there, around Brooklyn and just off Soto. it's where a lot of Eastside bands got started, you get some recording industry people hanging around."

"Including from Oriole?" Disaster has been forgotten, lust has retreated to its sordid den, proof of access again occupies center stage.

"It's a possibility. Or someone who knew Oriole was wanting to buy a song. For a lot."

"Of boola boola." He thinks: Clarence is smart enough to have figured out, as he was driving to L.A., playing Gilley's tapes, that he had a potentially lucrative property on his hands with the tape marked "Gilley 29-7-88." If he was in that live music club on Wednesday, August third . . .

And he realizes.

"August third. That was the day Long Tom Slider claims to have written the song."

CHAPTER

22

The engine of her Jaguar XKE whispering power, Tricia speeds them nimbly along the Hollywood Freeway through the swirling clusters of cloverleaf, at home in her adopted city, in its vastness. She spins past the bright, night streets of downtown, coming off the Stack onto Macy Street, past the Union Station, and crosses the Los Angeles River, truly, they call this a river, into Boyle Heights, entranceway to East Los, Mexico-America.

Tricia apologizes for her conduct. She doesn't want him to feel hounded, she just likes him a lot. She can't fathom the suddenness of her attack. Oliver's a nice man, he's cute, he's open and gentle and a little neurotic, all the qualities she likes, but to go overboard like this, to attempt to seduce him so blatantly, it's not her, honestly.

Oliver thinks she's trying to soothe the pain of his recent embarrassment. Taking blame on herself, she offers no reminders of the event that has so wounded his male ego.

Until, as they pass by a mountain of stacked cars, Junk Yard Row they call it, she throws in, "I was really extremely flattered, Oliver." She laughs and tousles his hair.

She's beautiful.

What has he on his hands here, a love affair on the field of battle? As bullets whiz past him and he prepares a final but desperate assault on his entrenched enemy, is he under risk of being captured by his own spy? A woman, it must sadly be recalled, who has danced the light fantastic with so many men she had to make a New Year's resolution.

"When you dropped your guard in El Cerro a few nights ago, when you cried out of love for your girls, I melted like a steamed sugar cube. When you told me you hadn't been with a woman in eight years I wanted to break the spell she placed on you."

"Who?"

"Madelaine. Your wife deceased lo these many years. Did you feel guilty almost betraying her tonight, Oliver? Why are you ashamed to let your daughters know you're human?"

"She died a very agonizing death. We were really in love."

A long pause as they cruise Brooklyn Avenue. She says, "Maybe it's because you're so safe that I'm pursuing you. Safe and scared, the kind of guy a woman can be comfortable with."

Buildings cluster more thickly here than most parts of L.A., it's an old and grand part of the city, probably passed through some ethnic changes, but currently it's Latino – California returned to its roots. There are actually *people* on the street. Strolling. Signs on the stores say, "*Se Habla Ingles.*"

"I'll get over it," she says.

Oliver wants to set some time aside to work this one out. What are these tiny, friendly shivers shooting through him? She is a flickering silhouette in reflected street lamp and neon. Her hands firmly grip the wheel and she smiles as if at a joke on herself.

Oliver returns to the reality of the street as Tricia pulls up in a no-parking zone in front of the club, Jose Pelicano's, whose doorman, a cheery Chicano, smiles at Tricia, holding the door for her. They know each other, and there's bantering, and he'll look after the car.

Oliver gets out and yawns and stretches, yearning for a coffee. The area isn't teeming at a quarter of two in the morning, but the embers of the evening still glow. A drunken soldier is pressed against the wall of the club, trying to keep upright. A teenaged couple walk by, hand in hand and sharing a joint. A prostitute in an obscenely short skirt makes eyes at him from the corner.

Tricia is asking the doorman about Clarence Boggs and an old Mercedes. The doorman is shaking his head.

"Did you bring his photograph?" she asks Oliver.

Oliver shows him the copy of the court exhibit, Clarence in his bow tie.

The doorman says, "Nope, sorry."

"Want to go in?" Tricia asks.

An old greasy-looking man slouches up to the prostitute. "Fuck off," she says.

Then another decrepit guy comes around the corner, and two more, then three, a parade of dirty old men.

"Movie's lettin' out," says the doorman.

"Just a minute," Oliver says, and leaves them and walks the fifty feet to the corner of the block, where the hooker stands.

Men are straggling from the exit doors of a theater called The Imperial.

"It's really lowered the neighborhood," the streetwalker says.

There's a big marquee over this theater, which once was maybe a grand dame but now is a bag lady, shabby. A determined-looking little man is up a ladder taking down big black plastic letters, which have been proclaiming tonight as the last night for the steamy double-bill "Nympho Terrorists" and "Come Like It Hot."

Oliver says to the prostitute, "This hasn't been a porno theater for very long?"

"Only a few weeks. Change of ownership."

"You, ah, been working this beat long? Ever see this man?" He shows her Clarence's picture.

"Never remember the faces."

Oliver calls to Tricia, who is giving the doorman some paper money to watch the car. She joins him at the corner, and they turn it and walk arm and arm to the box office of The Imperial Theater.

"You into dirty movies?" she asks.

"My Geiger counter says Clarence is near."

"I used to come here," she says. "You could get highbrow flicks from Europe." She looks up at the marquee. " 'Nympho Terrorists' – they specialize in blowing people to death? Aren't you interested in Jose Pelicano's, Oliver? They'll be closing."

Oliver goes up to the man on the ladder. He is Oriental, about forty, has horn-rimmed glasses and a Fu Manchu mustache. He's replacing the letters with "L.A. Premiere of . . . "

Oliver asks, "Is the manager around?"

"No manager. I manage." He looks placidly down at them. "No more show to three o'crock tomorrow."

"Who's the owner?"

"I own. With partner. Have ricense, all regal."

The little man finishes spelling out the name of the forthcoming movie, "Swap Meat," then comes down from the ladder, brushing off his smock. He smiles warmly.

"My name's Oliver Gulliver. I've come to see Clarence."

"Crarence? Who Crarence?"

"He's in trouble."

"No Crarence here. Prease, I rock up." He pulls keys from his pocket and bows and turns and walks toward the door.

"I have vibes," Oliver says to Tricia. "Clarence has some minor experience in the film industry."

Oliver follows the manager to the door, stopping him as he opens it, showing him Clarence's picture and giving him a business card.

"I'm his brother-in-law. Tell him if he doesn't agree to see me in two minutes, I'll bring the cops in."

The man hesitates, studies the card. "Prease you wait." He goes in but doesn't lock up, so Oliver hustles Tricia inside to the lobby.

Oliver and Tricia find a machine that coughs out a couple of plastic cups, into which plastic coffee is poured. Oliver drinks it down, but it doesn't improve the wine headache he's developing.

A staircase leads to what must be the projection room, where a radio is playing. Two voices begin talking over it. No mistaking Clarence's self-pitying whine.

Oliver beckons Tricia to follow, and they walk up the stairs and enter the projection room. There's a cot, where his brother-in-law is seated, and the radio and a hot plate and dishes, and a little fridge.

"I heard," Clarence groans, staring down at his hands. "I just listened to the news."

Oliver says, "Yeah, your good name has been sullied."

"You not say big trouble, Crarence. You say little trouble." Clarence's partner, arms folded, stands in the aisle, quite put out.

Clarence wears a sweat-stained white shirt and, for a change, a yellow bow tie. Above that he is ghost white, partly from a month of hiding in the shadows. Partly from discovering he's famous.

He looks wanly up at Oliver. "You met Saigon Jimmy, my partner? Jimmy and I put everything we had into this."

"Yes. Your contribution was Sybil McGuid's thirty-five thousand dollars."

"You not say fraud of record company. You say rittle trouble over missing money."

"It's nothing to worry about, Jimmy, it'll blow over. Oliver, I can pay everyone back, you especially. Jimmy and I'll clear a hundred grand this year, we're specializing in a genre that has a steady clientele."

"They keep coming," Oliver says. His brother-in-law, a porno pusher – if Oriole finds out, it will embarrass the plaintiff's case beyond belief.

"The former owners were going to close it down, the place was losing money, and, ah, they owed some gambling debts to Jimmy here, and . . . Jimmy and I kinda met in 'Nam, when I was doin' my thing for God and country."

"Yeah, I can imagine."

"He knew I used to be a projectionist. You want to introduce me?"

"Tricia Santarossa."

"I'm his right-hand man," she says.

Clarence says, "My picture's gonna be in the paper?"

187

"You bet."

"Look, Oliver, I'm sorry about all this. Maybe I should have phoned you." He turns to his partner. "Jimmy, I got family business. It's your turn to mop."

Jimmy rolls his eyes and makes a face. "What you have to do to make a riving." He turns to go and stops at the doorway. "Crarence, is it bad heat?"

"I'll figure out what to do."

Jimmy leaves, shaking his head.

"This record company's got me accused of a scam with you and Gilley."

"Yes, well who *did* you scam with? And what did you do with the tape?"

"Oliver, believe me, I know nothing."

Oliver reads his eyes, hoping Clarence doesn't speak truth.

"You don't want to involve me, it won't help the image."

"You've got that correct. I haven't figured out your immediate future. Jesse Gonzales happens to be in L.A. right now, he'd like to see an old face from home. Start talking."

"When the fire started I didn't know what to do. I just began to drink. I went down to the bus station, I was going to leave town, but some guys saw me there, and then I went up to your place, and I just couldn't break the news to you." He slumps back onto the cot. "I intended to parlay those premiums fast, Oliver, I had a real hot tip. I was gonna double my stake in a month. There wasn't supposed to be a fire."

"Gilley's tape is what I want to know about. It says 'Gilley 29-7-88' on the label."

"Look, I didn't play any of his tapes, I don't remember what he had, I was too drunk to figure out the stereo system, and when I sobered up I was more interested in the news. There was a wooden box with about fifty cassettes, but I didn't look through them. I wasn't into listening to any tunes, I was figuring out where to go. I knew only one guy I could trust – Jimmy. I helped him get stateside."

Oliver joins Tricia, who is looking out the projectionist's window at the scene below. Saigon Jimmy is working between the rows with a mop and pail. Tricia seems rivetted at the sight of the man patiently bending to this unpleasant if not downright disgusting task. "Yech," she says.

"He let me buy in equal for what money I had. He's a sweet man, Oliver, and I'll be paying you back, the loan you got for me – "

"Where are the goddamn tapes, and where's the car?" Oliver almost barks this.

"I don't know. They towed it, it was in the no-parking around the corner."

"And you haven't claimed it back?"

"Get myself in all sorts of trouble doing that," Clarence says.

"Was it locked?"

Clarence goes to a shelf, behind a row of paperbacks, and brings out a set of keys.

"I don't remember that the locks worked very good."

"Clarence, the car was towed on August third?"

"A couple of days after I came here. I'd been in the theater all day talking plans with Jimmy, and then I ran out at four-thirty to move it from out in front of Jose Pelicano's, and it was gone. I didn't care, the car was hot. I was gonna hide up here, Jimmy agreed to do all the front office biz and bring me food, he's an expert at smuggling people, and all that stuff."

Oliver assembles this. On August third, while the Mercedes, a car that lots of people in the music industry would recognize, was parked in front of a popular live music club, Gilley's tape was lifted and sold into Oriole's hands.

Oliver wonders if Louis LeGoff may have been hanging around this neighborhood that day. Or Long Tom Slider himself, it could be that simple. Oliver remembers: he may be cross-examining that selfsame person in several hours if Judge Willabee gives him a green light. The injunction hearing, however, seems distant, light-years away, the finding of the car is of ultimate moment.

Gilley 29-7-88 must absolutely not be found in that automobile. The absence of the tape from the car is a kind of negative evidence from which strong inferences can be taken.

Given the other circumstances – Oriole's last-minute plight, the fact their people hang out in this club, the high visibility of Gilley's old German car – it could be there's enough circumstantial evidence of access to win his case.

Unless the tape is in the car.

Oliver slips the keys in his pocket. "Where do we reclaim a towed car, Tricia?"

"This area, I'm not sure. Phone the police."

"Maybe find out from them why they never checked the city lots for a stolen car. I knew it would turn up under somebody's nose."

Oliver leans over Clarence as he picks up his bedside phone and begins to dial the police. Tricia joins them, snuggling an arm around Oliver's waist.

"Say cheese," comes a voice from near the door, and as Oliver turns his head he's startled by a flashbulb. After a moment of blindness, Oliver sees, holding a camera, the gay fellow from the bar at El Cerro's. He's caught Oliver, Tricia, and Clarence in a tableau of shocked expressions. She slowly withdraws her arm from around him.

"Aren't we the cozy little threesome," he says.

Before anyone moves, he takes two more photographs and bustles out the door.

In the awful quiet after, the impact slowly hits Oliver. Oriole had accused him of engineering a sting. Now they have proof. Pictures of him with his co-conspirators to be trumpeted to the press. Oliver huddling with Clarence Boggs, his wife's brother, a fraud artist and purveyor of pornography. Cozying up to counsel for the plaintiff is Tricia Santarossa, the company traitor. Her affidavit has suddenly lost its punch.

He sinks woefully into a chair. He remembers Tommy Klein's words. *They'll cut you up into cat food, Gulliver.*

*   *   *

Oliver dials the number of the *Times*' editorial office as the kid

190

looking after Babe's Towing rings up three hundred dollars in storage fees.

Inquiries had indeed located the car here. Oliver came by taxi, and he's sure he wasn't followed this time, no private eyes behind him as he was sped through a lonely backwater neighborhood of East Los Angeles.

This is a bad idea, coming here by himself, he should have brought a witness. Not Tricia, she's tainted. He sent her home, he was sharp, unpleasant, insisting on being alone. He could have called Jesse, but he doesn't want the fuzz here. He doesn't want a witness to the black deed his mind harbors. Is that why he's here alone?

If it's in the car, get rid it.

Tell the world he found the Mercedes and the tape wasn't in it. When last seen the vehicle was unlocked in front of a club where Oriole scouts hang out. The day Slider miraculously came up with his song.

The other side uses sharp practice. They stole the song somehow, no question about it. He's in the right and he'll be goddamned if he's going to lose this case. What is that nagging voice of conscience prattling on about? What do you mean, he's obsessed with winning at all costs? Justice is all he seeks, the court system isn't working for him, it needs a nudge.

Hold, on, he thinks, this is stupid, wrong, evil. He's an honest guy, there are Bolesteros in the profession and there are Gullivers. He's never cheated in his life, except a few minor deductions from his taxes.

But what if he does *not* find Gilley 29-7-88 in the car? He has no witness to prove its absence. Oriole will claim the plaintiff's crooked lawyer found it and got rid of it.

So it's obvious counsel for the plaintiff is not thinking straight, he's rattled.

Oliver has guessed right. Charles Loobie is at work, rousted from bed when Oriole delivered the photos and a report from their P.I.

"You don't want to see the breakfast edition," he says. " 'Oriole to File Proof of Gulliver Conspiracy.' Pictures of you in various poses with secret associates. They used a guy named Rock McGonigle, gay private, ah, dick from West Hollywood. Listen, if this is a sting to get a big settlement out of Oriole Records, I gotta give you credit, you almost pulled it off."

"Charles, don't be crazy, I turned down four million."

"You better tell me your side of last night. Won't make the next edition, I'm afraid."

"Meet me at my hotel."

It's now two AM, and a cold wind buffets him as he trudges between rows of automobiles jailed for their parking sins, two pit bulls grumbling behind him, the guardians of Babe's Compound. "Heel, you sons of bitches," says the kid. "They ain't et, unless someone climbed over the fence during the night."

Oliver finds the car at the back, near the far corner of the chain-link fence. Gilley's license plate and the sticker that says "Happiness is Coming."

The car is musty, the leather creaks as he enters and sits.

The boy comes up to his window. "Okay, you're away."

"The car was unlocked. Nobody can come sneaking in here and . . . " He looks at the pit bulls, who are snarling at a harried-looking gentleman waiting at the front gate. "No, I guess not."

The kid goes off to look after the new customer.

Oliver wearily studies the dashboard gadgetry, feeling flutters in his heart. A microphone is plugged in, its head sitting in the glove tray. Nobs and buttons, which one punches out the cassette that is in there?

He finds it, and the tape pops out and he's fucked. On a paste-on label on the plastic cover: "Gilley," and underneath, "29-7-88." He stares at it, mesmermized, for a long time.

Trash it.

▶ ▶ ▶

" 'I'm going to kill that son of a bitch.' Those were the words he used?"

"I took it as, you know, just angry talk."

"He said that just after he put the phone down?"

"Objection. Leading."

"Sustained."

"When did he say that?"

"Just after he put the phone down."

"He was lucid before then, he was making sense?"

"He was depressed, but yes, when I talked to him at lunch just before the phone conversation, he was normal."

"Not claiming to be code-named Sergeant Pepper?"

"No."

"Not talking about any organization sending him on a mission."

"No, sir."

"After lunch, Mrs. Magee, what did you do?"

"I went out and got some groceries."

"And what was the defendant's condition then?"

"He seemed a little dazed, otherwise okay. He was in his pyjamas when I went out. Pyjamas and slippers. He didn't say anything about going anywhere."

"And he was gone when you came back."

"Objection. Leading."

"Sustained."

"Where was he when you came back?"

"He was gone."

■ ■ ■

23

The engine grumbles reluctantly to life, and Oliver rolls out past the guard dogs, out the gate.

Toss it into the Los Angeles River ditch. Burn it. Bury it.

He put all his eggs in this basket, the theory of the tape being lifted. Now he has to go into court with these same eggs on his face, adding to the considerable omelet already there. How will he explain to Judge Willabee the events of his long and so far sleepless night, how disprove the circumstantial web of Oriole's evidence of connivery?

Turn the tables on them. Get an affidavit from Clarence, the whole story. Explain to the judge that he, Oliver, hastened to the towing lot in fear that defendants' investigator had overheard too much and was on his way there himself. Your honor, the tape had been removed, the vehicle is outside to be examined. The cassette was last seen in an unlocked car near a club which the defendant's agents habituate.

What could be more obvious, your honor? Murderers have been convicted on less.

Then Oliver thinks, I'm out of my mind. What are such thoughts even doing there? He feels bile rising, nausea.

He slides the cassette back in, pushes the play button. Nothing. It clicks off, he realizes it's run to the end. Oliver presses the rewind and it whirrs for thirty seconds, then finally stops. Again he pushes play.

Gilley's announcement first: *This is take one, 'Small-Town Girl,' July, what the fuck is it again, July twenty-ninth, three p.m. Instrumental on track one.*

Gilley has recorded voice over it, his raucous gravelings. Oliver remembers their vehicles crossing paths that day, as Oliver was returning from court, Gilley singing "Small-Town Girl," into his mike. The day he picked up Garson and Splint.

How to prove access now?

I'm a fool of the city, and I am to blame, don't laugh at my pain.

Oliver is the fool of the city.

What about a long shot? What if they borrowed the cassette, taped it, and returned it?

Give up, Oliver.

Oliver suddenly realizes he's speeding on Whittier Boulevard, there's a patrol car close behind him wib-wabbing the emergency lights. He pulls over. Gilley wails, *I am to blame, don't laugh at my pain.*

The patrolman sits in his car for quite a while, as Oliver lets the blues wash over him, Gilley's blues. He feels in tune with Gilley, he feels one with him. *Who's impressed by my fame, who can guess at my shame?*

The policeman surprises him by coming to the passenger side, poking his head in the open window, along with his Smith and Wesson. He's young, blond, a tanned Californian. Oliver turns the tape off.

"Can you offer an explanation of how you happen to be in possession of this vehicle?"

With his free hand, the officer fingers the butts in the ashtray, and comes up with a half-smoked joint. He sniffs it.

"It's a long story," Oliver says. "I've got to be in court tomorrow."

"On what charge?" The policeman pops open the glove compartment. A bag of green plant material, the Mendocino Mind-Fuck, stares out.

Gilley's Lawyer Charged with Transporting Dope. Gulliver Found in "Missing" Car. Planned to Get Rid of Evidence, Oriole Claims.

A night in jail to cap today's fine performance. Oliver feels like making a run for it, across the lanes of traffic, the copper won't dare shoot, there are too many cars.

"I've seen you somewhere," the officer says. "Are you famous?"

"You've heard of C.C. Gilley?"

"C.C. . . . Hey, that's where I've seen you. You're that *lawyer*. Doesn't the case have something to do with a stolen . . . yeah, this car."

"I just recovered it from a towing lot."

"And there was a tape, I didn't follow the whole story." He puts the gun away.

"I have the tape."

"Hey, great, I guess that sews it up for you. Listen, can I get your autograph?"

The officer obviously hasn't got the details right or heard the latest news.

"I get on an average one personality a night, you should see my collection."

The cop takes the pot but gives him a speeding warning instead of a ticket. Somehow this seems unsatisfactory. Oliver expected to be busted. This long, terrible night doesn't seem complete without that.

He climbs on board the endless L.A. freeway system, cruising on half a tank of gas, sleek California cars whispering past him in the night. Oliver drives and drives and thinks and plots, prepares for the court day. There must be a way to link Oriole in. But it doesn't come to him. The only way to win this case is with a miracle.

If he could only get that goofball Slider on the stand. Is Judge Willabee so unpredictable that in a manic mood - despite the bad press Oliver's getting - he might let him take a stab at Slider? The singer will be in court, he's subpoenaed. But if Oliver gets from Slider what he expects - a well-rehearsed script prepared by the Oriole promo department - and if Slider isn't caught out lying, it's nice try but goodbye. With the t.r.o. annulled, Oriole's song will be back in business, and no trial for a year, long enough for them to cover all tracks and beef up their witnesses' lies.

He should have taken the four million. He could have moved them up. Six, seven. Fat fee from that. Lindy could have gone to Berkeley or Stanford. He could have told Sybil McGuid to go jump, he'd just won a massive settlement, he's only taking federal copyright cases now, specializing.

A hint of dawn touches the eastern sky as he finally pulls up to the Beverly Wilshire. And a half dozen reporters, Loobie and some others.

"The missing Mercedes," Loobie says.

"And missing tape," says Oliver, removing it from his pocket, displaying it.

"Where'd you get it?" someone asks, sticking out a microphone.

"Does this mean you're going to withdraw your action?" another interrupts.

"Of course not."

A third says, "What do you say to Mr. Ford's charge you were meeting secretly with your co-conspirators last night?"

"Let's go into the lobby and sit down," Oliver says.

There'll be no hidden skeletons. Clarence will have to take his chances. After this press conference, he'll go up to his room, wake Jesse, and like the honest lawyer he is, he'll fink on his brother-in-law. Jesse won't leave L.A. empty-handed after all.

Oliver, exhausted, needing at least a few hours' down time, gives the press a chronology of his night's search up blind paths, the route to Clarence and the car. The defendants have employed desperate smear tactics, it's proof they're guilty.

"What about Miss Santarossa?" a woman asks. "They say you spent several hours in her apartment. You were seen on the balcony kissing. Is there a romance angle here?"

That dirty little snoop of a private eye, Oliver thinks.

"She's giving Oriole her notice. I can tell you she's convinced Oriole plagiarized the song."

"What about the kiss?" she says.

"We've become good friends. We only met a week ago. She's awfully nice."

"I like it," Loobie says.

*　　　*　　　*

In the courtroom, everyone's smirking at him, Oliver thinks, expressions that say, You almost pulled it off. He avoids eyes as he waits for the judge, who's in his chambers reading Tricia's just-filed affidavit. Willabee will also have looked at the pictures in the morning papers, Tricia hugging Oliver in a porno movie house.

Jesse Gonzales has gone up to The Imperial Theater to arrest Clarence Boggs. Oliver feels no compassion. Clarence could have saved him time and grievous pain and suffering if he'd contacted Oliver as soon as the plagiarism case hit the news.

Oliver is buoyed to see Tricia Santarossa smiling at him from a row near the front. She gives him an upright fist, go for it. He feels flutters of affection through his depression, he feeds from her, is made stronger. Maybe he can make it through this morning without collapsing.

He sees Bennie Ford glowering at Tricia. They must have known this was coming, they've coached Slider, prepared him for the allegations in her affidavit: *The defendant Slider informed me he was advised by the president of the defendant Oriole Records to remain silent about the circumstances of writing the said song, including the fact he was under the influence of hallucinogens.*

The said Slider is at the back of the courtroom, here in answer to the subpoena. He's dressed oddly, a ruffled pink-trimmed shirt. On his face glows a beatific smile. A grumpy-looking Louis LeGoff sits beside his property.

Here's Tommy Klein making a grand entrance, smiling and nodding, showing everyone that things have turned around. He confers briefly with Slider and LeGoff. Slider just shrugs and smiles. Klein joins Ford at the counsel table. He won't look

Oliver in the eye, he knows he's been playing in the mud with his reputation. He'll get his own bad karma back, somehow.

"Give up, old boy," Klein says to him.

"Fuck off," says Oliver.

Klein says, "You backed into it. It wasn't my doing, Bennie Ford hired the P.I."

"All rise."

Hollander Bainsley Willabee takes in the panorama of his packed courtroom and sits and stares down at Oliver V. Gulliver, twirls his mustache tips at him, doubtless repelled by the sight of this plumber of the depths of depravity. One of the papers, the *Herald Examiner*, has a photo of The Imperial's marquee: "L.A. Premiere of Swap Meat."

"Judgment," Willabee says.

Oliver thinks: he's throwing out the case, it's over.

"As to the motion to cross-examine the defendant Slider, my ruling is that this is not a trial and if the party objects to giving evidence he doesn't have to." He looks at Oliver, who wants to stick his tongue out at him. "As to the injunction applic – "

"But I don't object," comes Slider's voice from the back of the room, stopping Willabee in his vocal tracks. A hundred heads turn, including Oliver's.

LeGoff is talking low and urgently to Slider, who is shaking his head, getting to his feet.

At the counsel table, Bennie Ford, whose complexion has turned chalk white, leans forward as if to rise too, but subsides as the judge says, "Mr. Slider, you *want* to give evidence?"

Slider stands. "I gotta tell my story, man."

Klein says, "I wonder if we might adjourn briefly, your honor?"

But Slider is yanking his arm free from LeGoff, and is coming up the aisle, declaiming.

"Everyone's tryna make me look like I got something to hide. I think I been getting wrong advice, and I'm kinda tired of gettin' trashed in this court, man, your honor. I wrote that song and nobody's gonna take it away from me."

Paranoid, Oliver at first thinks this is another trick, they've set him up again. However, there's something quite unrehearsed about this scene, and an unhinged look is on Slider's face.

"Your honor, this is unexpected," Klein says, blocking Slider's progress as he comes before the bar.

"They told me not to say it in my affidavit, they practically told me to lie, I ain't into that any more. It's their game, man, I'm cashin' out." He scrambles around Klein, goes into the stand beside the judge. "This where I talk?"

Bennie has hold of Klein's arm, he's whispering furiously into his ear, and Klein is trying to pull free, and before anyone can react, Oliver is up and firing. "What did the lawyers tell you to lie about in your affidavit?"

"About my psilocybin trip."

"Objection!" Klein shouts, too late.

"Bennie Ford asked you to keep that a secret."

"Yeah, and – "

"Just a minute!" Klein shouts. "Nobody's called him to the stand, the witness isn't sworn." Klein is still trying to shake a frantic Bennie off, trying to concentrate on the crisis of the loose cannon in the witness stand.

"Then let's swear him," Oliver says. "Let's hear about this false affidavit and how he wrote the song while drugged. What is Mr. Klein trying to hide, anyway?" Oliver is hungry and forceful, he has to grab this last chance while the opponent is stunned and slow to react.

"Mr. Klein," says Willabee, "you object to this witness being tendered?"

"I guess I haven't made that clear," he says a little too caustically. "Yes, I do. He's my client, it's my duty to talk to –"

"Well, I ain't your client. I never hired you. If I did, you're fired."

Klein stands there open-mouthed.

"Swear him," says the judge.

After taking the oath, Slider looks out over the rows of press and public, all benches are filled. He nods slightly as if thinking,

Good turnout. His pupils are large and dark, Oliver notices, kind of googly.

"It's not that I said any lies, they just told me not to mention the 'shrooms."

"The magic mushrooms," Oliver says, nodding. "I hear they help the old creative juices flow."

"I don't know if you're being sarcastic, man, but yeah, you know, people get weirded out, like, wow, you did *magic mushrooms*? Like aren't they dangerous? Now amanitas – they're like, you know, don't play around if you got a weak stomach, but psylocibes gentle you out. Indians used them. They get your brain working in new directions, that's why they do it for me when I write."

"I see." Had they over-programed him, pumped him too full of a confidence he was the author of this song?

"I'm writing songs with psylocibin. It's a tool."

The courtroom is deathly quiet.

"Can I say something else about it?" Slider says. Oliver glances at the opposition benches. Klein and Ford are gripping the edge of their table, they look like coiled springs.

"I guess if you want to," says Oliver calmly.

"Like, I don't wanna sound pompous or nothin' but it helps you figure out where the truth is at, too. I mean, I'm not, hey, man, I ain't into kids using and stuff like that, I ain't into hanging' around street corners and signing people up like a cult or nothin', but I sat down last night, and I thought what was I gonna say to court, and if I'm gonna be straight with everyone, yeah, it can help you see through the lies that people live."

Oliver quickly breaks the silence that follows Slider's oddly rambling speech. "Before we get into more of that, just background me here." Ever so gingerly, Oliver, this guy seems to be whacked out on drugs right now. "August third, you took these mushrooms, now where was that? Let's set this in context so we can follow it better." Amiable ol' Oliver. Examining this witness is like meeting a grizzly on the trail, you don't know if he'll run or rip your face off.

"Okay, the story, man. I'm between homes that week, right?

201

I'm goin' up in class, movin' outa my old joint, I mean number forty-one, Cockroach Apartments, forget it. Meantime, the new place ain't ready, and I'm at Blinkie Smith's, he's in my band, black dude, used to be with Gilley, he'll back me up all the way. He's got this duplex down at Wilshire and Vermont, just off there."

Oliver thinks back to that poolside conversation Gilley had with Blinkie, the quisling. *I happen to know Long Tom wrote that song. That's all I'm gonna say.* And it's all he did say before Gilley shoved him into the swimming pool.

"And we're sittin' around with a few beer and we had some burgers sent in, and Blinkie says, 'You like mushrooms with yours?' I thought, okay, it's about noon, I don't gotta be at the studio 'til midnight. Can I have some water?"

Oliver is there quick as a rabbit with a glass and a pitcher. The rest of the court seems still and awed. Close up, Slider's pupils look like deep lakes.

LeGoff and Ford are conferring in the aisle. Jesse Gonzales has just come in, is looking about uncertainly.

"Anyone else there?"

"A girl, his girlfriend, Edwina. She didn't trip."

"Her last name?"

"I don't know, she's a looker, tall, good figure, real good dancer. We were jammin', and, ah, let's see . . . they kind of took off for a while, it seemed like a couple of hours, but it could have been five minutes because I was, like Blinkie didn't warn me, these were major fungi . . . "

As he rambles, Oliver goes to the front of the gallery and beckons Jesse.

Bennie comes up to him. "Get him off the stand, he's stoned," he says in a hushed, tight voice.

" . . . still noodlin' around with the guitar, and like I find this beautiful chord, like, where've *you* been, man? And you know, you dig inside the guitar, man, suddenly you find all sorts of interesting notes hidin' in there . . . "

"Looks normal to me," Oliver says. He brushes past him, meets Jesse in the aisle.

202

"Haul in Blinkie Smith."

" . . . it was like, hey, I'm inside my guitar, it's like I'm wandering in a field of flowers, plucking beautiful notes from all the little corners inside the guitar, it's like different notes have different colors, you pick a yellow note, a green one . . . "

"Clarence slipped the collar."

"Never mind. Bring in Blinkie Smith."

"How do I do that, I can't arrest him."

"Get a subpoena from the clerk's office."

" . . . I don't care if nobody believes me, I had a kind of, like okay, psychic thing there. Like I moved from this world we're all in now to a musical fourth dimension, and I saw myself from outside myself, like I was fifty feet across the room."

Bennie is bugging Klein hard again.

" . . . And suddenly there was a moment of absolute clarity when the song all came together – "

Oliver interrupts, "By the way, I guess there were stereo speakers in that room."

Klein pushes Bennie away and stands up.

"Yeah, of course." Slider stops, looks puzzled. "I lost my way."

"Your honor," says Klein, "I think the witness may not be totally with us."

Oliver finally looks at Judge Willabee, who slowly twirls his mustache. "Not with us?" he says.

Slider looks about blankly. "Who's talkin'?"

"Your honor," insists Klein, "I suspect Mr. Slider is under the influence of a drug."

"I just wanted to see what this whole farce really looked like," Slider says.

"This what?" says the judge faintly.

"My tune got ripped. It's, like, everyone's accusing *me*, and *I'm the guy wronged!*" He's becoming more animated. "It's a plot, that's what I come here to warn you, they wanna use you, your honor, to steal my song and my good name. I did a lie detector, okay? Writing a song, it's like giving birth to a baby, man, it's no mistakin', it's *yours* – "

"Witness," says the judge, "stop."

Oliver hears an air-conditioner hum, that's all.

"I think we'll take the morning recess," says Willabee.

Oliver has sensed more than a subtle reversal of the court-room winds.

CHAPTER

24

Reporters run a risk of getting trampled to death in the rush for the door. LeGoff leads his rock and roll star from the stand, the young man a little bewildered.

"How'm I doin'?" says Slider.

"I'm going to cut out your tongue," says LeGoff, pulling him out the side door.

"Hey, man, what's with this total animosity?" The door closes behind them.

Has Oliver recovered from the night's debacle? Maybe not completely, but surely he's turned the focus away from Oriole's spurious claims that crooks from Foolsgold engineered a sting.

A light must glimmer in the mind of Judge Willabee: Long Tom could well be an unwitting dupe of scheming mindbenders, a drugged pawn of a gang of song thieves including Blinkie Smith, maybe LeGoff.

But how to tie Oriole in? The plaintiff will not collect much in damages from Blinkie Smith. If Oriole Records comes out of this with clean hands and no *mens rea*, they may lose their copyright but they'll escape without paying a cent for their misdeeds. Maybe that will be their last-ditch stand, blame everything on Blinkie Smith, the big record label is an innocent victim.

Oliver turns to Tricia, who is leaning forward over the railing, chin on wrists, smiling. She puckers him a kiss and he feels like a hero. An exhausted, sleepless hero, a lone sailor navigating a sea of shifting advantages. Aboard the enemy's vessel, the loose cannon has careered wildly about the deck, causing injury and damage. It will take them a while to effect repairs. Time has been bought. Time, each minute more precious than diamonds.

Klein comes wearily up to Oliver at the plaintiff's table.

"They'll be along with a strait jacket soon. He must've been doing the goddamn mushrooms all night after we talked to him. Ate some before court maybe, because he's still accelerating. What a pisser. You were lucky, old boy, but you were good."

This is the first time he has heard honest praise from Klein. It raises him in Oliver's estimation.

Klein softens his voice – Bennie's at the next table. "They didn't tell me about this Blinkie Smith shit. Isn't he an old pal of Gilley's?"

"It's a case of no love lost."

"Slider brainwashed – it wouldn't have been hard. Bennie's having his own bad trip."

Oliver looks at the C.E.O. of Oriole Records, who is staring oddly at his upraised hands as if unsure he has the right number of fingers.

"My instructions are to let you talk alone."

Klein releases his seat and beckons to Ford and goes out to help LeGoff minister to Slider.

"There goes the Tinglewine campaign," Ford says, sitting beside Oliver. "Maybe my job. I guess there's always work picking fruit this time of year."

"What's the true story, Bennie?" Oliver doesn't try to fake a friendly voice. "How does Blinkie Smith fit in?"

"We've no alternative but to call him." Bennie looks at his watch. "We can bring him here this afternoon."

"What will he say?"

"He warned us, 'If I'm called to the stand, I'll tell the truth.'"

We were gambling it wouldn't get this far." He looks at Oliver with sad, bagged eyes. "When a case heats up sometimes people get their backs up, Oliver. I want to apologize. We pulled a cheap shot with that private investigator and his pictures. We'll make our apology public."

Oliver searches his compassionate soul for charity and finds none. "What will Blinkie Smith say?"

"We've been running on a kind of mindless adrenalin, Oliver. We just stopped thinking when you got that restraining order. Our brains went numb, it's like the power failed. Anyhow, the lights just came back on. I was sitting there listening to this asshole tripping on the witness stand, and then I was hearing another sound. The scribbling of many pens and pencils."

Ford grabs Oliver's wrist, he's suddenly earnest, pressing. "Oliver, we're *nuts*. With all this free publicity somebody should be selling a hundred million albums. This case has cooked up a big hot pumpkin pie waiting to be cut."

"I like pumpkin pie," says Oliver. What is this guy up to now? A few hours ago it was blatant character assassination. He pulls his arm free.

"So, let's cut the pie in half," Bennie says.

"Share the copyright? That's the offer?"

"Fifty-fifty on all song royalties. We put our product back on the shelves, and Gilley puts out his own version and sells his own hundred million copies." A pause. "We pay your share of accrued song royalties."

Oliver blinks. There is untoward generosity here. Oriole's running scared. Why have they hidden Blinkie Smith from everyone?

"The only problem I see is this pumpkin pie has to be eaten while it's hot. If it gets cold and moldy while we haggle over it for a couple of years we both lose a fortune. You can have his version waxed and out, the single anyway, in a week, it's the battle of the bands, lineups at the record stores. Meantime, we keep the agreement secret from the press, and pretend to carry on this action, the headlines continue to roll off the presses."

207

"Something about Blinkie's evidence you're afraid of?" Oliver hears his unfriendly voice.

"I told him he wouldn't be involved in this."

The court clerk approaches.

"Judge wants to see counsel in his chambers," she says. "Just Mr. Klein and Mr. Gulliver."

Bennie is noticeably not invited. As a member of the bar, he's been sitting at counsel table, posing, he hasn't practised in years.

"Also a Mr. Gonzales left this number." She gives Oliver a slip of paper.

When she leaves, Ford moves in on Oliver, close. "Okay, it was a little underhanded with the psilocybin and all, setting him up, and that's going to hurt us if we have to go to trial." A morose chuckle. "Blinkie was good, he really had the dork believing it."

"Where did Blinkie get the song?"

"Come on, isn't it obvious now? It's *his*. Blinkie wrote it. He played it for Gilley about five years ago. He says they worked it up a bit, but Gilley lost interest in it. That really hurt Blinkie. Gilley was always putting him down about his songwriting. Blinkie just put it away. He didn't even have much confidence in it when he brought it out, 'for laughs,' he said, just as we were going nuts here, a week before D-Day, an ad campaign about to fall on its fifteen-million-dollar ass."

"I don't get it," Oliver says.

"Sure you do. The idea was to build up this gork, make him a star. He's got to be singing his own love song. The kids think it's his own words, straight from the heart. It's part of the music game, done all the time. Maybe we can save the Tingle-wine campaign, make Slider a picture of fun, a kind of Harold Headloose." He shakes his head. "I guess not, using a dope-crazed, mind-altered maniac to sell coolers, it won't work. We can save the album, though. Hey, maybe we'll even save my job. What's the alternative? We call Blinkie, you lose your case, and I'm fired. Everybody can be winners, Oliver. Fifty-fifty."

"I need to talk to my client," Oliver says cautiously. He

should have guessed: Oriole has prepared a backup defense, a form of spin control. It's a good one, slick, Oriole may pull it off if Blinkie is a good witness.

On the other hand, Bennie is making this frantic offer. Why?

"We've got to do this fast, Oliver. Let's say deadline two o'clock."

"I've got to see the judge, Bennie."

"Okay, let's confab after." He straightens himself, tries to smile. "Let's do lunch."

Oliver has a moment with Tricia at the back of the courtroom.

"Tired?" she asks.

"I didn't sleep."

"I can get some . . . forget it."

"It's okay, I'm great."

"We're an official item now, Oliver. Is it awkward? Do you think we should cool it?"

"No. Can you stick around?"

*   *   *

"Dear gentle Lord," says Judge Willabee. "Do you think the music is the basic cause? The rock and roll? I read somewhere it affects your personality, this acid rock all the kids are into, it's what leads to the drugs and the permissiveness."

They're all three seated in heavy, businesslike chairs. On the wall facing Oliver is a Norman Rockwell cop-and-little-boy.

"About the most despicable excuse for a young American I've ever encountered," Willabee says. "Yet, oddly, you know I was thinking, you could probably write one of those rock and roll songs that way, getting high on dope."

Oh-oh, Oliver thinks.

"Mr. Gulliver can't finish his cross of this character until he's back in his right mind. How long will that be?"

Klein looks at his watch. "I'd say he'll be coming down about eight o'clock tonight."

209

"I was worried it might be a matter of days. Tomorrow morning, then?"

*   *   *

Ford corrals him just outside the Spring Street entrance.

"The Palm Restaurant? You'll like it, great crowd, it's where the big deals are made."

"Gee, Bennie, I've got an appointment. How about I call you? We've got to ten tomorrow."

"We've got to two this afternoon." Bennie's voice turns edgy, hard. "Or we tender Blinkie and take our lumps."

"You've talked to him today?"

"He's waiting in the wings."

Complete lie. Oliver knows that, he phoned Jesse. He suddenly feels buoyant, his fatigue forgotten. In the can Slider opened are more worms than Oliver saw on the surface.

But he'll be cautious until he gets the facts. "I'll try to raise Gilley. I think I know what he'll say."

"Persuade him for Christ's sake."

Ford's voice cracks. He grabs Oliver, a hand tight on his right bicep.

"We can work it out, let's talk, where the hell are you off to, what's so important? I offer the deal of a century, you've got an appointment? Let's go for the gusto while the song's still got legs." His eyes are wild and febrile, he still clutches at Oliver.

"We'll talk, Bennie. Later."

"There is no later. Where you off to? I'll give you a ride, we'll take a meeting in the limo, we'll talk."

Tricia pulls up and Oliver moves toward her Jaguar. "I have a ride."

Bennie strides up to the car. "You dirty little disloyal whore, you've got no more jobs in this town. You're a fucking *slut*!"

Oliver grabs at his shoulder with his left hand and turns him violently around, and his right fist is back and about to come whipping forward straight at Bennie's eyes, but Oliver holds

210

when he sees that those eyes are pumping tears. Bennie's wet with fear all over, perspiring and white.

Oliver knows: Bennie's pulled his last bluff, Blinkie is the torpedo that will sink his ship.

*   *   *

Blinkie's house is in the ethnic-rich Wilshire District, old and growing young, gentrifying, some black professionals and white Yuppies starting to thin out the melting pot.

There were no reporters when he arrived, but they're out there now. Oliver can see a TV truck from this room's one window. The room, on the second floor of Blinkie's duplex, is festooned with cushions, the walls baffled with blankets and thick cork, it's like a padded cell. No furniture, except for a pair of big speakers on ropes near the ceiling, their wires must feed from a source behind the wall.

It's where Blinkie and Tom Slider did their famous mushroom trip.

The cushion on which Oliver sits reeks of old, smoked cannabis. Blinkie, across from him, cross-legged, hides his crooked, scarred face behind dark glasses, and wears a serape. His father was a black bluesman and coal miner, Gilley had explained, his mother a Ute Indian princess.

"All he wants is amnesty," says Jesse, who stands at the window, his hands in his pockets.

"For me and Eddie," Blinkie growls.

"Who's Eddie?" Oliver says.

"Edwina Dill, my lady."

"No criminal charges, I can guarantee him that," Jesse urges. He's making too bold, he hasn't the power to make such a deal, he's a small-town cop in the city. "You agree not to sue him for damages."

"Me and Eddie, her too."

Tricia, who had driven Oliver here, would be meeting him for dinner tonight. If he could last that long. Events are fast unfolding, little explosions of good news that keep him awake and striving. Blinkie Smith had been an enemy agent easily turned. Oliver guesses the chief did a number, threatened criminal charges. Oliver wonders why Blinkie is so protective of his girlfriend Eddie.

"What do we get for that?" Oliver asks.

"You get all, man."

"All includes what?"

"He remains allusive to such questions," says Jesse.

"I want the immunity. We're on tape, okay? It's running now. I got microphones hid all over. I record here. It's where I play music."

"I think he's trading with hard currency, Oliver."

Oliver doesn't ponder much, though he doesn't like the microphones. "Okay, I'm in."

"No charges if you cooperate," says Jesse, making a brave promise he may not be able to back up.

Blinkie stands and pulls a panel of cork board from the wall. It opens on hidden hinges and reveals a reel-to-reel recorder. He pushes a lever and the reels whirr. "Bennie guaranteed me I wouldn't hear my name come up. I don't want to go to court, Mr. Gulliver, but I ain't gonna lie for them, no fuckin' way."

In the next room, a telephone rings. It's been going steadily, Blinkie says, he's ignoring it, refusing to answer knocks at the door, reporters.

He pushes the play button, and Oliver hears Blinkie and Slider, guitar strings being plucked.

"The microphones are always on," Blinkie tells them. "I flick a switch when I come into the house."

This fungus is way rad, man, Long Tom is saying, *you know what I'm doin' now? I'm goin' inside the guitar.*

"Silly Cubans, you call these 'shrooms," Blinkie tells them. "Grow outa South Texas cowshit. Way more vicious than acid. I did a little, Slider did a lot, only he didn't know how much."

Blinkie from the speakers: *Hey, what was that tune you were pickin', man?*

"I didn't have to do nothin' fancy," Blinkie tells them. "This dude comes pre-brainwashed. All I did is get him so loaded he didn't know if his head was on front to back."

Two guitars now. Playing Gilley's melody, Blinkie coaxing Slider along.

"That easy," Blinkie says.

The tapes whirr again.

"I didn't want to get into this at all, man." He's changing reels. "Eddie figured it'd be a lark. She's a kind of professional. Sometimes a record company wants to know what the competition's got. It ain't all just sneaking tape machines into concerts, she'll do your recording studio, the basement you rehearse in, the cat is wired for sound."

"Eddie's a song pirate?" Oliver says.

"I been eight months with her, we're happenin', I don't want nothin' to get in the way right now. I'm doin' this so we can keep it out of court."

"If this is good, they'll buckle."

"Oriole was wettin' their pants outa fear, they had no song, just shit. They gave us a hundred and fifty grand. Eddie bought a Porsche. I paid off the mortgage on this place." He slips earphones on, listens to the tape. "I was in San Francisco last month. You're in the music scene, you hear things. Like Gilley boasting in a bar he just wrote a song with the mother-fucking-est bitchin' hook you ever heard. And saying things like maybe he'll go up to his new girlfriend's place in northern California and put an album together."

"Where's Eddie now?" Oliver asks.

"We done a deal, right?" says Blinkie. "We turn state's evidence, nothin' is held against us."

Oliver and Jesse nod. Oliver worries: the chief is out of his territory here, the L.A. district attorney may blister him for this.

"Say it."

"You're protected," says Jesse, none too confidently.

Blinkie shouts through the open doorway, "Eddie!"

In a few seconds Eddie Dill comes in.

Only it's Raquel.

The last time he saw her she was refilling his cup in the Paradise Cafe.

Jesse's mouth falls open.

"Hi, boys," she says. Her hair is an orange tangle shaved at the nape and along one side of her head, what a desecration of beauty. The cocky smile. Endless glamorous leg beneath a mini. She perches on a cushion near Oliver.

"Every time I look at the TV, there you are, Mayor Gulliver, Call-Me-Oliver, David versus Goliath Records, the shy, lonesome, straight dude who used to overtip me, and I'm thinking, what have I done? For something that started off as just a hoot and a scam, suddenly I'm sick to the stomach and I've got reporters at the door. I asked Blinkie, get us terms and get us out."

Raquel. Many times had he bedded her in his dreams. Gorgeous sultry Raquel.

Oliver remembers wondering about her – what was this vivacious young city modern doing in Foolsgold, carrying trays of dirty dishes? After she stole Gilley's song, she must have decided to stick around town long enough to build up her cover.

"Play it, hon," she tells Blinkie.

He takes off his earphones and turns up the sound.

Bennie Ford's voice. *He's a total juicehead. We took a bath on the last two albums, Shit, I don't know.*

Blinkie will set it up so it'll look like Gilley copied from him, says Eddie.

No way, babe, I'm outa this.

Ford: *Play it again, Eddie. Maybe it won't sound so good a second time.*

"Monday night," Eddie says, "two days after the big fire, I sneaked by your trailer with a microphone. Easy as pie. Tuesday was my day off, I flew down here."

Gilley's voice, clear but distant. *Okay, Jamey, another take, let's catch a lighter groove and cut it off clean at the end. Da-da-da-dum.*

The drum machine goes into action. Jamey grunts, and he

214

beats out the bass line for "Small-Town Girl." Gilley's voice and guitar enter.

Oliver enjoys this song, he knows the words by heart and wants to sing along and clap his hands and stomp his feet and dance a jig with the chief of the Foolsgold P.D. The music cheers him, but it's blues for Bennie Ford. Now Oliver knows why he panicked at the courthouse. *Play it again, Eddie.*

After the song ends, a long pause, then Ford clears his throat.

I'm not going to ask how and where you got that.

We can change a few notes, says Eddie.

Change a few . . . I'm not going to admit I'm even here. Or that this is really happening.

Just a thought, says Eddie. *It's double platinum, it's a very smash hit.*

Another pause.

We couldn't cover our tracks, says Ford. *How would we say we came up with it?*

I have an idea on that. Blinkie's kind of tight with Long Tom Slider.

I'm not sure if I wanna be involved, says Blinkie.

"I kept sayin' that," says Blinkie live. "No one believed me."

"Bennie Ford bears Gilley lots of ill will, maybe that was one of the reasons he finally went for it," Eddie says. "He's was up shit creek if he didn't come home to momma with a hit, that's the main reason. I sold him on the gig with Slider, even provided the psilocybes." She's proud of herself.

"You're real good, ma'am," says Jesse, shaking his head, probably wondering how he got suckered so easily into letting her off the hook before getting the facts.

You bet this brilliant young confidence woman wanted immunity. She single-handedly assembled this, packaged it, tied a ribbon around it and sold it to Bennie Ford while buying her and Blinkie's safety by ensuring the whole transaction was recorded. And came away with a hundred and fifty thousand dollar profit.

I've got to clear it with people in New York, Bennie says.

Oliver's ears perk up. New York - that's the head office of Royalty Distillers, the parent. Clear it with what people? But the subject doesn't come up again, and Oliver can't tell whether Bennie meant that or was stalling.

I need time, he says.

Well, if you have to have that single out in a week . . . Eddie urges.

I know, I know, he interrupts. After a pause, *I'll tell you in the morning if we're go*.

She outlines her plan to convince a drugged Slider he wrote the song, Eddie wooing a nervous fly into her web.

Oliver watches Eddie Dill a.k.a. Raquel, who is smiling serenely, as if a good joke has been had on all. After a few minutes she turns to Jesse. "You like it black, right, chief? And Call-Me-Oliver, you're double cream." She gets up and wiggles her ass at Blinkie, and strolls out.

25

To duck the press the four of them will slip into Eddie's Porsche in the attached garage and race off down the alley. She and Blinkie will hide out, she has a place in Santa Monica.

While the young couple pack Oliver and Jesse meet in a hallway, murmuring low, the walls could have ears.

"You can't promise immunity for God's sake," Oliver says. "The writ of the Foolsgold police ends at the town limits, it doesn't extend down Wilshire Boulevard."

"It's my biggest collar, Oliver, the chief exec of Oriole Records." In Jesse's pocket are the originals of Blinkie's incriminating tapes. The relevant conversations have been copied to a cassette in Oliver's briefcase.

"The local D.A. will have you charged with obstructing justice, making deals you can't make. It may even be an FBI thing, it's under a federal act, those guys are heavy."

"I missed Ernie, I missed Arson Garson, and I missed Clarence. I'm not going to miss Bennie Ford."

"You can't put these two Good Samaritans in the spotlight by busting Ford. Keep a lid on it and let me handle everything."

Jesse is silent for a moment. "Maybe I went too far."

"I'll say. Let's just hold off making any collars, pal, until I talk to Tommy Klein."

A few minutes later, the four of them are in Eddie's car

backing out of the ground-floor garage, into the alley.

Charles Loobie, panting, having just raced around from the front, bends down and cranes to see who's in the car, and Eddie twirls the steering wheel, almost shaving the reporter's knees as she accelerates past him.

*   *   *

In the candlelight, Oliver drinks Tricia up as he sups his soup. Life is mellow. God is good.

Between spoonfuls he talks, recounting the day, glorying in it, success has made him immodest. She encourages him with enthusiastic smiles.

The rich juices of victory have burned reticence away, have dissolved the walls that protect his heart, and over onion soup at Le Dome, he wonders if the hot rush he feels is the real thing, the first time since Madelaine, since he was twenty-four. Or is it the blood heat of triumph, misread?

Oliver in love? The girls will laugh.

"I didn't see Bennie Ford at the courthouse. Klein told me Bennie was looking sick and went home. 'Caught some kind of bug maybe,' he said. I said, 'Let's talk about bugs.' I took him and Louis LeGoff aside and showed them the tape in my brief-case, and described generally what's on it."

"What'd they say?"

"Louis just about dropped his pants again. Klein started reciting the Twenty-third Psalm."

He pauses for a glass of wine, it's a Chardonnay listed for eighty dollars, what the hell.

"Klein doesn't want his professional reputation soiled by a messy, prominent loser. The upshot is we agreed not to talk to the press and put the court case over to ten AM. Tonight the chairman of the board of Royalty Distillers comes to town. Tomorrow, he and Klein and I have breakfast."

Gilley is on his way, too. Oliver phoned him excitedly after returning to his hotel. His client was blasé. *Knew you'd pull the gig off, counsellor.*

218

But Oliver is easily distracted from thoughts of business.

"You know what?" he says to Tricia.

"No, what?"

"I really like you."

"Like is good."

"Well, it's better than like. Beyond like."

"Where is beyond like?"

A foreign land, what are the conventions, the rituals? He can't say the word yet. Love.

"Do you think we're getting serious?" he asks.

"Serious. As in solemn?"

"You know what I mean."

"We should go somewhere," she says. "For a few days. Try it on for size."

The waiter interrupts with main courses, laying out plates while Oliver gropes in his mind for ways to be frank with her. Two divorces, unnumbered affairs: a masochist, he wants to know how many. He doesn't want to be the caboose on a train of broken hearts. How does one talk about it, how does shy Oliver find the words?

After the waiter goes, he says to his roast duck, "I'm a little scared. I haven't had a lot of relationships."

"Mrs. Harvey Sweet, the druggist's wife," she says. "Otherwise I have on my hands a nice old used car that's hardly been driven for ten years. A comfortable *safe* car in this era of immune deficiencies."

"I may need a few driving lessons."

She takes his hand, encloses it in her two, squeezes it. "Just step on the gas and go, Oliver. Let's shack up in your fishing shack. No radio, no phone, no escape, two alone against the wilderness. No music business and no music, only the sounds of bears crashing through the bush and the soothing drone of mosquitoes."

"You'll really get along with Lindy, she's got your personality."

She still holds his one hand with both of hers, and Oliver closes his other hand on the clump, fingers writhing, gripping.

"This is nutty," she says. "You're *so* nice."

A shadow across the table and a familiar voice over his shoulder. "I hate to tell you, Tricia, but he's got more buried lovers than Jerry Lee Lewis."

Four hands quickly untwine. "Hi, Gilley, long time," says Tricia.

Gilley draws up a chair grinning ear to ear. "Oliver Gulliver, my putative father-in-law, is suddenly a hot item with Tricia Santarossa, ex-A. and R. with Oriole Records. Holdin' hands like a couple of teenage pubescents."

"Yeah, how about this?" she says.

"Think I'll party with you guys tonight, what about it, Oliver, the three of us into the small hours? Just kiddin', I know how it is when lovers meet. I'll be out of your hair in two minutes."

"Elora okay?"

"Yeah, I left her at my manager's. Elora thinks it's neat you're having an affair, eh, but she's suspicious it's just some groupie wants your bod. I told her, it's Santa Tricia, I know her, she's as neurotic as your dad, they make a match."

"Oliver will introduce me to his daughters in due time. He's been screwing up his courage."

"Well, I hope he don't screw it up too bad, we need him in San Francisco. We're gonna be signing contracts. Argonaut Records. If you get me the song back, they'll go twelve million up front on a three-year three-album deal with a ten per cent royalty. Twelve million, Oliver. Ironically, that's what I'm worth thanks to all the publicity over them yobbos stealing 'Small-Town Girl.' I gotta get back tonight, eh, we're settin' up to record in Sausalito. Highwire Studios."

"They'll be offering terms of surrender tomorrow over breakfast," Oliver says. "I may need you around."

"Jeez, I can't, we've blocked time at six hundred bucks an hour. All I want is my song back and some reasonable coin in damages. Listen, I got no vendetta, magnanimous in victory even though Oriole screwed me on my old contract. They wanna save some face, we can keep the terms of the settlement secret. The evidence, too. Bennie Ford's got a wife and kids, why bring shame on them, eh? And Royalty Distillers may feel real altruistic if we don't embarrass 'em too hard."

Gilley is prepared to let Oriole save face? Just doesn't sound like him. But he's right, a corporate reputation is on the line, and Oliver could hold it hostage for a handsome ransom. It's his lawyerly duty, you get all you can for your client and feel no guilt.

"It could be worth two, three, four million, hard to say what the traffic will bear."

"Here's the deal, Oliver, and it's in front of a witness, your cut's a third of the damages plus your normal fee, which is already a million fish. I ain't gonna see my bride's father wearing rags to the wedding."

It feels wildly generous, Oliver's about to protest, but Gilley gets up, reaches a scrawny arm to Oliver's shoulder, the other takes Tricia's hand. "I feel the tantric energy pulsing through me. You guys are on major power load."

He wheels and prances off but suddenly returns.

"Whoa, Silver, back up." He kneels beside Tricia. "I forgot all about what I wanted to ask you. You're through toilin' for them corporate wrong-doers, right?"

"Quit today. I'm a lady of leisure."

"Lookin' to turn a fast trick?"

"Where?"

"Sausalito."

"Yeah?"

"Produce the album. We've got Highwire booked starting tomorrow night, six to midnight."

"Seems to me I swore I'd never work with you again. The last one, 'Deadpan Alley,' remember? You weren't getting your attacks and releases right and you called me a stupid bitch. You were soused."

"Have I had a drink today? I'm straight, Tricia. Please. I won't, like, mess up the cues, or tell you how to work the sliders, and I won't call you a bitch to your face, honest." He says to Oliver, "'Deadpan Alley,' I listened to my guitar solo

221

after she did the mix and told her, 'Jeez, I didn't know I could play like that.' She said, 'You can't.' "

"Actually, it sounds great."

"We'll need you tomorrow, Tricia. Call Jodie, she'll handle the contracts and stuff."

Oliver watches him saunter off. A different man from the embittered wreck that arrived last June on his doorstep. Demanding vengeance against Oriole Records.

"Why don't we have coffee at my place?" Tricia says.

*   *   *

Oliver soaks in her big whirlpool, bubbling away the aches and strains of this long September seventh. The eleventh-hour evidence seemed too easily procured, unearned. That wily young Eddie, she was awfully eager to please. But she bought a good deal for herself.

Glorp, glorp, glorp. The water gushed out secret nozzles, and Oliver, bouncing on a cushion of bubbles, sunk into it to his chin.

A million dollar plus fee, he has warm thoughts about Gilley. He'll be happy to get back to Foolsgold and pay off his debts and live fat for a while, hide out in the fishing shack with Tricia Santarossa. What is he going to do about her, are they talking long term? Elora and Lindy are wise, they'll give him counsel.

Naked, she slithers in beside him, and she smiles up at him, and he feels a woozy surge of energy, a powerful inner glowing. He can't remember, was it this way with Madelaine in 1962? Hard to breathe, blood roaring through the veins.

"Let's relate," she says.

For several minutes a pretence is played that they are two mature adults of the opposite sex who happen to be in a bathtub together. Sharing funny anecdotes. Oliver stares at her eyes, not her nipples, but seen peripherally, they're chocolate bumps, delicious and dark atop vanilla sundae breasts. The rest is mystery under the churning froth.

The talk dies, his last story fails, she's not interested, just that quizzical smile, those examining eyes.

"Oliver," she says finally, "I don't want you to get the impression that just because I'm in here naked with you gives you any special license. You will promise to keep your hands off me?"

She slithers toward him, thighs bump, fingers graze his hip. "Because I'm warning you, Oliver, if you get fresh I'll call the cops." Toss of her hair as her lips part and reach for his.

She rolls gently onto him as they kiss, and hands gently explore, her pianist's fingers playing him, his own hand touching her softest part, feeling it wiggle against his palm.

Soon they are splashing around as happy as otters.

CHAPTER

26

Breakfast is in the boardroom of Oriole Records, a sedate affair, catered. Royalty's chairman is General Wilbur Chillies, Ret., a Second World War hero, seventy, with the look of a rheumy old bloodhound, pouches under the eyes you could store useful small items in. He eats only dried toast and half a grapefruit, staring dolefully at the spools unwinding bad news from a tape deck on the table. Tommy Klein is here, but General Chillies kindly asked his retinue of v.p.'s to absent themselves. Fewer ears, fewer mouths, fewer well-founded rumors.

The v.p.'s were reading magazines in the waiting room when Oliver arrived. A surly Louis LeGoff was among them, looking ready to bust the place up. He's about to see his hot property turn worthless.

Oliver's loins are girded for battle, not to mention sore and painful. Last night, muscles were called upon that have not frequently been exercised. And with their closeness came his admission of . . . well, love. He felt released when he said the magic word, freed finally from Madelaine's distant pull.

When Bennie utters that deathless line about clearing things with New York, Oliver looks for expression from Chillies. His reward is subtle but real – the general raises his eyes toward heaven.

During a lull in the taped conversation, Oliver reminds them, "We have to be in court at ten."

It's nine now. The clock has switched over, befriended its former foe, it's ticking off the seconds in favor of the plaintiff.

After a few more minutes of the Eddie-Blinkie-Bennie show, Chillies asks, "Does this get worse?"

"The people in New York aren't mentioned again."

"So you have extended to us the courtesy of hearing the exhibit before you file it," Chillies says.

"The original is right now in the hands of Jesse Gonzales. He's the police chief up where I come from. He thinks there's a conspiracy to defraud, but he doesn't necessarily want to lay charges. Or even make a stink. He's my best friend. Discreet guy."

"Discreet," says Chillies.

"Yes."

The general nods. He's polite, the word holdup is not used. No ugly intimations of blackmail.

Oliver has to remind himself, he's a *lawyer*, forget Mr. Nice Guy. They've given no quarter, why should he?

Chillies smiles forlornly at Oliver. "I don't suppose you'd care to settle this by our offering up to you the testicles of Mr. Ford. We can arrange to have them coated in brass for an attractive fireplace ornament."

Bennie yesterday suffered some kind of n.b., they'd hinted earlier.

"You have to feel sorry for him," Oliver says. "He did it for the company, got nothing out of it personally."

"I think you can turn that thing off," says Chillies. After Oliver does so, the general says, "What is the solution you are seeking, Mr. Gulliver?"

"I dealt the cards, general. It's only in poker the dealer bets first." Oliver smiles. Chillies smiles. Klein smiles.

"Who else knows about this?" Chillies asks.

"I told LeGoff. Slider's manager."

The general nods and speaks carefully. "Mr. Gulliver, I

won't insult your intelligence by pretending we wouldn't wish to keep everything confidential as between ourselves and among the few people who know of the existence of this taped conversation. But I'm wondering how we could guarantee that?"

"Everyone has a strong motive to keep his silence. Blinkie Smith and Eddie Dill especially. I've explained about Jesse Gonzales. C.C. Gilley told me there's no reason to embarrass Bennie's wife and children. All he wants is the song back and a fair damage settlement."

Chillies, with his droopy dog smile, says, "Mr. Gulliver, believe me, no so-called people in New York are involved. If we have to we'll extract a statement from Ford to that effect. In fact if we have to, we'll bite the bullet over this, and dump everything on his lap." Still smiling. "If we can't work something out."

Klein says, "If we transfer copyright to your guy, damages aren't much, let's face it. Forty days' lost royalties."

"We can always let a jury decide the amount," says Oliver.

"A jury trial will take two years to get going and a fortune to pay for," says Klein.

"We'll have the injunction in the meantime. A record contract. You'll have continuing bad publicity. For two years."

They're still shadowboxing, no numbers are being mentioned. Klein looks uneasily at General Chillies. Oliver looks at his watch.

"So, what's a jury going to award anyway?" Klein says.

"Punitive damages," says Oliver.

The two words sit there like an evil threat on the negotiating table.

"Perfect case for awarding punitive damages. Major corporation steals love song to sell alcohol. It's getting on toward nine-thirty."

Chillies frowns at Tommy Klein, waits for some disavowal of this punitive damages business.

"Look what happened to Texaco," Oliver says. "A jury hit them with a ten-and-a-half-billion bill in generals and three billion in punitive damages and they nearly went bankrupt. Texaco. Used to be up there in the top half dozen industrial corporations." Oliver locates a fact sheet from one of his files. "Some of our jurors may remember Royalty turned a two-hundred-and-fifty-million profit each of the last couple of years."

"And what, Mr. Gulliver, do you suspect a jury might award in punitive damages?"

"Sky's the limit there, I guess." The idea is to force them to name a figure first. With the song returned, Oliver will be happy with two or three million, which means he should suggest four, but what if they start off with four, which means they'll pay five? Oliver's had hundreds of personal injury settlements over the years, he's learned the tricks. This isn't much different from a whiplash, you play close to the vest and take them to the courthouse steps.

"Maybe we should start moving on down to the Federal Building," Oliver says, getting up. "We can talk about it on the way there."

They see he is serious, he's taking the tape off the machine, slipping it in his briefcase. "Or I can just grab a taxi."

They go in a company limousine, Oliver comfortably in the back seat with General Chillies, Tommy Klein on the jump, leaning forward, doing most of the talking.

"We take a bath on the Tinglewine campaign, a jury will take that into account. We have to drop Tom Slider from the label, so we take another bath."

"Just think how clean you're going to be," Oliver says.

"Gilley's obviously got a recording contract. By the time the trial comes around, everyone will know he made a fortune from this case, a jury's not going to want to throw a lot more money at him."

The limo steals silently and swiftly along the Hollywood Freeway. Oliver can see the rectangular sculptures of downtown, the Federal Building where Judge H.B. Willabee awaits.

"Bennie was snookered by that dame into the scam, jury will think about that."

"Will they think about the people in New York?"

Klein gets a little hot. "Oliver, we'll take the hit if we have to, don't kid yourself. We're not going to be held hostage by that kind of threat."

"No need for any emoting," says Chillies calmly.

Chillies and Klein turn silent, words exhausted. In a few minutes they will be pulling up to a horde of reporters. Oliver worries, maybe they won't make any offer.

Finally, General Chillies says, "We will want to issue a statement immediately to the effect the company was hoaxed, but no names will be mentioned. We would also want to keep secret the figure we will agree on."

"And what is that, general?"

"Seven and a half million dollars."

Oliver swallows. "I was thinking more in terms of double that."

"That's roughly the amount we'd have to pay in advertising and public relations fees to repair a shattered image. If it's not acceptable, Mr. Gulliver, let's go to court. I have a reputation. I don't haggle."

"No, I'm at thirteen, fourteen, I can't see my way down from there. A jury might give thirty or forty." Oliver says this with a flushed face, trying to keep it straight. Seven and a half, it's fantastic, he'll get them up a couple more.

The limo wheels onto Spring Street, and parks among the TV vans. The three of them dash for the front door, hoping to make it before the press converges.

"Absolutely no comment, ladies and gentlemen," says Klein.

Loobie catches up to Oliver at the door. "Come on, what gives?"

"Sorry, Charles, I have things on my mind." Seven and a half million bucks, maybe more. He better not stretch the elastic too tight, it could snap back and hurt.

"I made you what you are today, Oliver, a fucking American icon. Where's gratitude? What is this iron curtain that's been rung down over this case?"

"Can't talk now."

Willabee's clerk meets them inside the front door. The judge wants to see them in chambers.

"I have to file an exhibit," Oliver tells her. "Can he wait a few minutes?"

"He's kind of anxious."

On the seventeenth floor, they escape the reporters, the clerk leading them into the anteroom of Judge Willabee's chambers. "I'll go and see if he's ready for you." The clerk leaves them.

"Nine," says Chillies.

"Twelve," says Oliver.

"I've made an honorable offer, Mr. Gulliver. If you're an honorable man, you'll take it."

The clerk comes out to fetch them into chambers, where the judge puts out his hand to Chillies.

"General Chillies, sir, you don't know what a pleasure this is, you're one of my heroes." He won't let the hand go. "Read that interview in *Forbes*, I want to tell you I think you're dead right about the mess we're in."

His effusiveness alarms Oliver.

"Gentlemen, what I want to know is, are we going to get this case over today? I have a judge's conference in Palm Springs starting tomorrow, Friday."

"Well, your honor, I have some evidence that – " Oliver begins.

"Excuse me," says Chillies. He whispers in Oliver's ear. "Ten."

"I think we have settlement," Oliver says.

Willabee sags into a chair, looks relieved. "Good, I was really hoping to get out there tomorrow afternoon with my old bag of sticks and balls."

Klein says, "Guess we should put this hearing over until after this weekend so we can tie up any little loose ends, get all the paper done."

"Tomorrow, ten AM," says Oliver.

"That's not much time," says Klein.

"It's enough," says Chillies.

He's in a hurry. The general wants everything signed and sealed fast to prevent leaks.

"Tomorrow at ten?" Willabee says. "There won't be any problems?"

"You'll be on the first tee by noon, judge," Oliver promises.

"Settlement satisfactory for everyone?" Willabee is prying.

Ten million, a third of that as fees. Thinking about it makes Oliver dizzy.

"The terms won't be disclosed," Klein says. "Tomorrow we'll simply ask for a consent order that the action be dismissed."

"And a further order that the questioned song be copyrighted in the name of my client," Oliver says, nailing things down.

The judge looks shocked. "Really?"

"What happened, your honor," says Klein, "is Mr. Tom Slider was innocently duped into thinking he was writing an original song. None of the defendant's employees are involved, so there's no wrongdoing on the company's part, but we're satisfied it's the plaintiff's song and should be returned to him."

Willabee stands up. "Well, I never quite knew what was going on, but I always suspected something fishy."

In court, the appearance takes fifteen seconds.

After the judge adjourns the case to tomorrow, a puzzled silence in the courtroom is broken by the sound of someone shuffling roughly down an aisle. Oliver turns and sees it's Louis LeGoff, who glances at him with murder in his eyes before banging out the door.

*   *   *

After a wearying afternoon and early evening at Klein, Ingle working out the settlement clauses, Oliver takes a next-to-final draft of the agreement on a late shuttle to San Francisco. Tricia flew up this morning, to listen to the band rehearse and to do a quick study of the songs before the first recording session tonight.

Gilley gave a gleeful yelp on the phone when he heard about the ten million. Oliver will hold jubilation in until he sees the check, to be handed across the table when the final papers are signed. Tomorrow before court. He swore Gilley to secrecy, nothing must imperil the promised payoff.

That General Chillies is a decent sort for an industrial czar. Maybe Oliver will switch from J.D. to Tennessee Jim, the Royalty label. Oliver enjoys the rich thrill of success, is pleased with his wily chaffering. An attorney less deft would have left money on the table, but not Oliver. At the end they were afraid of him, they lost stomach for the fight.

He tries to smother thoughts of the one-third contingency fee plus the additional million Gilley promised. It's too much to think of, too bulky to grasp, to get a handle on. Rags to riches in two weeks. He fears if he believes in it too much, it will dissolve like a dream, and he'll wake up in his bed to Gilley singing the blues outside.

Oliver is met at San Francisco International by an Argonaut Records limousine.

Elora is in the back. As the limo moves off, she grabs him by his lapels.

"All right, we're alone, talk."

"Talk. What's there to talk? She and I happen to get along."

"I hear you're going to shack up, you fraud." She grabs his chin and pulls sideways, forcing him to look at her and her impish grin.

"She told you that?"

"I spent a few hours with her this afternoon. We have no secrets. By the way, she's great."

"She really likes me."

"Yeah?"

Under her gaze, he wilts. "I think I'm in love," he says.

There's a moment when her expression doesn't change. Then she puts her hand to her mouth as if to hide a smile.

"Dad!" she says.

She bursts into laughter and stifles it. "But you only met her." She laughs and hugs him. "And here's the guy who warns

231

me about falling in love." She mimics with a low, masculine voice: "It's an infatuation, my dear, an adolescent fantasy."

And she laughs again, enjoying the delicious irony. "Sorry, Dad." She hugs him. "I'm so goddamn proud of you I could pop."

It's as they're rolling over the Golden Gate Bridge, a dazzle of harbor lights below them, that Elora whispers into his ear, "By the way, Dad, Gilley and I have settled on a date."

"When?"

"October fifteenth."

Oliver gulps. "So soon?"

"There's a reason."

"Oh, no."

"Oh, yes, grandpa."

Oliver's jaw drops. "Good God almighty."

"Results came in this morning."

She burbles delightedly the rest of the way to the recording studio while Oliver sits there stunned, letting the surprise settle, another life in creation, a Gilley-Gulliver, and he can't help but be melted by her joy, which eases his trepidation.

The gatekeeper at Highwire Studio – it's in an old country estate near Muir Woods – waves the limo into the grounds of a rambling stone mansion, and Oliver staggers weak-kneed out, Elora leading him by the hand.

After they are tagged and signed in, she takes him to Studio C where, behind the console, Tricia is in command. On the other side of the glass are Gilley and his band in their separate baffled spaces, Jamey McGuid smiling his guru smile.

"Gilley, you're flat on the first eight of the second verse," Tricia says over the talkback. "Buddy-Joe, let's bring the toms up on the la-las, then harder on the lu-lus. Take four, guys, let's do this for posterior."

She turns and greets Oliver with a kiss. The guys in the band whistle and cheer.

"How's it feel, gramps?" she says softly, winking.

It feels confused, he's a percolating stew of emotions. As he watches her work the boards, he flounders in the complications of love and interlocking genes. Gilley, the sire of his grandchild-to-be, seems welded to him now by an unbreakable bond of blood.

With Tricia, another bond – of love. This is a career woman, she will not want to settle in far-off Foolsgold. Maybe he's outgrown it. Maybe he should move Lindy to nearer the city, nearer culture. Nearer his grandchild.

"That's the keeper," Tricia says over the talkback. "Good work, guys. Take a break. There's Tinglewine or psylocibes in the cooler, take your pick."

She gets loud guffaws from the band. Tricia turns to Oliver and Elora. "The idea is to play a song until you can't stand it any longer. But everyone's up for it, we'll meet the mastering date."

"There's the great man himself," Gilley says, coming in. "His Lordship takes time out to visit the peons in the field. Just back from the fox hunt with ten pelts."

"Gilley," Oliver warns. There are engineers in here.

"Shut ma' mouth," says Gilley. "Nobody talks, everyone walks, as they say in the joint."

"Silence is golden," says Oliver. "Congratulations, I didn't know you had it in you."

Gilley grins and puts an arm around Elora's middle. "I did, but it's in here now. Future musical genius."

Jodie Brown comes in and hands Oliver some papers. "Contracts for the tour, like you to look at them. That reporter from the *Times*, Loobie, phoned to track you down. Wanted me to tell you Louis LeGoff spilled the whole bag of beans, and he wants a comment."

After a night of near-sleep with Tricia in her private cottage on the Highwire grounds, Oliver, worrying about his deal falling through, putting thoughts of grandfatherhood aside, flies back to L.A. and phones Loobie from the airport. But by then he knows the worst, it's in the morning first edition.

LeGoff's gravy train having been derailed, he resigned from the conspiracy of silence and is threatening to sue Oriole for breach of contract if they cancel Slider's record deal.

"The angry talent manager told this reporter that Oriole president Bennie Ford engineered the theft of the song early in August," the story says a few paragraphs down. "LeGoff claimed lawyers for both parties possess voice-taped evidence of Ford's dealings with an unnamed song pirate. Neither Ford nor any official of Oriole Records was available for comment."

What if they renege on the deal? General Chillies will feel he's been too generous now that the shit has hit.

LeGoff kept Blinkie Smith's and Eddie Dill's names out of it - he had to, he manages Blinkie's band - but everything else Oliver told him and Klein is quoted. Luckily for Oriole, perhaps luckily for Oliver's client, he had not told LeGoff about the people in New York.

"I should've warned you, Oliver, this is Charles Loobie you are dealing with, he's a digger. I, too, saw the way the ape man grouched out of the courtroom. Bought him a couple of beer and became his pal and confidant. How soon can I hear the tape?"

"For the record, I don't know what you're talking about."

"You and I should meet, Oliver. I think I'm on to who the thief is. Oriole's case collapsed after you visited Blinkie. A doll was driving when you pulled out of there. She was smiling as she tried to run me over. The face of someone who tries to kill you is a face you never forget."

"I'll talk to you after court."

"How much have you settled for?"

"Gee, Charles, I *can't*. My hands are tied."

"Not to mention your tongue, huh?"

"Anyway, everything's still a little up in the air."

He sees ten million dollar bills, little wings on them, flying away.

Oliver gets a bus to the airport parking lot, where he left Gilley's Mercedes. He drives off to Klein's office, keeping his fingers crossed.

*   *   *

"First time since this case began I haven't felt like there's worse yet to come," Tommy Klein says, and propels Oliver from his waiting room to his office.

General Chillies is there, sitting on an upholstered chair, smoking a cigar with a long ash, the newspaper spread out on the table in front of him.

"Can't keep secrets in this damned city," Chillies says. "Mr. Gulliver, do you think this reopens matters?"

"General, we have settlement."

The secretary brings in an ashtray and three cups of coffee. There is silence until she leaves. Chillies taps his ash into the tray, mashes it with the cigar tip.

"Louis LeGoff was out of our control," Oliver says. "He's your problem."

"It becomes a very onerous proposition now that tales have been told," the general says.

"No mention of any people in New York."

"There's that," he says gruffly.

"You said you believe in honorable dealing, general."

Chillies nods his head slowly, and lets out a sound that is half-snort, half-sigh. "I should have known we couldn't cover it up forever. It would be like burying a body in the garden. We'd always be worried. It's costly medicine, Mr. Gulliver, but best we take it early."

He reaches into an inside pocket of his suit jacket and pulls out a check and places it on the table in front of Oliver. Ten million dollars drawn on the Security Pacific main branch here in Los Angeles. Made out to Oliver Gulliver in trust.

"You'll wait until we've signed the settlement deeds before you cash it?" says Klein.

Oliver looks up finally, realizes he's been staring in awe at the check.

"You can sign for Gilley?" Klein says.

"I have written instructions."

Calm and easy does it. Act like you move sums like this every other day, Gulliver.

"How is Bennie, by the way?" The last Oliver heard, he was in a clinic being treated for nervous collapse.

"We told him last night we'd keep his soiled linen hidden from our voracious press," Chillies says. "He suddenly got better and went home."

"What happens to him now?"

"Dismissed immediately without compensation," Chillies says. "We'll be informing him of that today." He adds, "Poor bastard."

Oliver figures there'll be a public sacrificing of Bennie Ford followed by the traditional washing of hands.

*   *   *

Judge Willabee twitches his little mustache as he listens to Klein, whose remarks seem mostly intended for the press.

"I want to reiterate that Mr. Ford's actions were entirely his own, that he sought no approval from anyone at Oriole Records or its parent company, and he alone bears the responsibility. He acted in flagrant and deplorable fashion and my clients wish it to be known that his services have been terminated and that his former company may take legal recourse to seek remedy from him."

Oliver feels dampened by these words, he's helped ruin a man. No, Bennie brought this on himself, if he hadn't been so venal, Eddie's plan would not have worked. It's like entrapment, police do it all the time.

He'll certify that check at the main branch of the Security Pacific after court.

Klein says, "The parties are bound to mutual promises not to disclose any details of the amicable terms reached between us and the very able and honorable attorney for the plaintiff."

The judge smiles warmly down at Oliver. "Declaration of copyright to the plaintiff," he says. "Otherwise action dismissed without costs to either side."

"All rise."

Klein is upon him, shaking his hand. "Never trust your clients, it's a safe rule. Congratulations."

This Tommy Klein isn't such a bad guy after all.

Other reporters hurry outside, but Charles Loobie remains in his seat until Oliver is by himself, packing his briefcase, then he sidles up to him.

"I can't talk," Oliver says.

"You can listen. I'll be able to tell if I'm right by the expression on your face."

"It's not safe here."

"Your car. You got a lift?"

"Sure, okay." Oliver feels he owes Loobie something, and maybe he'd better find out what the reporter has learned.

"By the way, Bennie called. He wants to meet me."

*　　*　　*

Oliver picks up Loobie at a discreet corner a couple of blocks from the courts. "Edwina Dill," says Loobie, climbing into the Mercedes. "I did some checking."

"Hope you got your facts straight." Oliver heads to the Hollywood Freeway, toward the mountains.

"Got her name from friends of Blinkie Smith's, checked her out with people in the biz. I like it - she's known as the Thief of Songs. Responsible for that pirate tape of Springsteen that went like hotcakes under-counter before his last album was released. Bennie Ford turned to her in a time of need."

Oliver changes the subject. "Why does Bennie want to meet you?"

"I think he's going to name some names. You got any guess who?"

People in New York. Bennie's about to dump all over Royalty Distillers. Better certify that check or they might withdraw the funds.

"Guessing causes libel suits, Charles."

"I'm meeting him at the Palm Restaurant for lunch, it's near his home." He pulls out his notepad. "We've got an hour, I'd like to talk. I've got the feature article for the October *Stone*, Oliver. And what looks like a book contract. Hell, I'm there, I've got an agent."

Oliver exits at the Hollywood Bowl, and climbs up the Mulholland Drive switchbacks.

"Sure would like to hear that tape, old buddy, old pal."

"Charles, I'd be in breach of contract."

The tape is in his briefcase, along with the other one: Gilley's cassette, the object of that wild goose chase.

He flashes back to the morning when he awoke to Gilley fulminating in the orchard about the stolen car and tape. That morning of misery after the fire, after Clarence bankrupted him and ran. He recalls the tortuous false trail that led him to the car, this car, and to the tape that led nowhere, he remembers that bleak moment. It would have been mighty hard to convince Oliver as he sat in the Mercedes playing Gilley 29-7-88 that four or five days later he'd have the copied song back and ten million dollars in his pocket.

"You want background for the book, I'll play you a tape."

He wants to relive that despairful time, to enjoy more vividly his wondrous recovery. He eases to the curb and digs into his briefcase.

"Gilley's missing road-test tape. I thought it was the key to the case but it didn't fit any locks."

He plugs it in and turns on the machine.

"I think you're trying to divert my aim, Oliver. But okay, what the hell."

Gilley is singing the last verse of his song, the tape picks up from where it left off, when that patrol car stopped him. . . . *Ain't she got pity, for a fool of the city.* Oliver hums as he motors again through the mansion-studded mountains.

She don't sympathize with my disguise. Gilley's voice trails to a spoken stop. *No. That ain't it.* The instrumental track chugs on as Gilley ruminates into the mike, recording onto the second track, searching for words, maybe pausing for a toke. Oliver remembers the pungent whiff of cannabis as their cars passed on the highway.

My wailing cries, naw. How you tantalize, your eyes are like apple pies. A low, druggy chuckle, Oliver knows that characteristic Gilley sound.

"He was always changing his lyrics."

"Sounds a little blasted," Loobie says.

The singer continues to experiment. *I sang to your eyes, I played your eyes. No . . . I played your eyes while they plagiarize.*

A whoop, a throaty rumble of delight.

While they plagiarize? Oliver feels a slight tightening of his rectal muscles.

No way do you see past my disguise. Gilley laughing, then strangling on it, coughing smoke from his lungs.

You don't realize. Ain't you surprised?

It is then that a fireball flares in Oliver's head, a light radiant with terrible, iridescent truth.

Some part of Oliver is dimly aware he's driving up a winding ridge road, into the Santa Monica Mountains, holding his position in a slow parade of cars and trucks. Some part of Oliver stays the Mercedes to its lane, not off and down the banks of Coldwater Canyon. Some part of him prays that it isn't so.

Do you still believe my little white lies?

He should turn it off. But to do so would bring Loobie's antennae to attention. Oh God, he's bringing his notebook out. But he's smiling, surely he thinks it's just a joke in rhyme.

Oliver knows it's not a joke. What has been niggling most at him was Gilley wanting to keep the lid on, flying down here to tell Oliver he didn't want to ruin any corporate reputations. Too unlikely, a very un-Gilleyish empathy for the company he felt robbed him. He had his own friends to protect.

Blinkie and Eddie cooperating that way. For immunity. Too easy.

He dimly remembers a mission. Take that check to the bank. Drop Loobie off and get to the Security Pacific. And do what? Cash it?

He can't cash it.

"He was almost psychic there," Loobie says. " 'While they plagiarize,' that's a good hook, I like it."

Loobie hasn't unriddled it. Oliver glances over, the reporter is still smiling, scribbling. "Shit, I've run out. Got any paper?"

Oliver reaches numbly into his briefcase, gives him several sheets of his own office stationery. He prays: let the tape come to an end.

Gilley is now singing another of his songs, *Don't wake up, you're dreamin', the world has no meanin', you'll open your eyes to a fool's paradise . . .*

Oliver remembers him shoving Blinkie into the pool. Great act. In front of witnesses.

Finally Gilley's voice gravels to a halt and there's no sound at all for several seconds, and then . . . a car door opening and shutting.

A woman's laugh. Two persons outside the vehicle, he can't make their words out, but they come closer, and inner voices shout to Oliver, Stop the tape. The car door opens and shuts again, and Gilley is louder.

240

Tomorrow night, Sunday, if you come about midnight, I'll be rehearsin' there.

Why don't you just give me a tape? Eddie Dill says.

Oliver sags. It's all over.

Naw, it's gotta appear right, don't it? Like you came sneakin' around, eh?

I'm going to stay on at the café a few more weeks, looks lots less suspicious. You still off the booze?

I get drunk on love.

It's real?

It don't stop, I'm amped. How's Blinkie?

Missing him. I scored some mondo silly 'cibes. Interested?

Nah. I better shine outa here.

Cheers.

Silence after that.

Just Loobie scribbling away.

Oliver is in mental disarray, dimly aware he's been driving blindly, he's lost, down from the mountains, somewhere in the Valley in a confusion of busy streets.

"I think you better stop for a coffee," Loobie says after a while. "You look shaky."

He pulls into a drive-in fast food and they pick up two large coffees. He parks in the lot, under a clump of date palms. They don't talk. They don't look at each other.

All his illusions of his own cleverness, his brilliant prosecution of a case that became a cause, all his realized daydreams, are all coming apart and dissolving like smoke.

Suddenly Oliver is outraged, an angry victim. How damn stupid of Gilley to leave his mike on, to make a public fool of his lawyer. To ruin things for himself and for Elora and for their innocent child to be.

"I hate to tell you this, Oliver. It's a bullet. I like it." Loobie pockets his notes.

CHAPTER

28

The bartender pours Loobie a beer and Oliver a double straight bourbon. Loobie is waiting for Bennie Ford to arrive. Oliver needs a steadier or he won't be able to make it to his hotel. Gilley 29-7-88 enfeebles him, it sits in his briefcase beside him like a lump of kryptonite.

They're in the Palm Restaurant on Santa Monica Boulevard. The walls are festooned with caricatures of entertainment personalities, there's sawdust on the floor.

The whiskey rolls hot down his throat.

"You've been an innocent foil, Oliver. Blinkie and Gilley, they played music together for seven years, the sudden animosity seemed a bit unreal. I bet it started out as Eddie's idea. She knew Gilley had written a charter. She also knew he had a major hate on for his old record company. The two of them went fishing, and they cast their hooks and Bennie Ford bit. That's my new theory."

Oliver's almost back where he was a month ago, bankrupt. Worse. He thinks of Elora, the pain and the shame, her fiancé on trial for fraud. A scar to be borne by her yet unborn.

"I want to hear Bennie's reaction, I want to see his face," Loobie says. "The *Stone* piece will be heavy on the gonzo, ego-trip journalism. You still don't want to make any comment?"

He's reading over his notes, the pages of stationery spread on the bar in front of him.

"I don't think so."

"Listen, I hate to do this, I admire Gilley for almost pulling it off. I don't blame him, Oriole screwed him for millions of bucks. But I'm not getting beaten to this story, Oliver. I gotta. I can't not. It's the way it is."

Oliver will give him gonzo. He'll take the worthless ten-million check from his breast jacket pocket and rip it up in front of him.

He thinks he'll be ill and looks around for the men's and sees Louis LeGoff entering by the front door.

He walks over to them with an inquiring frown. "What're you all doin' here?"

"What are *you* doing here?" Loobie says.

"Bennie called me up. He ain't gonna be happy to see you all."

"You're not on his fan list either, Louis." Loobie gathers his notes, turns the pages upside down. "What's up, he phoned me, too."

"He wants to talk to me about a fuckin' mission."

"A what?"

"I don't get it neither, he sounded like the cheese slipped from the cracker. He asked me if I had a military code-name."

"Seemed okay when I talked to him. A *code-name*?"

"I'll buy y'all a drink. Gulliver, what's your poison, I got arsenic and strychnine." He claps Oliver's shoulder. "I'm a tough fuckin' Kentuckian, I can handle it. Way to go, you took them boys to the cleaners. Now I gotta sue 'em, too. Same for these gentlemen on my bill, a gin fizz for me."

"Comin' up, pal."

Oliver can't refuse this gesture of conciliation, but he wanted to drink up and go. It's time for an emergency call to Gilley. They have to confer, Gilley has to know what not to say to the police when he's arrested.

243

His heart aches at the thought of Elora, how will she endure her suffering? How will Oliver?

He gulps down his first drink and grabs up the next.

"Weird, I don't like it," Loobie says. Oliver sees he's looking at Bennie Ford, who stands inside the front door, lost, forlorn.

There is something impellingly odd about Ford but Oliver doesn't grasp it at first, then finally realizes it's the slippers. Bare feet and slippers. The bottoms of pyjamas are showing. Hands in the pockets of a khaki raincoat, it's been forty consecutive days without rain in L.A.

"Bennie, you dumb fuck," LeGoff says.

He's staring into the dining area, hasn't spotted them at the bar. All the customers turn silent, are watching.

"Bennie," Loobie says, "Over here."

Ford turns his head not in the direction of the voice, but slightly up, toward a wall, at a caricature of Humphrey Bogart. He moves closer to it, frowning, moves on to study Jack Benny. His back's turned to Oliver.

LeGoff nudges his elbow. "Told y'all, his elastic snapped."

"We better call his doctor," says Oliver.

"What can I get ya, pal?" the bartender calls. Bennie doesn't move.

"Bennie," Loobie shouts.

Ford slowly turns his body in their direction, but doesn't quite seem to see them. He stands with hands in pockets looking like he's about to throw open his coat in lewd display. Little Orphan Annie eyes, maybe he's on heavy medication.

"We don't allow weird in this place, pal."

"They said to come here," Bennie explains in a hollow voice.

"They did, huh?" The bartender calls to one of the waiters, a husky guy. "Ivan, little problem here."

"We'll handle it," Oliver says. "We know him." He gets off his stool and moves toward Bennie, who backs up and shakes his head.

Loobie moves Oliver aside. "You and Louis take the wings, I'll come up the middle," he says softly, and takes a position in front of Bennie. LeGoff moves in a large circle to his left side and Oliver starts edging around the bar to his right.

"Let's go for a walk, Bennie," Loobie says. "I think this place will be closing up soon."

"Who are you?"

"Hey, it's me, Charles. Loobie. *L.A. Times.*" He advances to a few feet in front of him.

Bennie now inspects Loobie much as he did Bogart.

"Loobie," he intones. "They said you'd be here."

"Yeah, and they said we should go for a little ride in a taxi, right?"

Bennie takes a couple of steps back, and he's against the wall, near Jimmy Durante. He glances over at LeGoff, twenty feet away, then back at Loobie.

"You're with the mind enslavers."

"Uh, I don't think so, Bennie."

"They said your brain is joined to mine."

"Who's they?"

Oliver hopes it's not the people in New York.

"You know who they are. The organization."

"Call somebody, a hospital," Loobie says to Oliver, who is still edging over to the other side of Bennie.

"We have Siamese brains," Bennie says. "They said there is only one way to disconnect."

He pulls his right hand from his raincoat pocket and with it comes a gun, a snub-nose .38.

Loobie, four feet in front of Ford, shows a look of wide-eyed shock and fear that cuts Oliver like a branding iron, a look of gonzo horror, his facial muscles in vibrating spasm, a last look from Loobie before he whirls off into eternity.

The gun fires twice.

A bullet in the central forehead that Oliver sees shatter the bone.

A bullet lower, between the eyes.

Loobie collapses in a tangled heap of limbs, like a raggedy doll.

Oliver watches as if from a nightmare in which he cannot

make his legs move. All around him waiters and customers are scrambling for cover.

Louis LeGoff is six feet from Bennie, as still as a tree stump, arms stretched tautly out, eyes bulging.

Bennie turns the gun on him. "Who are you?"

"Louis," he says in a thin croak. "Louis, your buddy. Stopped off for a drink, jes' leavin'." He takes one slow step back.

If Oliver can get closer, he will jump him. He inches forward.

Still looking intently at LeGoff, who is frozen with fright, Bennie points the barrel of the .38 at Louis' heart. "They said you'd be here."

Oliver takes a big step to launch himself forward, but throws himself sideways out of instinct, against the wall, as Bennie fires, sends three shots snapping into LeGoff's chest, and the big man jolts back and collapses in a shuddering pile, and the gun is suddenly on Oliver, who is clammy-cold against the wall among the smiling caricatures.

"Who are you?"

Bogart, Durante, come up with a name, who are Bennie's favorites?

The angel of death hovers, his talons out.

"Code-name General Custer. I'm with the organization."

Bennie squints at him.

They are five feet apart. The nearest table is overturned, facing him like a barricade, three men squeezed in behind it. One way to go, back to the bar, two leaping strides.

The waiter Ivan is coming up behind Bennie with a baseball bat.

"We have another mission for you," Oliver says, speaking with a steady, natural cadence.

"They didn't tell me you'd be here." Bennie licks his lips and lowers the gun to about testicle level, and Oliver feels the merest tickle of relief. Bennie glances quickly to his right, at Jack Palance, causing Ivan, still several feet away, to freeze. Bennie jerks his eyes back to Oliver but keeps the gun low.

Oliver tells him, "Your code-name will be Sergeant Pepper, and you'll be on a mission of peace. You'll have to go unarmed, of course." Oliver extends his hand, palm up, for the gun. He expects the hand to be shaking, is amazed that it's not, but he's been coldly deliberate for the last thirty seconds, having determined that he was damned if he was going to die.

Bennie, with agonizing slowness, takes his finger from the trigger and extends the gun butt first. Oliver takes it.

"I think I need to rest, sir," Bennie says, and slumps down onto the floor, staring vacantly forward.

A dazed moment of silence, before someone picks up a phone.

*   *   *

The first police arrive in two minutes, a young woman and younger man, who take charge nervously. She tells everyone to sit calmly, and examines the sour-faced, bloody corpse of Louis LeGoff and shakes her head.

The patrolman has his handcuffs out and looks uncertainly down at Bennie Ford, who sits on the floor, legs straight out, his back against the wall, staring up at the ceiling and sobbing.

Nearby lies Loobie, a towel thrown over his broken face.

Oliver returns to his barstool and drains his double bourbon. Then he picks up his briefcase. The policewoman comes up to him.

"Mr. Gulliver?"

"Yes."

"Afraid you'll have to stay until the detectives get here." She picks up Loobie's notes atop the bar, turns them over, sees Oliver's name on the stationery. "These yours?"

Oliver stares at the pages for a couple of seconds. "Oh, thank you very much." He calmly slips them into his briefcase.

29

Next morning, when he states his business at the bank, Oliver is ushered quickly into the manager's office, and after a few phone calls are made, he is told, yes, the check may be certified, but wouldn't he like to set up an account to start earning interest immediately, a special thirty-day rate if he likes, very wise. Terrible, terrible thing that happened, Mr. Gulliver.

Still improbably calm, Oliver goes about his task with cold efficiency.

Business concluded, the manager doesn't let Oliver escape his clutches, but escorts him down the street to the car park, hungry to be with one so nearly murdered, anxious for after-dinner tales. But Oliver is sombre and quiet, full of purpose.

Last evening was a ghastly collage of shocked and grieving faces. Superimosed on those were the flat, remorseless expressions of the L.A.P.D. and of reporters, awed and ashen. One of their brothers paid a deadly price for his exclusive.

Loobie's final scoop will be buried with him.

At the police station, Oliver met Bennie's home-care nurse, Mrs. Magee. She said he was lucid most of the day, read the paper in his room, made some phone calls. He did start using profanity at the end of one incoming call, she now thinks that was when he learned about his summary dismissal.

And that was when he came apart, Oliver figures.

Mrs. Magee didn't know he kept a handgun in a locked desk drawer. She was out getting groceries when Bennie left for his twenty-minute raincoat-and-pyjama stroll down from the hills to Santa Monica Boulevard. His kids were at school and his wife at the therapist's. A copy of the morning *Times* was later found spread open on his bed.

Later, two men from homicide visited Oliver's hotel room, gruffly polite but pressing a case of murder with motive.

What was your business with Loobie this morning?

He wanted my comments on his latest story. I think he hoped to meet Mr. Ford at the restaurant for a similar purpose.

But Loobie said Ford phoned him.

He said that, yes.

And he phoned LeGoff?

Apparently.

And this is the day LeGoff and Loobie put Mr. Ford on the front page of the newspaper. Mr. Ford was ruined.

All I can tell you is what I saw. He looked mad, as in mad, not angry.

How could you be sure he wasn't faking insanity, Mr. Gulliver?

If he were sane, he would have killed me, too.

They did not ask him about Loobie's notes. None are presumed missing. His full pad was found in his jacket pocket.

Oliver burned the pages of stationery before the police arrived.

When one has been a twinkle in time from death, life takes on significant new dimensions. What is paramount, vital, is seen in bold relief. Elora, her unborn, the seed of his seed, the stuff of reality, eclipse notions of law and ethics.

"Ghastly business. You talked him out of the gun, I hear, very brave."

"Thank you."

He escapes from the bank manager, from downtown L.A., heads for the airport in the old Mercedes.

Tricia talked to him on the phone last night. She wanted to come down with Gilley, but he told her to wait for him in

Marin County. After she finishes recording and mixing he hopes to escape with her to the monotonous safety of little Foolsgold.

The wreckage that is Bennie Ford is in psychiatric confinement, facing two murder charges.

"Poor bastard," Chillies had said. Before phoning Bennie to tell him he's been cashiered. Oliver feels no welling out of sympathy for Royalty Distillers. Their board chairman lit the fuse that exploded the bomb in Bennie's brain.

At the passenger loading zone, Gilley waves him down, then comes to the driver's door.

"Bet they needed a crowbar to unclench the anus afterwards, eh? You okay?"

"No. You'd better drive."

Gilley gets in and pats the dashboard as Oliver shoves over. "Mommy loves you, mommy wants her little sweetikins to come home with her."

He shifts into gear and they head for the San Diego Freeway, toward the I-5.

"I shouldn't joke, eh, I know you feel rotten, everyone does. We had to cancel last night, we were all too blown away to record. A maniac holding a gun on you, man, what does it it feel like?"

"It feels like you almost got me killed."

"I warned you they were dangerous."

It is several minutes later, as they are climbing into the mountains on the I-5, that Gilley, after glancing at Oliver a few times, says, "What do you mean, *I* almost got you killed."

Silence at Oliver's end.

"Why did you want me to fly down here to meet you, Oliver? I'm getting odd vibrations."

Oliver sticks Gilley 29-7-88 into the tape deck and rewinds it a ways and plays the damning evidence, the meeting outside Raquel's cabin.

Gilley listens in silence, his eyes holding to the road.

After Oliver pulls the tape out and replaces it in his briefcase, Gilley sighs. "Okay, mother-sticker, this is a fuck-up. Man, I must've been really blasted to leave that mike on."

After another silence, Oliver says, "Does Elora know any-thing about your sting?"

"No. Honest. I wouldn't involve her. I love her, man. Just Blinkie, Eddie, and me. There wasn't gonna be no leaks." After a pause, "Anyone else, ah, know about this?"

"Just me. It's enough."

Gilley takes a deep breath, fusses in the glove compartment for his stash, doesn't find it, groans, shakes his head. "It started as hilarious stoned joke. Elora was at the modeling school, and I went over to Blinkie's, and Eddie was there, and we got ripped, talking, laughing, making up scenarios, you know how it goes."

"I have tried to imagine."

"It still seemed kind of humorous the morning after. Eddie wanted to try it for fun, and she came up to Foolsgold and got a job in the café, and then me and Elora arrived a few days later. The whole carnival just took off. Court case and wild goose — chase and all."

He glances at Oliver's sombre face. "Didn't mean to send you runnin' in circles, it's the way things happened. Anyway, sud-denly there was headlines all over. I never expected to win no ten million dollars, but it looked like a pretty good way to hype my album, eh, and I guess I just played it out to see where it would end. When things got hot for Blinkie and Eddie, they figured it was time to make statements. That was the ultimate plan, Oliver, they'd come forward and make a deal for immu-nity, then bail out."

"Pulling their ripcords all the way."

"I never dreamed nothing like this would happen," Gilley says softly.

As they slip over Tejon Pass, Oliver sees the southern lip of the San Joaquin Valley spread open below them, baking in a merciless late-summer sun, a boundless plain disappearing into thick haze.

251

Gilley clears his throat. "I don't wanna sound crass or no-thin', and I got no doubt about your strong moral attitude to this matter, but, ah, did you cash that check?"

"I have everything in an escrow account."

"Includin' your three-and-a-third-million cut, like."

"I'm not taking it."

"Jeez, that's very high-minded, Oliver. But we can't really return all that bread to them, can we? Wouldn't they wanna know why we're actin' abnormal?"

Oliver doesn't answer and Gilley can't seem to find more words to say, and they sweep out onto the dry flatlands.

It is hot and barren and dry where Oliver asks Gilley to pull off the road onto the shoulder. "Can I see you outside for a second?" he says.

Gilley gets out and follows Oliver down into a ditch. "What's up?"

Oliver turns and faces him, sizing him up, then unleashes a stinging hook to Gilley's jaw.

"You used me, you son of a bitch!" he roars down to Gilley, who is on his back and blinking. "You came into my home and you played me the dupe! And two guys got killed out of it!"

"Goddamn, Oliver, I didn't drive Bennie over the edge!" he shouts back. "You can't blame me for that! Man, do you think I wouldn't undo it if I could?"

"Did you think about Elora? Did you think what you might have done to her? I ought to kick your teeth in, you scheming prick."

"They ripped me blind," Gilley shouts. "You saw the options on that contract, they stole triple from me what we just got back."

"There I was, the hot-shot lawyer, winning against odds, not knowing the fight was fixed. I played your innocent shill and I feel like a fucking asshole!" He stands all clenched and red, shouting.

"Hey, man, don't give me no bullshit, you came out a god-damn hero! I'm proud of you. Everyone's proud."

"Fuck proud. People have died! *I* almost died!"

252

"Aw, shit, I'm sorry, Oliver. It freaked me out, honest."

"Weekend visits from your kid, watching you grow old in jail, that's what you wanted? All our lives ruined? Out of some stupid, alcoholic idea of revenge?"

Gilley wiggles his jaw with his hand, sitting up. "I don't know, it all ballooned out of proportion. Oliver, you were so down, you'd lost faith in yourself, I love you, man, I wanted to see you come out smiling. I blew it."

"I have to live your lie with you," Oliver says softly. "I feel tarnished. Elora doesn't deserve you."

Gilley loses the last of his brave front as his eyes grow wet. "Don't say that."

"It's blood money, Gilley."

"I don't want it."

"And we can't give it back." Oliver helps Gilley to his feet. "We'll talk about it on the road."

CHAPTER

30

The thunder of sixty-five thousand clamoring voices and stamping feet, echoing and reechoing under a Teflon dome, is as much as the human ear can clinically withstand, Oliver has decided. He wants to plug his ears, but Tricia will make fun of him, a lone old fogey in this vast sea of kids less than half his age.

"Sounds like the siege of Stalingrad," he shouts to her.

She goes on her tiptoes and yells into his ear, "They're celebrating. They know they're at a wedding party."

He shakes his head. It's unnerving, what if the roof comes crashing down, the vibrations have to be shaking it loose.

The electric lights went out three minutes ago. Oliver sees Tricia smiling at him in the other-worldly glow of thousands and thousands of pin-pricks of light, extending for a distance of what seems many city blocks. Almost everyone in the indoor stadium is holding lit matches, and, from the smell, many of these matches are being put to illegal use.

The screaming and the clapping and the stomping and the whistling vibrate painfully on his ear drums. The epicenter is in front of the stage, hundreds of teenagers crushed together. He's seen at least six kids nearly pass out in there. They had to be hauled by husky young men in white T-shirts to a huge first-aid area backstage. Oliver was terrified for them, but was reassured by Tricia that this goes on all the time.

Before the concert has even started? "The first ones in are always the first to get packed out," Tricia told him. The hundreds of youngsters jammed against the wooden-plank barriers had lined up outside the stadium all night and all day, in brittle, cool October weather, for the privilege of being the lucky sardines in front.

Lindy and her friends from Foolsgold are safely up in the seats. He hopes.

Oliver and Tricia are standing close to the crowd barrier, near the musclemen who defend it, and they'll have a good view of the show from there. But where's the band? They'd better come on and get control of this crowd before his ears split.

He wonders how Sybil McGuid is managing. Maybe it's less noisy where she and Pastor Blythe sit, up high in one of the boxes. She was in the dressing room earlier, nattering about what a beautiful city Vancouver is. She and a few Foolsgoldians, Jesse Gonzales, Blythe, Oliver's grandparents, toured the city by limousine after the wedding. Vancouver, Gilley's hometown, his crucible, where he started playing music.

But the first musical instrument I ever played was myself, eh.

From here the tour drops down all the way to San Diego, then east, Texas and the South, up the Atlantic Coast, back across Canada, through America's heartland, then to Europe, Japan, Australia, and New Zealand. Tricia's tank top says, "C.C. Gilley, Around the World in 180 Days."

A man in the stands just above him whistles so piercingly that Oliver winces.

When does Gilley and Co. start playing music? Has his son-in-law got a sudden fit of nerves?

Oliver would not be surprised. The guy having got married only five hours ago.

Gilley and Elora flew up fifty-plus friends from Foolsgold and Frisco, all sworn to secrecy. It wasn't to be a media circus, but the press was somehow alerted, and they invaded en masse part way through the ceremony at the Unitarian Church, and it became a noisy but a joyful shambles.

The gentle and unflowery nuptials - a compromise between Gilley's vague agnosticism and Elora's concern about her grandparents' feelings - seemed to lift from Oliver the veil of wistfulness that had settled on him after that murderous Friday a month ago. Today was a day to forget blood and sadness, a celebration day. He almost became cheery.

His daughter looked so incredibly beautiful. No wedding gown, just an elegant formal dress. Gilley was in white tux, all the band members in black.

Oliver had a smile on his face but tears in his eyes as he gave her away.

She was so goddamn happy. Oliver will do nothing to destroy that happiness, and he will live with the fact of Gilley in the family. They're joined in unlikely orbit, maybe forever, joined in their uneasy secret. But they've regained their kwonky, kidding friendship, it's survived its angry crisis.

At the wedding, Oliver felt momentarily sad for Gilley, his adoptive mother didn't show. No one, apparently, knew how to reach her. His father came, however, a tough old brewery worker who boasted he's been on ten strike committees, a rather uncouth Canadian communist.

Making a guest appearance at the ceremony was uncle-to-the-bride Clarence Boggs. Yes, Saigon Jimmy's freedom train got him safely to Canada, a country that apparently takes American refugees. He called Oliver at his hotel last night, he had to be invited to the wedding, he's family.

So Oliver talked to Jesse, who agreed to turn a blind eye to seeing Clarence there. The heat is dying down anyway, the insurance company isn't pressing charges. What they shelled out on the Opera House policy will be recovered from Ernie Bolestero, they've stuck liens on everything he owns. Ernie's out on bail. Arson Garson did a deal with the People of California.

The crowd noise doesn't abate. The minutes pound by. Oliver wonders if he'll lose his sense of hearing. But as Tricia says, it's a wedding party. All being recorded live for an album.

He hopes there hasn't been a glitch, Gilley getting into the champagne. He went on one bat, just after finishing the album, but he came out of it fast, after a few days, and hasn't had a drop since. Maybe that is the best that can ever be expected. *I'm only an alcoholic when I drink, eh.*

Suddenly, and it seems from all around him, comes a sound like the thudding of God's heart, it makes his teeth chatter, he's going to disintegrate like glass. A high-pitched screech, a jungle cat noise of guitar, has him climbing from his skin, then drums and cymbals, and an Indian whoop that is the voice of C.C. Gilley amplified a billion times. Oliver, his ears snapping and pinging, realizes he's standing in front of a thirty-foot bank of speakers.

A spotlight stings stage center: Gilley and guitar at a stand-up mike, he's in tux and white tie, the tie askew.

"Don't mail me home," he screams.

The crowd goes into a blind frenzy, Gilley issues an ear-splitting screech, an avalanche of decibels burying Oliver.

" . . . in no plain brown wrapper!"

His voice goes abruptly silent. Oliver feels a hot shiver race through him.

Another roar from the crowd as spotlights zap the four band members. They stand silently poised in front of their instruments in their black tuxedos, as Gilley pulls an incredibly long, searing note from his guitar, and screams again, "I said don't mail me home . . . in no plain brown wrapper!"

And his arm whips down and the boys in the band blur into motion under colored lights that dance and blink to a violent, banging rock and roll beat, a cacophanous musical clamor, and Oliver staggers back, his hands to his ears, and his last vision before Tricia pulls him to safety is of Jamey McGuid bouncing around in a frilly silk shirt, looking for all the world like one of those white-skirted hippopatami doing the *Nut-cracker Suite* dance in *Fantasia*.

"I've suffered injury," he tells her as he slides into a chair backstage, near the first-aid area. They'll have oxygen there, he feels woozy. "That was *loud.*"

"Come on, don't be a poop, this is magic, you're watching

rock and roll in the grand style, these guys are on and it's a high. Gilley gets them up."

"I didn't catch anything you said, you'll have to speak up."

She bends to his ear. "Forget it. I love you." She gives him a tiny electric kiss. "We'll get up above the sound a little."

He gathers strength and she takes his hand and leads him like a little child up a ramp.

Oliver still feels quite in love. For the last two weeks, after she finished post-production on the album, Tricia has been with him in his cabin up the Foolsgold River, roughing it, a slow unwinding from recent madness. They lived on trout and blackberries and wine and rapture, and she helped heal his pain. They will take up living together, see how it feels, make no long-range plans. She'll rent her place in L.A., move a lot of her stuff to Foolsgold, freelance out of there.

Foolsgold is where Oliver intends to stay. There's a flood of work with Bolestero gone, there's Sybil's mess to clean up. He may have to hire someone to help Mrs. Plymm.

When he visited his office, she said, "Now don't get too pumped up with a sense of self-importance, Oliver."

Country living has become too gentle and ingrained a habit, city life is cruel and dangerous. He'll be financially comfortable. He took from Gilley just enough to pay his debts, maybe he deserved more, but he didn't feel right.

It looks like Gilley's boat isn't going to be rocked or even rolled. Gilley 29-7-88 is history, melted into black smoke in Oliver's back-yard burn barrel. Oriole Records has closed the books on the affair, all except the books of account. Their cash registers will, as a final irony, ring merrily, the back catalogues of Gilley's albums are selling like, ah, murder. And Long Tom Slider and the Joy Flakes are attracting reasonable crowds on their tour, a rock and roll oddity. They had to replace Blinkie Smith who, Gilley has hinted, is still holidaying in Mexico with Eddie Dill.

The dying faces of Loobie and LeGoff often still flash back to him, chilling images to replace the daydreams he no longer needs. Bennie Ford's expensive Texas lawyer has announced his client went around the bend and never came back. The D.A.'s office is sending out hints Ford failed to test insane at the state hospital.

But Oliver will give Bennie a reasonable doubt. He'll not help him to the gas chamber, his somewhat soiled and rumpled conscience won't allow it.

Sudden tragedy has made him fateful, less worried about the future. As the shock of events lessens, he feels scarred but calmer, mature, grandfatherly. The crisis of being fifty has been vanquished, all that self-absorption now seems silly and futile.

Tricia leads him to the third tier, high and to the right of the stage. It's where Lindy and three or four of her home-town pals are standing and jumping.

They watch Gilley oscillate in front of the band like a driven devil, belting his old hits into a hand mike, alternating with songs from his album. Which was released here just Thursday, two days ago and is already sold out.

Gilley from the speakers, "It's good to be home, man."

A cheer.

"Now we warmed up, we're gonna start cookin'."

A louder cheer.

"Want you to listen."

Bam, it's silent. Gilley has total control.

"Guess you all heard I got ten million dollars from Oriole Records." His words reverberate around the massive building. "I spent it all today. Me and some friends drew a list up. Greenpeace, 'cause the planet's going to hell. Nader, 'cause the profiteers are takin' it there. We got thirty names, we got anti-poverty and abused women, we got cancer research and alcohol. I just wrote out the checks. What a fuckin' rush."

A slow build, then the stadium erupts, and Gilley waits until they subside.

"Anyway, it's been quite a day."

Little Kelly LeGrange plays a few chords of Wagner's "Wedding March" on the keyboards.

"Got hitched today. A small-town girl I met in the city."

Before an eye can blink, Gilley and the band are on cue into their number-one single.

Oliver knows what they mean when they talk about high energy, he feels it lifting him. Everyone is standing, moving. The song weaves a celebration of love through his flesh, its wriggling little rhythms make his bones seem loose.

As Winston Ogumbo blows sax, Gilley disappears into the wings and comes back a few seconds later, pulling a resisting Elora by the wrist. She's shaking her head and laughing. Oliver feels a pouring out of love, an explosive joyful communion. He hugs Tricia.

The band whips into the chorus, Gilley singing and dancing with Elora and Jamey, and everyone around Oliver is dancing, Tricia and Lindy and the Foolsgold kids and the happy tens of thousands here, and maybe Mrs. McGuid and Pastor Blythe are dancing, and Oliver can't stop moving himself, can't stop his body from pulsing, can't stop his feet from stomping, and Tricia is laughing and shrieking and kissing him and Lindy is smiling and loving him, and he forgets clever plans and wasted lives and murder and deceit and joins in the song.

▶ ▶ ▶

"How do you feel?"

"All right, I guess. But I'm not insane, Mr. Gilchrist, whatever the jury said."

"That was by the skin of my teeth. That fucking pea-brained judge, I've never heard more biased instructions. Gulliver saved you. The jury liked him, he came across honest."

"He's code-name General Custer. He's with the organization. When they make contact, I'll see your bill gets paid."

"It's being looked after, Bennie."

"The organization?"

"Oriole Records. I think you should ease off on the secret organization bushwa. We can get you into the outpatient program in six months if you look like you're coming around."

"You're not from the organization?"

"No, I'm from Barch, Gilchrist, and Levinsky, attorneys-at-law. I'm Gilchrist. Listen, pardner, I've been in this business too long to be shucked by too many clients. But don't shuck yourself. The doctors at the state hospital aren't going to send you home if you insist you're in some group that gives out licenses to kill."

"Maybe I should resign."

"You're nobody's fool, Bennie."

■ ■ ■

71,500

A Selected List of Fiction Available from Mandarin

While every effort is made to keep prices low, it is sometimes necessary to increase prices at short notice.
Mandarin Paperbacks reserves the right to show new retail prices on covers which may differ from those
previously advertised in the text or elsewhere.

The prices shown below were correct at the time of going to press.

☐	7493 1352 8	**The Queen and I**	Sue Townsend £4.99
☐	7493 0540 1	**The Liar**	Stephen Fry £4.99
☐	7493 1132 0	**Arrivals and Departures**	Lesley Thomas £4.99
☐	7493 0381 6	**Loves and Journeys of Revolving Jones**	Leslie Thomas £4.99
☐	7493 0942 3	**Silence of the Lambs**	Thomas Harris £4.99
☐	7493 0946 6	**The Godfather**	Mario Puzo £4.99
☐	7493 1561 X	**Fear of Flying**	Erica Jong £4.99
☐	7493 1221 1	**The Power of One**	Bryce Courtney £4.99
☐	7493 0576 2	**Tandia**	Bryce Courtney £5.99
☐	7493 0563 0	**Kill the Lights**	Simon Williams £4.99
☐	7493 1319 6	**Air and Angels**	Susan Hill £4.99
☐	7493 1477 X	**The Name of the Rose**	Umberto Eco £4.99
☐	7493 0896 6	**The Stand-in**	Deborah Moggach £4.99
☐	7493 0581 9	**Daddy's Girls**	Zoe Fairbairns £4.99

All these books are available at your bookshop or newsagent, or can be ordered direct from the address
below. Just tick the titles you want and fill in the form below.

Cash Sales Department, PO Box 5, Rushden, Northants NN10 6YX.
Fax: 0933 410321 : Phone 0933 410511.

Please send cheque, payable to 'Reed Book Services Ltd.', or postal order for purchase price quoted and
allow the following for postage and packing:

£1.00 for the first book, 50p for the second; **FREE POSTAGE AND PACKING FOR THREE BOOKS OR
MORE PER ORDER.**

NAME (Block letters) ....

ADDRESS ....

....

☐ I enclose my remittance for ....

☐ I wish to pay by Access/Visa Card Number

Expiry Date

Signature ....

Please quote our reference: MAND